M000211828

defenseless

CORINNE MICHAELS

Defenseless
Copyright © 2016 Corinne Michaels
All rights reserved.
ISBN: 9781682306253

No part of this publication may be reproduced, distributed, or transmitted in any form or by any means including electronic, mechanical, photocopying, recording, or otherwise without the prior written consent of the author.

This book is a work of fiction. Names, characters, places, and incidents either are products of the author's imagination or are used fictitiously. Any resemblance to actual events or locales or persons, living or dead, is entirely coincidental and beyond the intent of the author or publisher.

Editor:
Brenda Letendre, Write Girl Editing

Proofreading:
Ashley Williams, AW Editing

Interior design and formatting:
Christine Borgford, Perfectly Publishable
www.perfectlypublishable.com

Cover design:
Sarah Hansen, Okay Creations
www.okaycreations.com

Cover photo © Nicole Ashley Photography
www.nicoleashley.ca

dedication

For my readers. Thank you for the unending love and support that you show me every single day. You've kept me going when I wasn't sure I could. Thank you for loving my characters, and my evil ways. I love you infinitely.

And to show my appreciation . . . NO CLIFFHANGER! You're welcome!

one

Mark

"EVERYONE LOCKED AND LOADED?" Liam Dempsey draws our attention. There's a part of me that wants to slap him, but then I remember: I'm the guest. It would probably be frowned upon.

"Ready," Jackson says and bangs the magazine into the rifle. "What's the plan?"

"We have the location where Aaron's being held captive. We'll split into two teams, surround the building, and get him out. The helo will be on standby for extract. Muffin, Twilight, you guys will handle meeting with the CIA agent." Liam lets us know the plan.

He's the big cheese of our small team. Commander was fine with allowing Muff and me to go on the rescue. First, we know what the hell we're doing; I could be the damn commander at this point. Second, if it isn't Aaron, we have the best chance of knowing quickly. I know it is, though. The code word that the CIA agent communicated was the one we've used for years. She relayed his area and the best way possible to enter the compound. Of course, deciphering her instructions was difficult, and it left us to make plans for the plans.

"Let's get this shit done and get back in one piece this time, okay Muff?" There's no hiding the sarcasm in my voice.

"Fuck off, Dixon."

"So touchy." I grin and double-check my gear. As funny as it is, it's also not funny at all. Jackson Cole was once leader of our SEAL team when our mission went really wrong. We lost three teammates that day, and all of us suffered injuries both mental and physical. Then we sent Aaron to deal with a lost shipment of weapons and he was killed. Well, possibly not, but still. Each time one of our asses touches down in this fucking place, some-one ends up shot or killed. I'd love to be able to forget, but the truth is, I never will. The guys I've lost reside in my heart. The memories take hold in all of us, and for some, they torment us. The wondering if we could've done something different, remem-bering their last moments—it's a heavy burden to carry.

I've lost too many friends and too much blood to this hell-hole.

"Okay," Liam says through our earpieces. "Two minutes out."

Everyone stands, heads toward the back of the plane, and readies for the ride. We're parachuting in, and there's a part of me that's alive for the first time in a while. I live for this shit. The command of the sky, the adventure, the danger—I love it. It's a part of who I am, and while I don't regret getting out of the Navy, I miss the fun. Being a SEAL was everything to me. I was damn good at it, too. While Aaron and Jackson had no problem getting out and starting Cole Security Forces, I would've been buried in my uniform. However, my arm had other ideas and made the choice for me.

Jackson slaps my shoulder. "Ready to be badass again?"

"I never lost it. Unlike you other pussy whipped assholes."

"At least I get pussy, unlike some shithead who talks a lot of crap," he mutters under his breath.

"Keep it up, fat boy. You're starting to earn your call sign again, Muffin." I pull my goggles down and watch for the light to turn green. There's no hesitation as I jump out the hatch. The plane fades away as I plummet to, once again, do what I live for.

We all reach the ground safely a few miles from the I.E.D. site where this whole shit show started.

Liam gives the hand commands as we split into teams of two. If I ever felt like a piece of shit before, it was nothing compared to now. Aaron is possibly still alive and nearby. We didn't search before, partly because Muff got shot, but I never even considered coming back. They claimed there were no survivors, and we listened.

If it were me, would I be pissed? Fuck yeah, I would. We should've looked.

"See that, up on the building?" Dempsey's voice cuts through the silence.

My eyes dart to where his hand is pointing. I can't see it clearly, but hanging from the antenna is a red scarf, the go-ahead signal from our contact.

"Charlie better not be fucking us around," I grumble. I've missed the way my body feels right now. Everything inside me is awakened. My mind knows there's danger and my muscles are tense so I do my best to relax. I can't be on edge or someone could get hurt. I remember how it felt to lose our teammates on that mission. I remember carrying Brian, Devon, and Fernando's bodies out. I remember watching the life fade from their eyes. Then to think of all the other drama we've dealt with being in the sandbox—this fucking place gives me anxiety.

"She's on our side. Head in the game," Jackson snaps as he creeps forward. He's in the zone. I need to get there before we kick in the door.

As we approach the entrance, Liam comes through with the green light. "Petunia." His tone is clear. This time we're using flowers for code names. I liked it better when we used liquor or tobacco . . . more manly. Shows just how much the Navy is breeding pussies now.

Jackson braces his hand against the door, ready to push through, but someone pulls it open first. All of our guns raise, and my gaze locks on the bluest eyes I've ever seen.

The woman's hands slowly raise, and she casually removes the hijab that covers her mouth and hair. "Check out the garden, boys. Petunia." Her accent is clearly American. "He's down the hall and knows you're coming. There are three on guard by his cell. The others are out doing errands. I'm leaving with you, so don't fuck this up."

I stand there, staring, unable to form a fucking coherent thought. This is the CIA op? This five-foot-four, drop-dead gorgeous woman? No wonder she gets information. I'd sell my soul if she asked. Her hair is almost black and hangs straight, her eyes are ice blue, and don't get me started on what I imagine her plump lips doing. I've never seen anyone like her. I've never reacted to anyone like this before. I want her—any man would—but I want to *own* her. Every part of my body, especially one in particular, yearns for her. I want to see if her skin is as soft as it looks, if her hair feels like silk, and her voice—I'm fucking done for.

Jackson lowers his gun and then addresses her. "Which door, Charlie?"

"Second on the left. I need a gun." She puts her hand out.

The need to protect her calls from deep within. "Maybe you should stay out here."

"And watch you guys get lost? I don't think so. Gun. Now." She doesn't look my way when she replies. She just waits for Jackson to hand her his pistol.

I don't like this. She may be trained by the CIA, but that's not saying she can handle combat. "Are you sure you know how to use it, princess?" I ask.

Her eyes meet mine and narrow. *Oh, that got her attention.* A storm's raging in those baby blues. She recovers quickly, though, when Jackson places his nine mil in her delicate palm. "Thanks. I'll let that slide since you obviously aren't aware of who I am," she says without taking her eyes off me. "We don't have a lot of time. Where's the rest of your team?"

"We are the team," I reply. Who *is* this girl? Maybe the CIA needs ten people, but Jackson, Liam, and I could handle this entire thing on our own—the six-guy team we brought is more than enough.

Jackson smirks. "They're approaching from a different entrance. Let's go."

"I'll lead," Charlie says and lifts the hijab over her hair.

"We know what we're doing." I speak just so she'll look at me again.

"Wouldn't want you to get lost or hurt. Don't worry, I'll protect you." Her voice drips with sarcasm. My cock hardens. It fucking hardens on a goddamn mission. I am so fucked.

She opens the door and I push Muffin out of the way. No way is he going to be behind her. Charlie turns to relay a message, and notices he's not the one following. Her eyes roll, she holds up two fingers, and then she points to the room. The way her ass sways is hypnotic. I lock down the sexual urges flowing through me and focus. The two men trailing me let off two silent shots and then return to following us. We slink through the dirty hallway and come face to face with another guard.

I don't have a moment to take the sight. Charlie doesn't hesitate. No more than a breath passes before she raises the nine and shoots him in the head.

I'm in love. It's official. I'm going to blow my fucking load right here.

This woman is going to be mine.

She turns her head to face me and lifts her lips. The words

that come from her mouth go straight to my groin. "Don't be afraid to pull the trigger next time, princess." Charlie's eyes glimmer, and I know right then that this woman will not be owned, but she sure as shit will own me.

two

One Year Later

I TOSS MY LEGS up on my desk as I lean back in the office chair. I close my eyes with the phone against my ear. "Well, there are answers somewhere, Muff. I'm not sure what the hell to think anymore." I swear it's like talking to a brick wall. After the mission to save Aaron, I went through hell trying to find answers, but I came up empty.

Jackson sighs. "You've gone over our competitors?"

"No, I figured I'd leave them out," I reply sarcastically. "Of course I looked at all of them."

It's been almost two years we've been dealing with this bullshit. Charlie and I worked together using the intelligence she gathered along with what little I had. It went dormant for a while, and we thought the threat was eliminated. Then she left on assignment, and we had no more problems. Seemed whatever it was had eliminated itself. But sure enough, it's happening again.

Things are starting to go missing again. There's no way I'm letting this go. Jackson and I will spare no expense to figure this out. I won't lose another brother, and I sure as fuck am not letting whoever this prick is get away with it.

"I'm just as frustrated as you are, Mark. Don't be more of an asshole than usual. There's a reason all of this is happening and why it's happening now. The first shipment encountered issues around the time Raven Cosmetics came back into my hands. I had just hired Catherine. See what else happened around that time. Any new clients we took on, anything that was a shift." Jackson lets out a deep breath.

I know this entire situation haunts him. Aaron lost a year of his life and his family, and Jackson almost lost his now fiancée, Catherine. She had a hard time when he got shot. Hell, we all did. Jackson is the reason we're all here in so many ways. He and I are closer than the other guys. I see how heavily this weighs on him.

However, his suffering doesn't stop my need to piss him off for fun. "Weren't you the damn intelligence officer? You should've figured this out already. Apparently, the Navy spent too much money training a dipshit."

"You're fired."

"You can't fire me. I'm the only one who will put up with your shit."

He's silent for a moment. Then I hear the dial tone.

Dick.

I lean back and think about what he said. It's true, all of this happened around that time, but I've been over this so many times. I really could use another set of eyes, someone who was with Aaron, because it seems the key to all of this is in Afghanistan.

"Hey," Lee says softly from the doorway, breaking me from my thoughts.

"Sparkles! Back from your honeymoon so soon? Liam couldn't get it up, huh? The juice will do that to you." I grin as I taunt her.

They got married a few months ago, but decided to hold off on a honeymoon until after she had Shane. Liam's dad was all too happy to watch the ankle biter while they went off to the islands. Aaron, her ex, has been really good with everything, thank God, especially about their daughter, Aarabelle. Any time he can get with that kid, he takes. I don't blame him; she makes all of us behave a little more.

"Why are you so hell-bent on making people want to punch you in the throat?" She pops her hip and narrows her eyes. She's so cute when she's hostile. I love having her working here. Cole Security Forces has been thriving with Natalie's help. She gets things done that the guys just can't seem to take care of.

I shrug as she enters. "How's Liam handling going from bachelor to father of two?"

Her eyes light up and I have to force myself not to puke. "He's on diaper duty and doing well. We're doing good though, since I think that's what you're asking. And I guess the 'roids are what caused your shrinkage?"

"Oh, good one." I stand and start unbuttoning my pants.

"What the hell are you doing?"

"Proving mine is bigger. I figure you must be in need since you cut the trip short. I can satisfy you." Instead of flushing or giving a hint of embarrassment, she grabs the closest item off the table and chucks it at me.

"Sit down, you dipshit."

"I'm just making sure I don't have to kick his ass."

She puts the paper on the desk with a smirk, "Oh, Twilight. You're old. I'm pretty sure he could kick your ass with his eyes closed, but thanks for the sentiment."

"You forget who taught these younger idiots how to handle their shit. And fuck you very much. I'm not old. I prefer 'seasoned'."

"Same thing."

"I'm not even forty yet."

"Yet."

Natalie is one of the few females I don't mind being around. Thankfully, Catherine is the other. They both can verbally spar with the best of them. It also helps that they're both hot. Not that I would ever touch them, but there's something about a sexy woman mouthing off.

"Is that how you should address a man of the cloth?"

"Oh, for the love of . . ."

"Do not finish that sentence, my child." Her eyes roll as I fight back a laugh.

"Mark," she huffs. "You have issues."

As if I didn't know that. I've had issues for a long time, but my friend's issues were far worse. I was able to take some of the stuff, put it to the side, and focus on functioning. There's not a part of me that doesn't think I fought hard to save those guys. Jackson and I have always been close, but Brian was like a brother to me. We went through hell together during jump school. I was there when his wife left him, when he lost his house, married again, and then when he took his last breath. To lose him of all the guys was hard, but you can't do anything except move forward.

"Only issue I have is being in love with you," I joke.

Lee raises her hands then let them fall. "I give up."

"What's this paper?" I ask, bringing the conversation back to whatever led her here.

She sits with a sigh. "I can't get hold of the contact person in Egypt. It's a small team that's guarding a diplomat. He didn't trust his last company, so he hired us. I worked really hard to secure this account. Assured him that we could handle it. No one is able to get hold of anyone in their group."

Fucking shit. "How many checkpoints have they missed?" I keep myself under control. Could this be another blip? Sure. It could also be shitty reception on a satellite phone.

"Two."

"How the fuck is this happening?" I grumble.

Lee shifts. "I wish I had answers, but Liam thinks some-thing is really wrong. I've put him at ease because he trusts you guys . . ." she trails off.

If she were my wife, I'd be telling her to leave, too. Before I can say anything else, Aaron knocks.

"Hey," he says. "Lee, can you give us a minute?"

The former spouses smile their fake smiles, and she gets up. I gotta hand it to them. They both act way more mature than I would. Aaron really fucked up. He hurt Lee more than any of us probably know.

It was a mess.

And really awkward.

At the end of the day, she made her choice and he made his, but for Aara they keep their crap together. He always makes sure he's there for her, and Lee does her best not to make him feel alienated. I wish more divorces were like theirs.

That being said, if my wife marries my former best friend, can't say gloves would be off.

"What's up dickface?" I ask.

"I assume she told you?"

"Yeah, she did." I stand. "Jackson know?"

Aaron walks to the door, pulls it closed, and then releases a heavy sigh. "I don't think we should tell him."

"Have you lost your mind?" I'm not sure I heard him right.

He walks toward me with his hands up. "We don't have any information. Why would we go to him? Let's spend the next week doing what we're trained to do. I think all of our instances are related. Missing shipments, me being taken, Muff being shot, the mission in Egypt . . . it all centers on Jackson."

I know where he's going, but this is Jackson's company. Sure, I practically run the operation from here, but he funds it. He's in constant contact, monitors everything from California. He's even opened a field office out there to expand our reach. There's no way in hell I'm keeping things from him. I like my paycheck.

"I'm not saying you're wrong. I'm just not saying you're right."

"I need to *do* something," Aaron says while he cracks his knuckles. "I'm asking you to put me in charge of investigating this. Let me go back and figure out this whole thing."

Now I know I heard him wrong. "You're asking me . . . to send you back to Afghanistan?" I'm stunned. "Voluntarily?"

"I'm asking you to let me do what I know how to do."

Aaron was an interrogator. A damn good one. There's not a part of me that doesn't think he gathered something while over there. Something he's been harboring and festering over. I sure as hell would. A year of captivity is a long fucking time of quiet reflection with nothing to do but use your mind.

"What do you know?" There's no point in beating around the bush. It's like a meeting of the minds with us, each of us working to outsmart the other, all the while pissing each other off.

For second he looks stunned. "Same thing you know."

"Don't lie to me. Of all the people in this world, not me."

Aaron knows why. I've saved his ass more times than he can count. I've covered for him more than I ever should. I'm also not an idiot. I'm sure he knows something.

"All I know is a name."

I wait for an answer.

And wait.

Finally, I give him what he apparently needs. "And what name is that?"

"Al Mazir."

That just happens to be a name I've heard before, and I know just who my next call is going to be.

three

Charlie

"I UNDERSTAND, BUT I felt the mission was too far gone. I couldn't return to Afghanistan without being made," I explain to my handler for the third time. Debriefs are the worst. The conference room is large, but you feel so small. You go over every single angle, all the things you did right . . . and wrong. Of course, they tend to point out your errors more than anything. But I'm good. I'm damn good, and they know it.

"Charlie, there's a great deal of intelligence collected, but what about where the leader is hiding? That was your mission. You were supposed to relay the location of Al Mazir, report any suspected terrorists he was working with, and get the hell home." He flips through the very thick file I handed them. "I figured you would've gotten it after the first six months, not over two years. Instead, you come home, continue working and saying you're close by tracking him, but in essence you're in the same damn spot." Thomas looks up with disappointment.

If there's anything I hate, it's that look. One from not fulfilling the job I was sent to do. Did I get the info? No. But not for lack of trying. I spent over a year in that camp trying to gain access to the files I needed. I had to keep an injured American's location quiet because the mission comes first. I knew he had a wife and child who thought he was dead. My job was bigger than either him or me, though, so I did the best I could to keep him from dying, and then got us both the hell out of there. I sacrificed a lot and was so deep undercover that I started to miss check-ins, code words. I embodied Fahima Salib. I was *her* in every way, all to get what I needed—answers.

Some of the other members of the terrorist ring were becoming suspicious. I started to notice hushed voices when I came around. It became more difficult for me to move among the groups, and I wasn't sure anymore how close I could get. I figured they were meeting in other locations to discuss strategy; the safe house where they held Aaron was no longer their meet up.

"I gathered a lot more information than your other op did. Let's remember that I also managed to find an American hostage who was presumed dead, collected files no one else could, and managed to gain more intel in the last year than anyone else who has boots on ground there." My frustration grows, mostly at myself. Thomas would have a better chance of cutting my tongue out before I admit that, though.

"Your father would be—"

"Fuck you, Tom. You don't get to talk about him."

"I want you to take a few weeks off."

My jaw would drop if I weren't trained so well. "I'm sorry, I thought I heard you say *weeks*."

He stands, pushing the papers on the desk so they align. "I did."

I leap out of my chair. "I can't. You can't be serious. I'm one of the best you have. You can't let Al Mazir get weeks ahead of me."

"You're off his case. You need to take some time to get your head on straight. The operation went on too long. I should have taken you off when you got back with the hostage you found."

Tom strides out of the office, leaving me stunned.

He's been my supervisor for five years, and I've never once been removed from a case. I know everything there is to know about Mazir. No one in this office could pick up where I left off. I have deep-seated contacts. This is a mistake. It has to be.

I rush out after him but stop short.

"Hey, Charlie." Vanessa shifts in her seat, twisting her hands. I wish people would use the damn training we went through. I read her body language and the little nuances tell me she's nervous.

"What can I do for you?" I look past her to see if Tom is at his desk. If he refuses to listen, I'll go above his head.

She places her hand on my arm to bring my attention back to her. "I just wanted to say I'm really sorry about your dad. I know it's been a while, but we haven't had a chance to talk since it all happened."

"Thanks."

I don't do small talk or fake empathy. My father was the most brilliant mind that ever worked for the CIA. He was an asset to this country, a patriot through and through. He betrayed his homeland to protect this one. Then he was brutally murdered and left for dead at the hands of Al Mazir. There's no one in the entire world who wants Mazir more than I do.

"I know you still have a few more things to do with debrief, but I'd like to go over the case file and really pick your brain."

"Why?"

"Oh." She shifts again. "Didn't Tom tell you? I'm the new op on the case."

I close my eyes and count to five to calm myself.

1. He wouldn't.
2. He couldn't.
3. Would he?
4. He did. Motherfucker . . . he did.

5.   I need a vacation.

I look back at Vanessa, who now appears as if she's gloating. "I can't talk now. I need to just think, okay?"

She nods. "Sure thing." Her smile grows before she walks off in the other direction.

Tom isn't at his desk, my co-workers refuse to make eye contact, and my mind won't stop spinning. None of this makes any sense. I've seen people do way worse than not gather one small piece of information and still be left on the case. Even though this "small" thing is really a large gaping hole, but that's beside the point. I've invested so much time. I know the area, the locals, the entire backstory, and with the help of the ground operative there, I'm so close to figuring out where Mazir is. My asset has been guiding me, which has allowed me to guide him. This is either personal or they don't want me to uncover something.

Director Asher and I are going to have a meeting. There's no way in hell I'll just go quietly into the dark. My gut tells me there's way more to this than meets the eye.

The phone rings at my desk.

"Hello," I say, still trying to wrap my mind around being pulled from a case.

"Charlie?" I recognize the voice instantly. Mark Dixon. As if this day couldn't get any more complicated.

"Hello, Mark. What can I possibly do for you?" I smile despite my shit mood. He and I had spent the entire flight home talking. He's funny, sexy as hell, but more than that, he just makes me smile—something I haven't done a lot since I lost my father. I worked with Mark for a week when we got back from Aaron's rescue but it yielded nothing. Then I had to leave for Dubai to track down an informant, and things returned to life as usual. Except he still calls randomly, and I smile despite myself.

"Don't ask questions you don't want answers to, princess."

Good mood gone. "You want your balls in a vice? Call me

princess again and see how fast I get to Virginia Beach and you lose them."

"You just want to touch my balls," he retorts. "Besides, maybe that's my plan. Get you here."

"If you had any." I smirk.

I picture him leaning back in his chair, longish blond hair pushed back, scruff painting his face, and his green eyes filled with mischief. Mark Dixon would bring any woman to her knees. Good thing I'm not just any woman. We've interacted a bunch of times since the Aaron rescue. He came up with Aaron once to talk, and then I travelled down there. It's not normal protocol, but after all Aaron went through, it was important. My handler urged me to help him through it, since no one else really could.

"Anytime you want to play with my balls, you just call me."

"Why did you call me?" I try to bring the conversation back on point. I have no idea what he could need. It's been over three months since we last saw each other.

He pauses. "We need your help."

That had to take a lot for him to admit. "How so?"

"Another shipment of ammo was sent, to Africa this time. It's . . . well, missing. I personally set up that transport. I double-checked it. And some of my guys aren't checking in. Someone is still fucking with us, and I can't seem to uncover it. Aaron made mention of something, and I thought of you."

"I'm sure you think of me more than I think of you."

He laughs. "Doubtful. I'm always on your mind."

"Anyway," I draw the word out. "What are you thinking?"

On the flight back with Aaron, I had overheard them speculating. There were too many variables that all seemed to lead back to the head of the company. Jackson Cole was a good man from what I observed, but red flags were everywhere.

First, they had issues in Afghanistan, which lead to Aaron going there in the first place. Everyone but him was killed when his convoy was attacked. Then, when Jackson and Mark went out to assess the incident, they were shot at. Jackson sustained life-threatening injuries and was flown out immediately. However, after following a ton of leads, nothing ended anywhere solid. Everyone checked out, so we let it go.

"Aaron mentioned a name," he says cryptically. "Jackson wants this shit to stop. And to be honest, I do too. It doesn't make sense, though. I've used all my contacts in the FBI and they say everyone within the company is clear. Nothing has surfaced or been suspicious. So, that leads me to think it's someone outside the US."

It's definitely a possibility, but what name would Aaron know? "Maybe, but why Cole Security Forces?"

"Why not? We're all former SEALs, we've all killed, and we've all been involved at one time or another with taking down terrorist shit. Plus, we still do. We protect bases and take missions that others are too scared to accept. I mean, you can tell me where you're confused on why they wouldn't want to stop us." His deep voice only grows deeper in his anger.

Before I can say anything, Tom walks by. "I gotta go. I'll call soon." I disconnect the call and run to save my career.

MY PHONE HAS BEEN ringing non-stop. My brother and mother won't leave me alone. We all knew what my father did. He recruited me when he noticed I had a knack for the business. Now, it seems to be the excuse used for every mishap in our lives. Dominic didn't get into the college he wanted because Dad was a spy and refused to move. Mom didn't get the head of the last charity she was involved in because Dad was a spy and it wouldn't look right. I'm not married because Dad was a spy, which is totally untrue. It's because the men I've dated are idiots.

Dad was a good man and a good father, despite his absences.

I always had the feeling when he was gone that he was doing something great. To most girls, I'm sure that's an impossible idea. I knew, though. I always felt as if he spent his time away doing something to protect us. I pretended he had covert missions to save the world one bad guy at a time. By the time I was old enough to realize what he actually did, he was recruiting me.

I love my job. I love my life. I sure as hell don't need a man to try to bring me down a notch. Being a female in this industry isn't easy. I'm always looked at as lesser than the men, so I work twice as hard.

"What?" I yell into the receiver.

"If you answered the damn phone when I called the first ten times, I wouldn't need to keep calling," my mother practically whispers. Her voice never raises an octave. She would've been a kick ass spy.

"I didn't want to talk."

"Clearly."

"Yet, you keep calling." I tap my foot. There are very few people in the world who can scare me. She's one of them. However, I still instigate fights with her. My mother is somehow able to twist me into believing everyone else is wrong, even if there is photographic evidence that proves otherwise. It's the most amazing thing to watch, but never fun to be on the receiving end of.

She sighs and I picture her running her hand through her onyx hair. "Don't test me." She pauses. "I'm hosting a gala in memory of your father. You're to be there this time. I don't care if the president orders you to Timbuktu, you're coming."

"When?"

My father's cover still has to be kept for appearance's sake. My mother's really the strongest woman I know. Having to carry on the façade for our entire lives wasn't easy, but she did it with a smile. I'm sure my father paid heavily for it, yet her place by his side never waivered. My brother and I grew up with more love than two kids could ask for. We were happy, considering our father did a lot of things we may never know about.

"In two weeks. And Charisma?" She's the only person alive who is allowed to call me by my name.

"Yes, Mother?"

"Bring a date. No one likes to see you walking around and drinking alone. It makes me second-guess not setting up that arranged marriage," she says and then disconnects the call.

I swear there are times I contemplate making an anonymous tip to Homeland Security that she's a terrorist. However, I'm sure she'd find a way to swear I defected against my country.

The loss of my father did a number on her, no matter what she shows. She loved him more than anything. He left a void in all our lives, but my mother—I can only imagine. I'm still amazed by the fact my father had it all. A wife, children, plus the job he lived for. I, on the other hand, can't seem to manage any of it.

My phone pings. It's one of my most favorite people in the world, my brother Dominic.

> *Dom: You're going to this stupid thing. I'm not going to keep pulling your weight.*

> *Me: Or what?*

> *Dom: Mom is killing me! She's up my ass, asking when I'm going to marry. She knows you're a lost cause.*

I roll my eyes. I'm not a lost cause, I just haven't found anyone man enough.

> *Me: I'll think about going.*

> *Dom: I'll tell her you want to go shopping for a dress.*

Me: I'll tell her you're running for senate.

I can imagine his face. The fact he's taken a few minutes to reply tells me he's staring at the phone with his jaw slack. Of course, there are only three people who know about his plans, and I'm not supposed to be one of them. I toss the phone and head into my home office.

This room gives me peace.

Once I'm inside, I close and lock the door, unstrap the gun from around my thigh, and pull the laptop down from its hiding place. To the normal person, this is simply an office. It has light-blue walls, white eyelet curtains, and a huge white desk. It's clean, neat, and deadly. This room is wired so I can see and hear anything in the entire apartment.

There are also more trap doors than anyone can image. Slowly, I pull the file that sits hidden between two others—the one that haunts my dreams; the only case I can't solve—and hesitate to open it. I know every detail. Each word is engrained in my mind, but I can't stop myself. I look every single day, hoping that maybe I find something I missed, and I can finally put a bullet in the asshole responsible for killing my father.

Mark

WHAT A DAY. I key in the alarm code and grab a beer from the fridge. My house is quiet, exactly the way I like it. This place is my only retreat from the crazy. I don't take work home. I don't even have an office. Just a man cave that all my friends hate me for.

I bought my bungalow in Sandbridge on the outskirts of Virginia Beach when I was stationed here years ago. It's small, but it's just me. The Sandbridge area is a hike to work, but it's like living on my own private island.

With my beer in hand, I head off to the beach. Once I get to my favorite spot, I sit watching a few surfers and the sea stretched out in front of me.

The conversation with Aaron replays like a loop. So many things don't add up, which makes me skeptical about his hunch. What the hell does Al Mazir have to do with any of us? He wasn't a target on our missions. I don't even think that terrorist ring was in action back when I was a SEAL, or if it was, it didn't have the same leaders. The region we were in during our active time was more Iraq or Libya based, although I don't know that it matters. Each time I think I have a handle on it something else throws me off.

Then, there's the fact he wants to keep it from Muff, which I'd never do. There are some lines you don't cross. Jackson would never get over being betrayed by one of us.

"Hey, Mark!" my neighbor Tiffany yells from the surf.

I should've brought my board. I always think better in the water.

I stand to greet her and push my hair back. "Hey, Tiff." I smile. "How're the waves?"

Her wetsuit clings to her body like a glove. She's beautiful with her long dark hair, brown eyes, and killer curves. But we've already had that dance, and I've learned not to put your dick in places it can get slapped again. Luckily, Tiffany is cool and never wanted more than one night. According to her, I was a conquest, which works just fine for me.

"It's good surfing! Go grab your board, there's still time before the sun sets."

I look up at the sky and I could get in maybe an hour. "Let me—" My phone cuts me off.

Charlie. This woman is one I'd give my left nut to tame—or try to.

"I'll catch you later. I need to take this call," I call off to Tiffany as I trudge up the beach.

I double-time it over a dune where the wind isn't so bad. "I knew you couldn't resist me." I grin. She's probably already wishing she didn't call.

"Oh, yes." The sarcasm is clear in her phone sex operator voice. "You're just always on my mind, Dixon."

"I'd be happy to make you the next Mrs. Dixon."

She scoffs, "I'm good."

I smile at the opening she leaves. "That's still to be determined."

"You'll never know."

"I'll take that bet."

Charlie is the type of girl I would never imagine hooking up with. She's definitely not my usual flavor. I like them tall; she's tiny with an attitude the size of Texas. I like them blonde; her hair is practically black. Then there's her body. I've always gone for the more Twinkie-type girls, but Charlie has curves. Her body is a weapon, one I'd like to take apart and get to know.

"Are you done now?" she asks. "I called for a reason."

"Of course you did, Charlotte," I joke.

She groans, and my grin spreads. "My name isn't Charlotte, you asshole. Do you want my help? Or would you rather the company you work for continue to get screwed with?"

That got my attention. "Yes, Charleston, I want your help."

"Fuck you."

"Anytime, baby. All I need is a time and place."

"I would destroy you." Her voice drops low and menacing.

"I have no doubt. You're one of those black widow type girls. A man-eater. But I'd gladly take the kill."

Charlie doesn't respond. She just let's out a long breath.

"Okay, I'm sorry. You called because you have info?"

I can almost hear the internal struggle. The want to help, the want to not help, and then finally the resolution of what's the right thing to do. We're alike in that way. We both are willing to die for the greater good. I'm just way more badass than she ever could be.

"I'll let you help me under one condition," she finally warns.

"What's that?"

"You understand who's in charge. This is my case, I'm bringing you in, and therefore, I call the shots."

I smile because the bottom line is that I'll tell her anything she wants to hear. This has been my life for years, not some case. Whoever is responsible for all of this has destroyed the lives of people who matter. I consider Aaron and Jackson to be family.

You fuck with my family and all bets are off.

Instead of playing my hand too early, I simply reply with what I need to say. "Deal."

"Then get up to DC and I'll read you in."

"Thanks, Charlize."

"I regret this already," she mumbles, then disconnects the call.

"THAT'S ALL YOU'RE GOING to tell me," Jackson grumbles through the line.

Needless to say, he's not happy about me leaving for DC. However, he doesn't have a choice. "Want me to make stuff up?"

"I want you to tell me what you know."

"I know nothing more than you know. She wants to help, thinks we can work together and find out what the hell is going on. What else do you want to know, Muff?" I can't give him information that I don't have.

"I'll talk to Catherine, we'll head back east. I need to be in the office if you're not there."

I laugh. I know how that conversation will end. Jackson's balls will be comfortably sitting in her palm, where they are now, and he'll still be in California. If the company wasn't growing as fast as it was, it wouldn't be a problem. I run the Virginia office while Jackson expands into an office near San Diego. We're each positioned to run side by side near the closest naval base. Plus, it's where the SEAL teams are based. It makes sense, makes recruiting easy, and makes us a lot of money.

"Stay where you are, man. Natalie is here, and she can manage more than we give her. Aaron is fully capable, too." I laugh at the idea of leaving them together. "Plus, Erik has been taking on more. He'll handle the communication system since Aaron is tied up with other stuff. Besides," I pause. "There's no way Cat will be on board with this. She's got her clients and can't leave. Let's not forget, your office is barely even up yet. What will you do here that you can't do from there?"

He huffs. "I want to be kept informed."

"No."

"No?"

"You heard me . . . no."

"This is my fucking company, in case you forgot." I can hear the anger rolling off him.

He needs to keep his hands clean. If this goes south, which it could, he needs to be completely clear. "Listen, I'm not going to explain all the reasons you need to have no knowledge of the shit I may need to do, but I'll sum it up in two words: plausible deniability."

"Mark."

"No. I'm not telling you shit. I'm doing this my way so you can be happy in California with Catherine. I'm the only one in this goddamn group who has nothing to lose."

"I'm not okay with this."

"I really don't care."

"As your boss I'm ordering you to keep me informed."

"Eh . . ." I pause. "I'll think about it."

"You're a fucking pain in my ass."

"And you're ugly."

Jackson sighs. "I'll hold tight until I need to. Look . . ." He pauses. "We need to talk about what you keep avoiding."

"Not now."

"Mark," he chides. "I'm serious. I want you to buy in, become my partner."

"Good bye, Muff."

I hang up the phone and push back from my desk. I should be happy—thrilled, ecstatic even—that he wants me to become his partner, but I'm not. It's not because of the issues that seem to plague it. My entire post-military life has been about Cole

Security Forces, but that's just it. How much more do I need to make this my life? Is this all I'm destined to have? Jackson has Catherine. Liam and Natalie are married and making babies. Even Aaron has moved on and started dating.

I'm just here.

Stuck.

Stagnant.

Mark the eternal funny guy. Yet, I'm the one they all come crying to because they can't keep their lives together. People get shot, divorced, screw up because they can't just tell each other the truth. I'm not sure if I want to do this for the rest of my life. I may want to open up a surf shop in Hawaii, but if I buy into this, I wouldn't be able to. Typical Jackson, though, he's on his time-line and is pushing me.

I spend the next few hours wrapping up anything I can here. My e-mails are cleared, now I just need to meet with the team.

Everyone sits in the meeting room with weary eyes.

"Welcome, my people!" I boom as I enter. Natalie smirks, Aaron looks unimpressed, Erik laughs, and the rest of our team just appear confused. The only thing that shocks me is Liam standing in the back of the room with his arms crossed. "Well, it seems we have a new employee."

Liam tips his chin down and eyes me cautiously.

Interesting.

"I'm just here to pick up my wife. She informed me that you were addressing the team. I figured I'd save her the hassle of re-playing everything."

Half of me wants to kick his ass, put him in his place be-cause we're not in the Navy here. The other half wants to clap him on the back and congratulate him on his balls dropping.

"Okay." I clap my hands, loudly drawing their attention back. "I have some information to go over, and it's going to be a while."

Charlie

"YES, I UNDERSTAND." MY mind is at war with my mouth. I can't seem to say all the things I want to. It's years and years of perfecting my self-control, now coming to bite me in the ass. The truth is . . . I don't understand one single thing.

"We're not fully removing you, Charlie." Tom sounds as though he actually believes the bullshit he's spewing.

"I'm not sure we have the same definition of 'off the case'."

My debrief lasted an additional four days. Since Vanessa needed to go over all of my notes, I was required to play more of their mindfuck games. It's the one part of this job I truly hate. It's hours of questioning, a polygraph, and then more interrogation about what you already said. It's easy to lie, but when you're forced to remember each detail of a lie, you're likely to screw up. They know this. We all know this, but I've been trained since I was a kid to believe the lie. To make that my truth. It's the reason any of us can pass a polygraph with flying colors. It's true to me, because I've made it so. With that, though, comes loneliness.

Even after I told the actual truth—no spin, no half stories, no chance of slipping up, even though that would never happen—they remove me from the case completely. I want to lose it.

"It's a break. A chance to recharge."

"Don't insult me, Tom. Placating me isn't really your style." I sneer.

"You're too close to the target, the case, the entire thing. You missed check-ins. Your handler was left in the dark too often. You were reckless. You lost Mazir and compromised your cover. There are more minuses than plusses in these columns. The Director wants you off the case. That's the end of this discussion."

I hold myself together. There's a bigger picture, one they fail to see. So I'll take my lumps—for now.

My mouth forms a thin line. "I can't say anything because you've made your decisions. I'd like to take leave from the agency."

Tom is good. He doesn't flinch or appear at all surprised. His eyes don't shift or widen. But his cheek twitches. It's a small sign, but it gives me a tiny thrill that I was able to catch him slightly off guard.

"Charlie," my handler, Mandi, says calmly. "Don't."

She's been my partner, so to speak, for six years. I've been fortunate to have Mandi since the beginning. My life has been in her hands. She's guided me, made my covers reality, and now she's turning her back on me.

There was no question as to why I had to stay quiet. I wasn't dark; I was playing a part. My cover had been carefully crafted. When my father was killed, it was imperative I *became* Fahima. I had to become an orphan who wanted to serve and belong, as well as help with the missions of her country. I needed to hate freedom. I needed to hate my country in order to infiltrate them. *Any means necessary* was what I was told. Apparently, that included rules I was unaware of. But her testimony sealed my fate.

I stand with new life flowing through my veins. I didn't think the decision would be reversed, which is why I already put plans in motion. Mark should be here later today, and I'll continue my work without the agency behind me. "I've already filled out the paperwork." I hand the leave request over. "I think I've earned a vacation in the sun and sand, don't you?"

Mandi's eyes give too much away. It's why she couldn't be in the field. She knows me, though. Our jobs required us to trust each other. I don't think for one second she believes this is over.

She would be right.

"Charlie, I think you're making a mistake." Mandi's voice shakes at the end. "I know you feel—"

"You have no idea how I feel," I cut her off. "I'm taking some time to spend with my mother. I need to grieve the loss of my father. My life has been this case. My life has been this job. You decided I failed; therefore, I'm going to take some time for myself. I'll be out of the country, which is on the paperwork. I plan to enjoy the sun." I say it with such conviction that I almost believe myself. Almost.

Tom stares me down without giving anything away and signs the document. "We'll be waiting for you to come back. I urge you not to miss the check-in. Forty-five days, and if you miss a single one for any reason, I won't have options. I can grant you an extension, but I have a feeling we'll be seeing you prior to the first six months."

Meaning that if I don't check in, I won't be able to come back at all. I'm fairly certain he has his suspicions as to what I'm up to. Any spy would do this. He would do this. There's more at stake than just finding my father's killer. It's also about taking a very deadly and blood thirsty terrorist down. Even though there's nothing connecting Mazir to my father's death, I'm certain he was. Call it a hunch. Call it intuition, but either way, I'll have my answers soon.

"Thank you." I stand, grab my clutch, and walk away, completely on my own.

Well, except for the former Navy SEAL who's on his way. What was I thinking when I called him?

One Week Later

HE'S LATE.

I don't do late.

I check my watch for the tenth time, then my phone, and my watch again. He's got exactly one minute.

My phone rings and Mark's name pops up.

"You better have some fantastic excuse planned," I warn.

"How many more times are you going to check your watch?"

I scan the area.

"You're spying on me." I laugh.

"I out-spooked the spook."

He seems genuinely pleased with himself. I'm impressed. Well, and irritated with him—and myself.

"I didn't know I had to be on my A-game with you." I fight the smile that forms knowing he's watching. Last thing I need is him to have a read on me.

But the reality is that I like him. He makes me laugh, which isn't easy. The adrenaline rush wore off on the plane, which caused my impenetrable armor to develop a small gap. He found it and used it. I'd be lying if I said I didn't enjoy it a little. Feeling like a woman, allowing myself to laugh, joke around a little, just have fun. Mark knows who I am. I don't have to lie and use my alias. There is no need to talk about antiques, which I hate. They seriously gave me the worst cover story ever. I would've rather had to study biology over antiquities.

"I'm more than just a pretty face, Charlene."

This is going to be when I kill him. My real name is *my*

secret. My mother still feels the need to use it but never around anyone else, and sometimes not even in private. There's something about my name. It's sacred to me, and the only piece of me I've never given away.

"You guessed it." I roll my eyes.

"Nope, you just told me I didn't." I continue to look around for him.

I grab my coffee cup and put my earpiece in. Once I stand, I go on autopilot, trying to look like the antiquities dealer I'm supposed to be. My long black hair is in a low bun. My knee-length pencil skirt clings tightly to my legs, and my pearls adorn my neck. I smile to the cute little girl sitting with her mother who's too busy on her phone to notice the chocolate all over the girls face. I hoist my Michael Kors tote over my shoulder and scan the area as I walk. "Are we going to play this game or are you going to be a man and face me?" I ask.

"Well, Charity. If I'm going to work with you, I need to see just how good you are. So, if you can find me, I'll be happy to let you have me . . . and my skills." His deep voice is layered with the challenge.

"Mark," I say as sexily as I can. I hate using the female card, but I want him slightly confused. "What do I win if I find you?"

He groans softly, yet loud enough for me to hear. Almost as if he couldn't help himself. "What?" he starts to say then stops. "Well . . ." Mark chuckles.

"Marco," I tease.

"Polo," he replies.

"I'm not new at this."

"Neither am I."

"Seems the question now is: who is better?"

Mark doesn't answer. I start to peek my head out of the alley I ducked into so I could survey the area more discreetly. Arms wrap around my torso and pull me back. I raise my foot, prepared to stomp.

"Ahh, you wouldn't want to do that, Charlie." Mark's voice is against my ear. "I'm just as well trained at self-defense, and I don't have any issues with kicking your ass."

I let my muscles relax. His strong arms hold my back effortlessly against his brick wall of a chest. Instead of fighting him, I try to pretend being in his arms doesn't feel good. I tell myself that he's part of the mission, he's a liability, but the warmth of his body blankets me and makes me want to stay here.

I need to get out of his arms, but I can't seem to get my body to cooperate.

This is going to be a problem. A big one.

Shut it down, Charlie.

"You should put me down before you get hurt."

"You should never let your guard down if you want my protection and skills."

I scoff. I don't need him. Mark releases me but keeps his hands on my hips. I shove his arms down and step forward. "Let's get one thing straight." I turn and point my finger in his face. "You called me. You asked for my help. I'm not the one having my men shot and kidnapped, who has things going missing and people running into issues." I raise my brow and wait for him to protest. That's what he should do. I wait for the words because I'm goading him to react.

But he doesn't.

What is with this guy? Does he do the opposite of everything he should? Why can't he just act like a typical person? *Because he isn't one.* He may not have undergone the training I did, but he's still highly trained. Mark and I are both reading each other, only right now . . . he's doing a better job.

"You done? Feel better? Assert your bullshit idea of dominance? Because you're going to see really quickly that I'm always on top. I'll top you even from the bottom, princess. You should get used to it."

I want to put a bullet between his eyes. "Think what you need to. I've never been on the bottom, and I never will be. So buckle up buttercup and get ready to be second in command." I'm half joking and half testing him. I need to really gauge him. I don't trust him fully. Then again, he probably doesn't trust me, either. "I'm . . ." I pause. I don't know what I am. "*Ugh!*" I groan.

"Sorry is the word you're looking for."

"We're going to have to check our egos for this to work, Mark. I don't know you and you don't know me. But we have one thing tying us together." We stand in the shadowed alleyway in a standoff.

"Love?" he jokes.

I laugh despite myself. "No. Let's be real and talk."

"Fine, talk to me."

I look around because the hair on the back of my neck prickles. "We need to get out of here." Someone is here, watching, listening, and now it's time to do what I do best. "I've missed you." I smile while I use the tip of my finger to trace his jawline.

Mark's eyes shift over my head as he pulls me flush against his body. We're both facing exits. "I've missed you more," he plays along.

This might just work. He's on alert as well and senses something awry. His fingers splay across my lower back as he holds me close. "Maybe we should head back to my place so you can show me just how much." I glance over his shoulder. His long blonde hair falls in his eyes as he dips his head into my neck. I know the move, but a shiver runs down my spine.

"You'd like that, wouldn't you?" I let out a very low moan, which I didn't give permission to escape. Mark's lips glide across my skin.

I'm not sure he's acting.

I'm not even sure that I am.

Then Mark reminds me this is serious. "There are two guys behind you." His voice is low enough that only I can hear him. To anyone passing, we're two lovers reacquainting ourselves. "One at my two o'clock, and the other just moved out of my view."

"One just passed behind you twice. I think going toward my exit is best." I snuggle closer. "I'm ready when you are." The double meaning is meant for anyone to hear, but Mark should know it means I'm ready to disappear. "You'll have to keep up, though."

He leans back while cupping my face. His lips hover over mine. "I don't have any problems keeping you satisfied, princess."

My pulse spikes. I know he can hear it, feel it, see in my eyes that I'm affected. My breaths are shallow as his hands slowly make their way down my arms.

"Arrogant prick," I mutter.

I can tell he'd be an incredible lover. His overconfidence would only play to my benefit. We're both cut from the same cloth, ready to fight for dominance. He'd win, though. I can see it in his eyes. There would be no battle, Mark has already won. Right now, he controls me. He determines whether we kiss, what it'll be like, and for the first time in my life—I surrender.

His lips come closer. "They're closing in," he whispers, his eyes locked on me. "Charlie?" he asks.

"What?" My voice is barely audible.

"This will happen again when we don't have to fight off people, and you'll be mine."

I don't have time to reply. His lips crash down on mine as he spins me around so he leads our exit. The second our mouths collide, my brain disconnects. My fingers tangle in his long blonde hair, grabbing it to pull him close. Mark's hands hold my face to his and he continues to guide me. I know we're moving but I have no idea to where. In this instant, I don't care. Never has someone made me feel so desperate for them. I never lose control, never feel so lost, yet right now, I am. I'm raw, exposed, and completely vulnerable.

And it's only a damn kiss.

Mark pulls my face back all too soon as we slip into the crowd. He takes my hand, pulls out a ball cap, and slips it onto my head. To disguise his clothing, he removes his button up shirt while he pulls me along. "Damn, you're a good actress. I almost bought that," he says, only wheezing slightly. "They got close enough I could hear a word or two, but nothing I could make out."

I can't get air into my lungs fast enough. "Yeah," I say half-heartedly. My walls go up fast as I shut down. "Did we lose them?"

"Let's keep moving. Were you able to get a description of the guy behind me?" He pulls out his phone. "Six-foot-three, short black hair, tattoo on the left arm, wearing a white shirt and black shorts. Mediterranean descent, spoke in either Italian or Spanish, but couldn't hear enough." He speaks into the recorder.

I just stare, trying to process what the hell just happened.

We were kissing, or I was kissing him, while he was watching the person following us and guiding us away.

I'm the CIA agent.

One of the *best* CIA agents.

I'm the daughter of the former Director of the CIA. I was born and raised to be the best.

Mark just did my job. He was in control, acting.

But I stopped acting somewhere back there, and that's a problem.

A very big problem.

six

W E GET BACK TO my apartment and I check for anything out of place. My house is a map—everything leads me to something else. I follow the exact same routine each day, and if something is missing or even a half an inch off, I'll know.

"So the guy moved too fast for you?" Mark asks me again.

"Are you hard of hearing?"

"Why didn't you ever bring me here before? This place is different." He looks around at my things and adds, "I'm just surprised. I figured you'd have his name already. Aren't you like a super spy?"

"I don't have X-ray vision. Plus, you were spinning me and moving me. It's kind of hard when I'm not leading." I turn and glare at him. "Stop touching things!"

"Oh . . ." he nods. "You're one of *those* kind of girls. Got it."

My jaw falls slack. "What kind of girl is that?"

"Tell me again how you failed to get the description of the other guy."

I want to slap that damn smirk off his face. Instead, I decide to focus on what we know and what I need to do. First, is to learn why I'm being tailed. Second, find out who it is and if it's the agency behind it, which wouldn't surprise me. My father had me shadow people after they took leave. We needed to be sure they weren't doing, well, exactly what I'm doing.

I can't screw this up.

"Mark," my tone is serious. "We need to talk. In here." We enter my very seemingly girly office.

"Never pegged this one."

"You make an awful lot of assumptions, buddy."

I know I'm not the typical girl. I don't give off the make-up and hair vibe, but I'm the fox in sheep's clothing. I should buy stock in Sephora with as much as I buy. I love to feel like a woman, especially because I live in a man's world. It's my one indulgence. Well, that and shoes. And purses. Okay, I'll just say I have a serious shopping addiction. Just because I fight like a man doesn't mean I can't feel like a lady.

He steps close, and I defend myself against his presence. The fact that he affects me at all doesn't bode well. I'm not sure why this man out of any can make me slip even a little. Could be because I haven't gotten laid in far too long. Sure, I'll go with that. I just need sex, and then I'll be over this little . . . whatever it is.

"I think you'll be happy to know I've been wrong more often than right. You're nothing like I expected. I imagined your office would be colder, sterile, like the illusion you give off." His eyes don't move from mine. "Instead, it's warm, beautiful, and comforting, which is what I think you are deep down. You have a tough exterior, but inside, I think there's more."

"Don't pretend like you know me."

"I know more than you'd like," he jeers.

"You think that."

"Princess, there's a lot a man can tell about a woman when her tongue is in his mouth. I know you wanted me. I know your breathing was shallow, your heart was racing." He steps closer. "You loved fisting my hair, pulling me more into your body. You kissed me like I gave you life." He shifts even closer. "I could do it right now, and you'd let me."

I move closer to him this time. I see in his eyes that he'd be all too happy for another round. I'm not playing this game, though. I'm here for one thing—to avenge my father's death. To destroy the people who've made my life miserable. This is an assignment I can't lose, and Mark won't be the variable to thwart my plans.

"I'll tell you what I want." I smile and then take my lip between my teeth. Seduction is a game I'm very good at. "I want you . . ." I pause, closing the distance. "To let me show you . . ." My body moves sensually as I push nearer. My hand presses against his chest as I move him back.

His eyes darken. "Show me what?"

Putty in my hands.

"Trust me?"

He smiles and wraps his fingers around my arms like a vice. "Fuck no, I don't. I see through you, Charlie. You may be good at playing this game, but you don't know who your opponent is." Mark pulls me against his body. "You underestimate me, but I sure as hell don't think you see me as a threat." His lips close in.

Fuck me. This isn't what the hell should be happening. Again.

"Which is your biggest . . ." He glides closer. "Fucking . . ." His lips ghost across mine. "Mistake."

He can read me. He sees through it, but I'm the world's best actress. It's time to play as if I expected this. "Ahh!" I lean back, smirking. "And you just played right into my trap. If we're going to work together, you'll need to be better at figuring out the end game."

He releases me and bursts out laughing. He clutches his stomach as it rolls through him. "Okay, Charlie. Whatever you say."

This new emotion runs through me. I'm not sure if it's embarrassment or fear, since I'm not acquainted with either. He terrifies me, though. The fact he can sense when I'm bluffing seeds doubt. What if Mark is somehow involved in all this?

"Maybe we should talk another time." I start to second-guess reading him in.

"What?" he asks in disbelief. "You're joking, right? Because I didn't drive up here and save your ass to have you back out." Mark's arms cross as he plops himself on my chair. "You want me gone? You're going to have to drag my ass out."

"We can't cross lines. There's too much at stake to even re-motely play games with each other." I go for honesty. Maybe if he sees, he'll stop pushing the buttons I wasn't aware I have.

"I agree. You'll have to keep your hands to yourself." He raises a brow.

"Is everything a joke to you?"

"Pretty much."

"This won't work," I huff out.

"Start talking, Charlie. We have a mutually important issue here. I don't know what yours is, but you know mine. If anyone is at a disadvantage, it's me. I came on your terms. I would've much rather had the upper hand."

That's partly true. I have the cards and the information he wants. Mark, Jackson, and Aaron are the ones who are trying to wade through the dark. Of course, I don't have anything con-crete on who's pulling the strings, but I have a hunch. I know Al Mazir is involved. They tortured Aaron for information he didn't have. And if Mark knows a name that Aaron figured out, I would bet my house that's why he's here.

I know bluffing. I know dying before giving up anything. I also know very subtle things the human body can't lie about. But as well trained as I am, and as damn good as I am, I have a tell.

"I have to be able to trust you, Mark. I need to know that no matter what, you're in this. One hundred percent."

Mark stands. "I will find out the information I need with or without you. I think if we work together, we'll accomplish a hell of a lot more and a lot faster. Trust works both ways. How do I know the CIA isn't somehow involved in this? What if you're trying to gather something from me? I don't know if you are, so I have to trust you. You're not the only one taking a risk, but answer me this . . ." He seems to weigh his words. "You know everything about me, I'm sure. You know how long I was a SEAL, my service record, the medals I've been awarded, and the people I've killed, but what do I know about you?"

"Nothing," I answer, because he's right. "It's meant to be that way."

"Exactly. So again I ask, who is taking the real risk?"

"We both are."

"Wrong answer," he says and turns to head out the door.

"What are you doing?"

He stops at the threshold. "Leaving. When you're ready to tell me everything, no holds barred, feel free to call me. Until then, good luck, Charlie."

My mind is at war. I have choices, we all do, but hesitation isn't something I have time for. Mark is my best shot at having someone smart, cunning, and ready to do whatever needs to be done for answers. He won't flinch if we have to do something unethical.

The choice is mine, and maybe I'm playing into his hands. Maybe he isn't being transparent, but my gut says he is. "Stop," I command. "I'd rather save you another trip up."

He turns, walks back in the room, and resumes his last location. Mark doesn't gloat or rub it in my face. Instead, he sits quietly and waits.

I turn on the monitors behind the one-way mirror, press the button that engages the steel door, effectively locking us in and ensuring no one can overhear, and activate the high frequency noise in case someone planted bugs. The trap door under my desk opens and I pull the file out.

"You're going to share the name of your decorator," Mark jokes.

I can't say I don't enjoy the awe in his eyes. I have more safeguards in this space than anyone could guess. But I needed a place where I could escape, hide, and sometimes lock myself away. "You're not high enough on the food chain."

"I joined the wrong government agency."

"It's okay. I'll let you look at my toys."

His gaze shifts to my breasts.

"I'll play with them, too." His green eyes deepen. "Your toys, that is."

"Sure, that's what you meant."

He shrugs as if it was only natural to be caught staring. "They're eye level."

I shake my head and sit next to him. It's time to get to work. Each minute we spend doing this is a minute my finish line gets farther away. "So, how much do you know about Al Mazir and the cell that held Aaron?"

"I know this isn't the first time I'm hearing that name." Mark's voice is smooth as glass.

"Well, allow me to enlighten you."

"First, I need to know something."

"What?"

"What's your first name?"

"Not on your life, Dixon."

"YOU LOOK GORGEOUS, DARLING," my mother appraises as I enter the ballroom. I'm a little late, so I expect the zings to start very soon. It's not within her to hold back.

"Not nearly as breathtaking as you."

She pushes the orange satin between her palms. "It was your

father's favorite color."

The one thing I have taken after my mother in is her love of clothing, especially designer fashion. Priscilla Erickson doesn't dress in anything cheap. Her purses are all coveted, and don't even get me started on the shoes. I've requested all of them be left to me in her will. I could sleep in her closet and be happy.

My dress is a deep navy-blue silk ball gown. It has thin spaghetti straps and a plunging neckline, which I had to tape to ensure I don't have a wardrobe malfunction. But the back is where the magic happens. The hemline has a small train—the entire reason I bought the dress—and there's practically no material all the way down to my butt. It's luxurious and sexy, yet it still appears classy. To finish it off, I wore my strappy gold heels.

"Your hair would've been better up." Zing number one is out of the way.

"I thought it would be better down, but thanks for the suggestion."

"I just don't see why you wouldn't want to show off your neckline," she continues. "You'd look so much prettier if we could see your blue eyes. But you keep them covered by your bangs."

I sigh and close my eyes. I wish we could just stop. She's all I have other than Dominic. We don't have a large extended family. Both my parents were only children, and my grandparents passed away before I was old enough to remember them. But my mother insists on keeping me at arm's length.

"Mother." My knight in shining armor appears.

"Dominic!" she squeals in delight. "You look positively perfect. Unlike some people."

Zing number two. I've got at least four more to go.

"As do you." He smirks knowingly. Bastard. "Hello, my gorgeous sister. Kill anyone today?"

"Only you in my dreams," I snicker playfully.

If looks could kill, Dominic would've never lived past his eighth birthday. He chose not to follow into the family business. Instead, he's in politics, the equivalent to killing people to our father. He wanted to make a difference, a real one, he said. I believe he knew he couldn't hack it in the CIA, which is unfounded, but it helps me tolerate his choices.

Dominic laughs and leans in to place a kiss on my cheek. "You owe me."

"Put it on my tab."

"Come," Mother calls our attention. "Charisma, I expect you to behave like the antiquities dealer you are. None of your bullstuff tonight."

"Shit, Mother. The word you're looking for is shit."

"Watch your mouth!" she chastises me. "And where is your date? I told you not to show up to this party alone."

"I left him at the morgue."

"You're going to send me to my grave."

It's so easy. However, I just earned myself some more zings.

Our mother gives us both a look, turns, and heads into the ballroom, which is the indicator that we should follow. Like the good, obedient children we are, we do. Dominic and I smirk at each other while we play the part we've been groomed for. Being socialites hasn't always been easy, but together we created games to make it fun.

"Ten bucks each time someone tells you that you look like Dad." I try to get him to bite. I'll make at least a grand if he takes it.

"Five," he counter offers. "And five each time someone tells you that you should really eat more."

"Done."

No one will ever say that to me. They don't think women can ever be too skinny. If anything, they'll tell me I should really start seeing their personal trainer, whom they're probably fucking on the side.

"Be ready to pay up, sister."

We enter through the double doors, and now I'm in awe. The décor is more lavish than anything she's ever done. Crystal is everywhere. The lighting is low but catches every facet of glass in the space; the room sparkles. The tablecloths are burnt orange. It's a far cry from her usual white and black style.

"Holy shit," Dominic mutters.

"Did she hire a new party planner?"

"Or maybe she had a lobotomy and we didn't know?"

"Would explain it," I say before our mother spins and levels us both a death glare. "Nose goes," I say with my finger on mine.

"Brat."

"Loser."

I love my brother. He accepts me for who I am, makes me smile, and keeps me human. With him, I never have to pretend. He stalks off toward the devil incarnate as I grab a flute of champagne off a passing tray.

"Keep these coming," I say to the waiter. He nods with a knowing look on his face. Yup, it's going to be an alcohol-required kind of night.

My natural instinct is to scan the room. It's habit, and it truly comforts me. I gain a sense of control when I know the enemy is lurking. I see a few family friends and our nosy neighbor who attends everything so she can build her case that we're into something illegal. I love that my mother indulges it, almost provoking her to try it.

"Charlie!" Kristy squeaks as she rushes toward me. "It's been forever. How are you?"

Kristy Tubb is my childhood friend. Her father Dean was an agent for twenty years and my father's handler. Naturally, they pushed us to be friends, and it was a blessing we got along. We grew up having only each other to talk to. Our "family vacations" were always spent together in some remote place with nothing to do. We had to entertain ourselves with made-up worlds and games. Kristy suspects I'm truly a spy, but I'll never trust anyone outside the CIA.

"You!" I smile. "You look amazing!"

She scoffs. "Hello! Look at you! I mean, do you eat?" My face falls. I'm not telling him about that one. She doesn't count. "I was hoping you'd be here tonight. Is Dom here?"

I chuckle. "I think your ship sailed, my friend." I loop my arm in hers as we walk toward the bar. Where, of course, my brother happens to be talking to someone.

"Not until I get one sailing trip in," she jokes. "I'll never lose hope on him."

I laugh and roll my eyes. She's a mess. You'd think after twenty years, she'd give up. But instead, she just keeps trying. "Look what I found, Dom."

"If it isn't Kristy Tiny Tubb." Dominic slips into politician mode. I watch as his body tenses, but he uses the nickname that drives her insane. "Been a while. You look great."

She nods and then downs her champagne. "It's been a long time, and I really hate that you still call me that. I'm not so tiny anymore."

His eyes peruse her for far longer than I'm comfortable watching. "I'll let you two catch up," I say a little too loudly. "Come find me when the deejay shows up!"

"Not a chance in hell Priscilla hired a deejay." Kristy giggles.

"But I might have." I tip my glass with a grin.

I saunter off to find that waiter with the drinks. I'll need to keep a full glass if I'm expected to stay for any period of time. Of course, Mom spots me before the nice man can refill me.

She gives me that mom stare that pins me to the floor. If I could read minds, I'm sure that look would say, *Move and I'll kill you. Don't test me, Charisma.* So, like a good daughter, I stay put.

"There you are, Charlie." This woman. She actually sounds as if she just stumbled upon me. Maybe she really is in the agency.

"Yes, here I am. Just standing here hoping that my new best friend makes his rounds."

"His?"

I lean in. "I like the waiter."

"Anyway," she decides not to play along. "I want you to meet someone."

Oh, this can't be good.

"Mr. Dixon, this is my daughter, Charlie Erickson."

My mother steps to the side, and sure enough, Mark fucking Dixon is standing before me.

seven

WHAT THE ACTUAL FUCK?

How in the hell did he find me? This makes no sense. I haven't talked to him in two weeks while I've been working on my own things. I didn't tell him I'd be at my father's gala. I didn't tell anyone. This is completely unacceptable. Stalker much?

My entire body is tense as my mother beams at us both. She has no clue that we know each other. My blood is boiling. He shouldn't be here. This is *my family*. He's gone one step too far, but at the same time a thrill rushes through me. No one has ever gone through trouble to find me. In the past, any man I dated brushed it off. There was no hunt, no excitement, just a nod and a kiss on the cheek. However, Mark'll never know that I find this a little exhilarating—he'll only see fire.

He steps forward with a grin. "Nice to see you, Charlie." He extends his hand and waits for me to stop trying to kill him in my mind.

"Same to you, Mr. Dick—" I pause, "—son." I tip my flute filled with my courage. "How absolutely lovely it is to see you."

My mother's eyes blaze. "Charlie!" She takes the glass from me. "How many of those have you had?" Her words come through gritted teeth.

Shit.

"Just one." I try to grab it back, but she places it on the table.

"Well, Mr. Dixon has made a rather large donation to your father's education fund. I know how much this charity means to you, as well," she says with a pointed stare. In other words, *You care more than you'll ever admit or I'm cutting you out of the will and selling the shoes.*

"Thank you so much for being such a thoughtful man," I say, laced in a sugary sweet voice dripping in venom.

My mother turns her attention, and I use my finger and make the gesture of slicing my neck. Mark gives a loud laugh, drawing her back to us. "I'm glad it makes you happy," he says.

"Do you two know each other?"

Oh, this might actually be good. Priscilla isn't to be toyed with. She makes me look like a daydream. I stand there with a smile as she waits for Mark to answer.

"Charlie and I have a mutual friend. We've met before. I manage a security firm and our paths have crossed with work."

Instead of becoming the slightest bit skeptical, she beams. It's as if light glows from around her. "So, you work for the government?"

Mark chuckles. "No, ma'am. I'm a former SEAL who runs a private security firm. So I make a lot more money and get better toys."

"He's also a giant pain in the ass."

"Charlie!" she reprimands. "I think he sounds like a wonderful man."

"Well, Charlie brings out the best in me." He grins as she falls under his charms. "I enjoy spending any time I can with your daughter."

I can see the thoughts churning in her head: a man, wanting to talk to her daughter. "Oh, how perfect." She turns to me. "Charlie, you can show Mr. Dixon around and escort him for the night since you didn't bring a date."

Zing number three.

"I'm sure Mark would much rather mingle."

"Actually," Mark chimes in, "I would love to spend the evening as your fill-in date." He grins like the Cheshire cat.

"That won't be—"

"A problem," my mother finishes my sentence. She saunters off with a little more pep in her step, leaving me with Mark.

"Why are you here?" I cross my arms over my chest.

"Because you want me here." Mark's green eyes glimmer. I take a second to study him from my hostile stance. Could he be any hotter? The black tuxedo looks as though it were cut specifically for him. His broad shoulders are wide as he fills out every inch of this space we're in. His hair is swept back but still has that almost messy look. The tux cuts his waist, giving him a large and powerful appearance. As I make my way back up to his face the amusement is plain as day.

"Admit it," he goads me.

I lean in close, inhaling his salt and fresh air scent. "Never."

He chuckles while he pulls me against his chest. "One day, princess. One day."

Mark steps back, but his hand stays on my back. It feels . . . natural. As though we've been casually touching our entire lives. Anyone who knows me is aware I don't like my personal space invaded. Even my mother respects that. Mark, though, doesn't seem to notice or care. We walk toward the bar, where Kristy is still vying for Dominic's attention. My brother lifts his gaze to me, and his eyes practically fall out of their sockets.

"Mark Dixon, this is my brother Dominic Erickson."

I swipe a flute off the bar and drain half of it.

"Representative Erickson, it's a pleasure to meet you."

Dom doesn't miss a beat. "Seems I'm more popular than I knew." He gives a short laugh. "Are you a reporter, Mr. Dixon?"

"Far from it."

Dominic's brow rises. "Good to know. How is it you know my sister?"

"Stop talking like an idiot." I slap Dom's chest to get him to loosen up. As soon as he thinks there's press or someone watching, he slips into being a tool.

He pinches the underside of my arm and I squeak. "Oww! Asshole."

"It's called proper English. God forbid I sound intelligent. Now, where did you guys meet?"

"Mark and I met over a year ago, through a mutual friend," I explain.

Dominic studies me. "It's the first I've heard his name."

I cock my head to the side and refrain from sticking my tongue out at him. He makes me behave like a child. "You don't know everything."

"Obviously, I didn't know you had friends," Dominic jokes.

"I'm her friend." Kristy smiles, her hand extended to Mark. "Kristy Tubb, Charlie's oldest friend." She leans in conspiratorially. "Which means I have the most dirt."

"Really?" Mark smiles.

"Oh, yeah."

I drain the remnants of my glass, and try to get every last drop. I need to search for someone with a tray—preferably with hard liquor.

Mark smiles and then glides his hand up to my shoulder. He pulls me against his side. "Seems you need another drink, huh?"

"Excuse us, please," I say. Dominic gives me a questioning look while Kristy looks as if she's ready to start shopping for bridesmaid dresses.

I've never been seen in public with a man. I don't do personal touching, yet here Mark is, breaking all my rules. It damn well needs to stop.

My feet travel quickly, but I hear him behind me. We exit

the ballroom, but then I turn abruptly and let out a heavy breath. "Why are you here?"

Mark stands with his hands in his pockets, unaffected by my anger. "Since you probably know my social life I felt it was only fair that I have a bit of a leg up, too."

"You think this is a damn game?"

"No." He removes his hands and steps forward. "I think you don't know how to have a partner. I also haven't heard from you in two weeks, after several phone calls. All I got was a damn e-mail saying you'd be in touch. We were followed by someone, or did you forget that? I wanted to make sure you were okay."

"I don't need your protection."

His eyes bore into me. "The hell you don't."

This guy must have the biggest balls in Virginia. I've never met a man so cocky and full of himself. Then, on the other hand, he's sweet and thoughtful. He confuses me, and I don't like it. I need to get a grip. There's been a lot on my mind from having the case taken away, and the loss of my father still weighs on me.

"You thought manipulating the situation to gain information was the best way to gain my trust?"

"Says the woman who lives for manipulating to gather information," he scoffs. "I'm not sure how you can say that to me with a straight face." Mark swipes his hand down his face. "I came because I'm heading out tomorrow. I had to fly out of a base undetected, so I figured I'd pop in and grab you."

I narrow my eyes. "How did you know I'd be here?"

"One day you'll realize I'm not a fool, and I'm damn good at what I do, too. Don't leave notes on a dry erase about being in hell and then put Ronald Reagan Building on this date on your calendar."

Something he said causes me to pause. "Why do you have to fly out undetected?"

Mark steps close and I retreat. "Why didn't you answer my

calls?" he counters.

He pushes forward again as I go back. "I wanted to have something useful to tell you when I did."

Again, we continue this dance. "That doesn't explain why you couldn't talk to me."

The space we're in isn't big. My back is now pressed against the brick wall and Mark's arms cage me in. The rough, cold bricks cause me to shiver, but Mark's heat ignites me. My mind is firm on getting answers from him, yet my body wants something else. I shut down the part of me that wants him. The woman in me has to wait. "Why are you flying out?"

"Leave with me tonight and find out."

"Answer the damn question," I demand.

His ivy-colored eyes bear into me. "Trust me."

I search for some sign, a reason to say no or insist I'm doing this alone—all I see is honesty and trust. He could've left on his own and used the information I gave him to do what he needs to, but he didn't. While I don't appreciate the fact he now knows my mother's name and my brother, there is a piece of me that feels—normal. While trust is something earned over time and not given on a whim, that time isn't something I have.

"I need another hour before I can cut out or Priscilla will morph into Maleficent," I murmur.

Mark presses his lower body against mine and traps me between him and the unforgiving brick. Yet, when he shifts his leg, he gives me a clear out. It shows me respect. He doesn't want to cage me or make me feel imprisoned. He's showing me that while I can go, he clearly wants me to stay.

"Remember what I said?"

"You say a lot of crap."

He laughs. "I made you a promise, Charlie." Mark's already deep voice is layered with desire.

Once again, my control begins to slip. "What's that?"

His hands drop a little lower beside my head. His lower body shifts so his knee is between my legs. I feel his arousal against my thigh.

My traitorous body shows its own awakening. My nipples hardening through the silk material don't go unnoticed. Heat pools in my core and my breath hitches. I want him. There's no use denying it.

"I told you I'd kiss you again. If you don't stop me now, there's no getting away."

I should stop him. I need to stop him. There's no way in hell it's going to happen, though. I'm craving his lips again.

He gives me one second before he crushes his mouth against mine. His entire body leans forward, and now I am trapped. There's nowhere to go. Nowhere to move that's not Mark. He takes every part of my mind and body. Our hands roam each other as his tongue slides against mine. Passion ignites between us; it sets the room on fire. His fingers cup my neck and then glide down the front of my dress. His hand brands my skin as he takes his time exploring the open skin between us.

My fingers grip the lapels of his tux, holding him, molding him to me. I can't get close enough. Our mouths stay fused as we both lose control.

Then my mind snaps.

I push back and my hands fly to my lips. They're swollen, bruised from the force of the kiss. His hands brace against the wall. I keep my eyes downcast. I can't believe I just did that, against the damn wall, at a ball commemorating my father.

I shift my dress, rake my fingers through my hair, and pull myself together.

"Charlie . . ." Mark finally speaks. It sounds like shouting even though it's only loud enough for us to hear.

"That was the last time that will ever happen," I say with no tremor to my voice. "Tonight we become partners. It's not about whatever this is." I shift my hands between us. "It's about finding the information we're both searching for."

"And what if we find something else?"

"We shut it down. There's not room for feelings in this world."

Mark pushes back, giving me space. I instantly feel cold. "Okay, then. Have it your way."

This is what I wanted, what we both need, but suddenly I wish it wasn't. I wish I could pull him close, kiss him, fuck him, and just *feel*.

But wishes are for little girls.

eight

Mark

SHE'S SO FUCKING STUBBORN. She's right, but that's beside the point.

I wonder if she's ever had fun. Does she even know how to let go? Even during that indescribable kiss, she held a thread of restraint. I could feel her fight from within her body, until I touched her bare skin. That's when it disintegrated.

One touch of her perfect skin and I almost came in my pants. Every inch of her skin I've gotten to see is unmarred. I imagined myself running my tongue down the same path. I'd spend hours doing nothing but tasting her, kissing her, and then I'd claim her. She'll ruin me for all women, I can just tell.

Charlie isn't the kind of woman you move on from. She draws you in with the brightness of her sun and then leaves you fucking blind. There's something deep and dark inside of her. She's trying to keep it locked down, but I can see it in her eyes.

"So, where are we heading?" she asks.

She doesn't know I have the private jet. It's not as if we can fly commercial. I do need to fly out of a military base, though, to avoid the customs bullshit. The number of favors I had to call in isn't even funny. We need to be at Andrews Air Force Base before one in the morning.

"We'll talk after the party," I inform her. I don't know if someone here is watching us. Considering she was tailed after leaving the agency, I'd bet my ass there are ears. This city is full of corruption, and it's always the innocent looking ones. Hell, no one would suspect a woman like Charlie would be an agent.

She nods. "I get it. You should mingle."

"I'll stick with you." My hand presses against her back and her muscles clench. I love knowing my touch creates an involuntary reaction. It's a huge ego boost that as good as she is at her job, when it comes to me—she sucks.

"Of course you will," she mutters under her breath.

"Dance with me."

She gives me the evil eye but takes my hand. "I'm only doing this because we have time to kill. Touch me wrong one time, and I'll make you pay."

I laugh at her empty threat. Even though I have no doubt she'd try . . . it'll never happen. I'm on guard with this woman. Takes the term sleep with one eye open to a whole new level.

Out on the dance floor, I pull her close and we get lost in the movement. Her body presses against mine in all the right places, and I fight my dick not to embarrass me. She rests her head against my shoulder as I survey the room. The party seems a little too pricey for my tastes, but it seems to be going well.

"See anything?" she asks without moving her head.

"Nope. Your mother has a huge grin though."

"She's probably already naming our children."

I stiffen, and I'm sure she notices. "Umm . . ." I stammer for words.

"Relax," she half laughs. "We'll never have sex, so there will be no children."

Charlie lifts her blue eyes to mine, and my chest tightens. Something about this girl makes my head spin. Her talk of kids didn't make me pause because I'm afraid of commitment or kids. It was because I *could* see it. I could see a life with her, or at least a shit ton of fun.

We dance through another two slow songs while the world goes on around us, but all I see is her. She's one of those women I have to look at. I can't believe that someone like her exists. Charlie is an enigma—one I plan to make mine. I watch the men rip their gazes away from her when I catch them. I successfully convey my message without having to say a word, *Yeah, step the fuck off, motherfucker. I'll rip your arms off and feed them to you if you try to touch her.*

Her hands rub up and down absently as we dance. My fingers rake the length of her open-back dress. I'm gonna get hard again if she keeps this up. Needing to stop before I create a rather embarrassing situation, I push her back slightly. "Come on, let's mingle. I need a drink."

We step off the dance floor, rejoin her brother, and spend time shooting the shit. I like Dominic. He's a stand-up guy who chooses to work around a constant state of scandal but doesn't engage. You can see the protectiveness he feels for Charlie. I don't blame him. I would kick anyone's ass who looked at my sister. Unfortunately, I only have Garrett and he can take care of himself.

The closest thing I have to protect is Aarabelle. And God help that girl when she steps into the dating world. Between her father, stepfather, and two godfathers, any boy who comes around her is fucking screwed.

Charlie and I circle the room. I keep my hand on her the entire time as if she'll vanish. She is a spook after all.

The waiter passes us twice. Each time she grabs a glass, downs it, and grabs another. I watch her smile, hug, and then almost glow as she floats through the room. Charlie is polite, but cautious. She's aware, but seems to be enjoying herself. She starts to sway a little as she tips her glass back, emptying every drop.

"I'll wind up carrying you out of here soon." I'm only half joking.

"You wish. I outdrank a Russian mob boss once. However—" She smiles. "You should play along. If I'm drunk, my mother will want me to leave. This is my plan." She slurs her words slightly.

"I think you should stop drinking because you're lit."

"Lighten up, Twilight." She steps forward and grabs yet another drink. "I'm not even buzzed. I'm just feeling the fun."

"You just said 'feeling the fun' and you don't think you're drunk?"

She leans forward against my chest. "I thought you liked fun?"

"I'd prefer you lucid when I fuck you unconscious."

Charlie leans back and smirks before the waiter magically returns.

I swear he's zeroed in on Charlie. As soon as her glass is empty, he just happens to reappear. I hold back my growl and glare at him. There's something about this guy. He rushes to the other side of the room as she gulps the drink. "Wow, these drinks are amazing. Want one?" she asks.

"Were you drinking water shots with the mobster?" I joke, but I'm really curious because she's hammered.

"This one time, I was dating this guy, even though I don't really ever date," she rambles. "I mean, I could date, but I disappear a lot. Apparently, guys don't really like being number two in a woman's world. Anyway, he was trying to convince me that he was better at shooting because he grew up hunting. I remember laughing in his face, which of course didn't bode well for his teeny tiny ego." She holds up her fingers as if she's pinching. "Which wasn't the only thing teeny tiny." Charlie nudges my side with her elbow. "If you know what I mean."

She's fucking adorable. And toasted. I need to get her out of here before she starts really talking.

"Anyway, he didn't know I'm a, you know . . ." She starts to tilt but I grab her.

"Okay, no more talking." I grab a water bottle and shove it in her face. "Drink."

"Bossy prick."

"Just drink."

She had about four flutes of champagne, but there's no way that would make her this drunk this fast.

"Mark," she murmurs. "I'm sleepy."

I remove the drink from her hand and sniff, but I can't tell a difference. However, with her loss of motor skills and the way she's slurring, this isn't just champagne. It hits me like a ton of bricks. "You're drugged. We need to get out of here. Hold on, don't let go of me." She wraps her arms around my waist and I start to walk her out.

I look around for that waiter now, but he's missing. What the fuck did they put in her drink? It could be anything. She could be out for hours or for days. I have no idea which drug they used or how much.

Anger flows through me as I peer down at her slumping form. Once I find out who was responsible for drugging her, we're going to get a lot of answers. Someone's head is going to roll.

"I'm gonna take a nap," she slurs.

I stop and turn her so she's looking at me. "Stay awake, Charlie. You need to stay awake. Okay?"

"Okay, then I can nap."

"Yes, then you can nap." I give her a fake smile and pull her tight as we begin to walk. Each time she slips, I fight the urge to haul her in my arms where she'll be safe, but that would draw too much attention. So I hold her against my side and keep her moving.

Of course, as luck would have it, her mother notices me hauling her drugged up CIA daughter.

This is going to be a shit show.

"Mother!" Charlie perks up as she lets go of me. She bumps into a chair as she walks over. "You look ravishing. Did I ever tell you about that time?" She starts to slump a little and I pull her tight against me.

"Charlie," her mother cuts her off. She says her name but shifts her gaze to me, then back to Charlie. "Darling, you don't look so well."

"I'm great!" She giggles.

"Mr. Dixon?" She addresses me with questions in her eyes.

"There was a waiter. He was feeding her drinks. And she's not feeling well." I hope she understands.

"Of course, she would drink too much." She shakes her head with disapproval.

The need to defend her arises. "No, ma'am. Something was added to her drink."

"Oh!" she says as her hand touches her chest. "Pretty brazen considering where we are, but I'm not surprised. Would you mind helping Charlie return home?"

"I'm not going nowhere," Charlie slurs. "Mother. I'm fiiii-ine."

"Of course, I'll watch over her. But we're not going home." I look into her mother's eyes. Priscilla doesn't move or flinch, but her eyes say she knows there's more behind my words.

She steps forward, "She's very important to me."

"I understand."

"She has a bag in the trunk. Always. It'll have everything she needs."

I nod.

Charlie grips my arm with both hands and I wrap my arm around her. When I inhale her honey scent filters in. My hand glides up and down her arm as we stand there. I won't even let go of her for a second. I can't believe someone drugged her. I was with her the entire time. I'm going to murder someone.

"Don't worry about me, Mom," Charlie says in a hushed voice as her eyes start to drift closed. "Keep the coffee on."

I look at Charlie, and then at Priscilla quickly, and catch her nod. Her code for a mission? Her mother wraps her arm around her waist before she kisses her cheek.

"I love you, Ch—" she stops, looks at me quickly. "Charlie."

Not another word is said as we head out the door.

Now to find out who that fucking waiter is, cut off his balls, and feed them to him.

We get to the car and she starts to get sick. "I'm sorry," she says as I hold her hair back. "I'm so tired."

I hold her body up as she lets it out. "I know, beautiful. Puking is good, get it out."

Once she's finished, I scoop her into my arms and load her in the backseat. She can't even hold herself up. I rush to car and grab her bag, head back to my car, give the driver our destination, and climb in. Charlie leans against the glass, but I want her closer. As soon as she's situated in my arms, her eyes close, and we head off.

We're silent on the drive to Andrews. Charlie sleeps in my lap as I try really hard not to consider all the things she spurs me to feel. I've never been so goddamn possessive, or protective. Her being drugged causes me to literally want to go guns blazing and take out everyone who came near her. No one should've gotten that close. No one should've had an opportunity to slip something in her drink.

So instead, I let my mind wander to my own parents and how they've fared with my and Garrett's choices. My brother is doctor in Virginia. He had it all and lost it. He had a successful practice, made a shit ton of money, slept around on his wife, and was the most miserable son of a bitch I knew. His gold-digger wife Michelle caught him banging his nurse and took every penny she could. He packed up, moved to Virginia, and is now dating Annika. She's fine, but a carbon copy of Michelle—she only wants his damn money. Each time we talk, I wonder, why? Why the hell would he live a life he hates so damn much? We only get one, might as well make it the best we can.

Which then brings me back to Jackson's offer.

It makes no sense why I put it off. I love this company—clearly. There's just something about making it permanent. As of now, I can walk away at any time. If I become his partner, I would be tied to this forever.

Before I get too deep, I grab my phone and set some things in motion.

"Hey, jackass." Liam's voice fills the line.

"Why did we become friends again?" I wonder aloud.

"Because my wife told me we had to."

"You know there was a minute I thought that kid was mine. She and I had a moment," I tease. My relationship with Liam really turned after the mission to rescue Aaron. I saw how hard it was on him, but he manned up and did what was right. He earned a great deal of my respect. Plus, he loves my goddaughter as if she were his.

He scoffs, "Yeah, by immaculate conception."

"She slept with me in her mind."

"What do you want, asshole?"

I gaze down at Charlie sleeping in my lap. I called Liam because I trust him. I also know there's no chance he's involved in all the shit that's been going down with Cole Security. When you feel threatened, you tighten your circle. Liam is about to be one of two people who know anything.

"I need you to find out who the waiters were at the party I attended tonight."

"You couldn't get his phone number on your own?" he jokes.

Charlie shifts and lets out a moan as she clutches her stomach. "Funny. No, Charlie was drugged."

Liam shuffles, and I hear a door close. "Is she all right?"

"She's fine. I was with her, but this our second close call."

"I take it this needs to be done without anyone knowing?"

"Yeah, man. I need the office left in the dark about what's happening. That way I can rule that out."

Liam sighs and then takes a long pause. I can only imagine what he's thinking. His wife, the woman he'd die for, works there. The last thing he needs is to worry about her safety when he's deployed, but if she leaves, it could shift the balance. "Natalie is my priority. I need to know she's safe."

"Liam, I would take a thousand bullets before I would let anything happen to Lee."

"I know, and Aaron already told her that when he says it's time to leave, she needs to leave. I don't know what the fuck you guys got going on there, but Lee loves you guys and the job. So, I'll do what I can. I have some buddies up in DC. Let me see what I can dig up. Send me the info and I'll be in touch."

"You'll have a secure e-mail soon."

"Don't do anything stupid."

I laugh and brush the hair off Charlie's neck. "I never do."

"Right. Gotta run. I swear this kid only shits when his mother is gone."

Liam disconnects the line right as the driver opens the door. I hoist Charlie into my arms. She's so light, I wonder if she ever eats. She curls into my chest, and rubs her cheek against my shirt as I hold her tight. She's calm, docile, and sweet, which will only last until she wakes up. A part of me wishes she'd stay like this instead of turn into the hostile jungle cat that tries to claw my eyes out.

Then I remember the way the waiter hovered. The way he

was so attentive to her and how she really didn't drink enough to make her pass out.

I get her and all our gear loaded on the plane. There's a small bedroom in the back; I debate whether I should strip her down, but she'll probably knee me in the balls.

"Ready to go, Mr. Dixon?" the pilot asks.

"Yeah, just get in the air and then I'll let you know where to," I command.

He nods and heads out. I leave Charlie dressed in her gown and sit on the bed next to her. She's so fucking beautiful, but there's more than that. She's smart, funny, and can obviously handle herself. She's everything I've ever wanted in a woman. She's right that being together while doing this is a dumb idea, but I've never claimed to be all that bright.

Once we're airborne, I lie back and close my eyes for a few.

"Where the hell are you taking me?" Charlie's unhappy voice wakes me. She's pointing a knife in my face. Well, that's one way to wake up.

"Good morning, princess."

"Fuck you. Why am in the air and still in the dress I was wearing last night?"

"Anyone ever tell you that you curse a lot?"

She glares.

"You have less than a second to explain." She shifts and I wonder if she would really stab me. Yeah, she would.

"You were drugged."

"What? No. I couldn't!" She presses the heel of her hand to her temple after getting a little too loud. "Ugh!"

"Headache?" I ask. I'm sure she's been drugged before in training; she knows how it feels.

"How? Who?"

"I fucking knew it! Son of a bitch! The waiter, did you get a good look?" I ask as she walks the floor.

"The waiter?" Her brow furrows as she shakes her head. "How am I okay right now?"

"I gave you an IV when we got in the air. Just one bag of fluid to flush your system. There was no way you would go from sober to that drunk just from champagne."

"I don't remember much. Shit! How did I not notice?" She throws the knife and it impales the wall.

"That'll cost me," I mutter offhandedly.

"How could I be so stupid?" she asks more to herself than anything. "You!" She turns to me. "You do this to me! You mess with my head and then I suck at my damn job. It's you!" Her eyes close as her hands fly to her temples.

"Sure, blame the guy. That's new." I smirk, and lean back against the headboard. I'm beat. I start to catalogue everything in my mind, replay it. It couldn't have been the same two ass-holes who followed us before—I would recognize them. So, either it's new people, or it's the agency watching her. However, it wouldn't make sense for them to drug her.

"My head," she groans before flopping onto the pillow.

"We'll figure it out. I've got someone looking into it and he'll turn something up."

She sits up, placing her head in her hands before she turns to me. "You'll never find anything if they're after me. These people aren't small time, Mark. To go after an operative isn't a child's mission. They're skilled and more than willing to do what they need to."

I know she's right, but I'll try. Liam isn't a child or unskilled. He knows this is important. He knows Charlie as well. He'll come through.

"We'll see. I'll check in with them when we get there."

"I need to know where you're taking me, why, and what the plan is."

Her hand rests on her lap while her mouth sets in a pouty

face. I want to kiss her lips, demand her to submit to me and just do what the hell I tell her. But that's not her. She'd probably bite my tongue off.

"We're going to Bahrain to meet up with a buddy who's a SEAL. The plan is—I don't have one. We do whatever we need to do. Chances are we're heading to Egypt too, so either you choose to work with me and do it my way, or I'll tie you up and leave you here."

"The hell you will. I'll knock your teeth out."

I let my voice drop. I use the one that gets all the panties dropping. "Sounds like foreplay." She scowls. Talk about infuriating females.

"You need to fly into another country. We're not flying directly to Bahrain."

I lift my brow. "I'm sorry." I look around. "There's no way you're telling me how we're running this. I didn't have to bring you in."

She shifts forward slowly on the bed. "Mark" Her tender tone goes straight to my nuts. Her tiny hand rests on my forearm. "I'm telling you we can't fly in where anyone knows we were planning to go. I'm saying that if it's someone we know or someone who knows your plan . . . we can't."

Why the fuck does she have to be so good at her job?

"Tell me your name," I plead.

Her head snaps back. "What?"

"Tell me your name and I'll go anywhere you want."

"You're ridiculous."

"You'll eventually tell me."

She lets out a deep breath. "Let's go see the pilot, shimmer boy. I've got to plan."

Charlie squeezes my forearms and then stalks off toward the cockpit. She may have won this round, but we have a very long flight—time enough for another bout. Time to see who comes out victorious.

"WAKE UP, TWILIGHT." SHE slaps my stomach to wake me up.

"Good morning to you, Chastity." I groan, rolling over. "Sleep well? Or do vampires only use coffins?"

"You're the expert, I hear."

I groan while I sit up and pull the drawer open next to me. I pull out the contents, and toss an envelope at her. "Here's a passport and new ID." She opens it up, looking suspicious—as always. "Memorize it. We don't have time to get tripped up because you're unable to remember."

"I don't have a problem keeping my cover," she snaps.

"Talk to me once I've had my caffeine. Right now all I hear is *wah, wah, wah.*"

We head into the main cabin where I smell the coffee. I grab a cup, take a few gulps, and sit at the table across from her.

"As I was saying," Charlie says impatiently. "I've heard all about the SEALs and how big their muscles are, but their brains . . . not so much. So if anyone should be worried about their cover being blown, it's me with your tiny pea brain."

"There's nothing small on me, princess." I smile and lean back with my hands laced behind my head.

"We'll be landing in Egypt soon. I assume we'll use that cover to figure out whatever we can about the issues you're having there and then change into the new identities when we leave. You trust the pilot?"

"I trust him."

"I have a plan."

It's way too fucking early to think, but no way is she leading this. I down the rest of the coffee sitting on the table. "That's great. I have one, too."

After Charlie and I talk about the missed checkpoints from our guys in Egypt, she and I decide we need to investigate it a little more. We're in agreement that Mazir is somehow connected to Cole Security Forces. There's nothing substantial, but enough coincidence to make me question it.

Nothing with this woman is easy. It takes me two more cups of coffee before we finally come to some kind of understanding regarding how to handle this. Of course, she argued so much that I now have a splitting headache.

The pilot comes over the intercom, "We'll be landing in about fifteen minutes."

Charlie and I share a brief moment of resolution. We're both committed to seeing this through. Neither of us is willing to allow failure as an option.

She clears her throat and looks away. "He needs to leave and fly home as soon as we land."

"He already knows." I smirk. "I took care of it while you were napping earlier."

She scowls. Even her dirty looks make her seem hot as hell. I don't think she could be unattractive if she tried. It's when she's a bitch that makes it impossible for me not to want her. I love her ability to argue, except when it comes to me touching her. Then I seem to affect her more than she likes.

Charlie sits in her chair, racks her nine millimeter, and slips it into her thigh holster. My cock strains in my pants as she pulls her skirt down a little. She looks up and gives me a look. I just deepen my stare, challenging her to say something. I could give a flying fuck if I get caught looking. I'd do a hell of a lot more than that if she weren't so hell-bent on fighting me off.

"Stop looking at me like you're going to eat me."

"Stop looking so damn delicious."

"You know you don't have to say everything you're thinking."

I laugh. "I'll remember that." I don't say close to half of what I'm thinking. I'm pretty sure she'd have kneed me in the balls if she knew the things I plan to do to her.

She quirks her eyebrow. "Good." Her mouth sets as if she's battling saying something more. Of course, she can't resist. "Even if I don't believe you. You're a major pain in my ass."

"I'll be happy to rub the pain away."

"Point made."

"You know," I stand up and walk close to her. I study her face, and watch for any small indicators to let me know she feels what I'm feeling. "You've probably never had a real man." My body presses forward as she stands her ground. "No one was strong enough to deal with your penis envy."

"Penis envy?"

"Yeah, sweetheart." I reach my hand to cup her cheek. "You live in a man's world. You fight harder, stand straighter, and battle for your place." I see the flash in her eyes that lets me know I hit a chord. "I don't need you to assert your shit, babe. I'll own you. You won't want to have control because I'll make it so fucking good that you'll beg me to take it."

Her lips form a perfect 'o' and she just stares at me. I exploit this moment of speechlessness and crush my lips against hers.

nine

Charlie

GODDAMN HIM.

Goddamn him for being the world's best kisser. Each second our lips touch feels like heaven. I want to tear my mouth from his, but I can't. The truth is—I don't really want to stop. He gets me. He knows what I need even though I've never wanted this. I need control; it's power, and without it, I'm weak. But Mark takes that power. He steals it from me, but it doesn't feel like theft. It's a gift.

Our tongues dance as his hand grips my ass. Mark's kisses aren't gentle. There's no give and take. It's take and take some more. He growls and grinds his cock against my leg. His hands are relentless holding my face as he controls the kiss.

He demands this kiss.

He possesses this kiss.

He possesses me.

Mark's teeth pull at my lip as he breaks away.

My hearts beats loudly against my ribs. I'm torn between pulling him on top of me and never stopping, or beating the ever-loving shit out of him for this.

So I go with option three. My hands press against his chest

as I throw him back. "Don't think you're winning anything here. You're an arrogant asshole who thinks he has it all figured you. You don't know shit." I push him back as the light in his eyes grows. "I hate you."

"But your body doesn't."

"Screw you!" I glare at him.

"In due time."

"In your dreams. I'm here for one thing only, and it isn't to put some I-once-was-a-Navy-SEAL-and-I-think-I'm-still-someone in his place. Because this," I point outside the window. "Is bigger than you, me, or anything else. People are *dying*, Mark. Your friends are being shot, taken, and their lives are in danger."

He grips my arms, pulling me close again. "You think I don't know this? Every single day I watch people around me suffer because of choices I made as well. I'm well aware of the bigger picture. But you . . ." his tone softens, as do his arms, "Make me forget for a minute. You're like some goddamn addiction I can't shake. I'm known for my self-restraint, so what the hell have you done? Why the hell do you consume my fucking mind?"

My breath hitches from his words. If I'm honest, he does the same. I think about him, and I wonder what we could be if our lives weren't so fucked up. Before I can respond, his phone rings.

"Dixon," he says, not removing his eyes from mine. "No, we're off the grid." A pause as he listens. "I'll relay what info I can, when I can," he huffs. "I'm alone, I'll be in touch, and keep Muff at a distance. I'll be in touch." He hangs up, looks at his watch, and then back to me. "Under twenty seconds. I wish they'd remember this isn't my first rodeo. Now . . ." He steps closer. "I'm warning you, Charlie. For some reason, I like you. There's something that keeps me coming back, even when I tell myself to stay away."

"Mark."

"I'm telling you, something's going to give. It's been a

goddamn year and you infest my mind."

"Mark."

"There won't be a way for you to avoid me forever."

"Mark!"

"You and I will happen."

His eyes never leave mine. He stares at me, letting me know that isn't a threat but a promise he will fulfill. It's not just on him, though. I'm fighting the tie between us. Since the first time I saw him, I knew there was something there. Yes, he's annoying and cocky. Yes, he needs someone to knock him down a few pegs, but God, he's sexy. He's funny, smart, cunning, and he sees the woman in me. Not some agent who can be used in a way to get a job done. No, he sees me, and oh, how I need that. And he saved me when I was drugged.

"Mark," I say again. "I can't—" His thumb presses against my lips.

"We're not having this out now." He drops his hand lower and hooks it around my neck to press his forehead against mine, which isn't easy to do since I'm so short. "We have work to do." His lips press against the top of my head and then he releases me.

I want to say more.

I want to make him understand there won't be any having it out. I can't be involved with someone and work like this. It's too dangerous, and we're not dealing with an amateur. I don't know how to work through this. Never before has anyone made me feel uneasy. I decide to do what I do best: put it away. There's no time to deal with this crap while we both have to be on our A-game. I don't even want to imagine what dealing with it means since I'm not exactly a relationship person. Yet, he makes me contemplate what it would be like.

Mark gathers his papers, throws his phone in the back of the plane, and grabs his bag.

"Do you have a burner phone?" I ask.

"I'll grab one when we get in town."

I don't say anything about the safe house I have here or the contacts that are easily at my disposal. There's a reason this is a good place to start. I have an asset here I can call on if I get in trouble. I should tell him, but I won't. Not yet. There's so much of me that doesn't know how to trust. I've been alone in this mission from the beginning. Bringing Mark in is dangerous, not just to me, but to the assets I have all around. If any of them become exposed, they'll die. There're no questions, no trial. Terrorists are judge and jury, and they don't hesitate to kill. The more I keep from Mark, the more I wonder what he's keeping from me.

"How much did Aaron tell you?" This question has bothered me for a while. Aaron debriefed with me when he returned. We went over anything he possibly heard while I wasn't in the compound.

Mark turns and studies me for a moment. "Everything."

I decide to test him. "He told you about the arms dealer they caught?"

He smirks while he walks closer. "I know what you're doing."

Here we go again.

"And what's that?"

His stupid sexy smirk grows. "Testing me."

Right he is. "Nope."

"Liar."

I snort. "I don't think you should call me a liar. I've never been caught in a lie." This is true. I've never been *caught*, but that's because I'm good at my job. While I may be testing him right now, I also want to know what Aaron held back. Because no one ever gives up all their information. There are parts that he kept for himself. Maybe not because he wanted to, but because it's in our blood. We're hunters. We want the kill and we'll stop at nothing to keep our prey off guard. Aaron is no different.

Mark's closeness rattles me. I want us to remain profession-al. "*Caught* is the word I hear in your statement, Charlie. I'm aware of your ability to dazzle and confuse. Not working this time."

"I dazzle you, huh?"

"Every fucking minute."

I take a second as his words seep in. It's kind of exciting to have him admit that he's affected as well.

Then he ruins it. "Until you open your mouth. Then I won-der what could possibly be wrong with me."

"I'm sure the list is long."

He laughs and grabs my hand. "Come on. Let's go to work."

Knowing we'll be without air transportation leaves me feel-ing a little uneasy. There's comfort in knowing you can get into some heavy shit but are able to get out of the country quickly if you need to. We head toward the outskirts of Cairo. He has a contact he wants to meet to learn about the mission where his guys have missed their checkpoints. He explains their last com-munication, where it went down, and what he thinks happened. I'm not sure I agree, but right now that's the last thing he needs to hear.

Once we get a little farther up, we buy the burner phones, change, and scout out a place where we can get a room. We agree to play the role of husband and wife on a Middle Eastern adventure. It's the best cover, considering he seems hell bent on kissing me all the damn time.

He tilts his head to indicate a rundown hotel. It's central enough for us to see and scout easily but far enough out of the way that it won't seem conspicuous. "Let's check that one out. I'd like to have a room facing this side of the street," he says as he takes my hand. "Don't you think the view is great, darling?"

"I already regret this."

"I think we should consummate the marriage."

"I think you try it and you'll have a new nickname, and it won't be about vampires or glitter."

He laughs and pulls me close. "You're going to admit how much you love me really soon. I can feel it."

"You feel something all right."

"Charleston, you and I will be married one day. Mark my words."

He's so insane it's beyond normal. I never plan to marry because my life is too unpredictable. There's no way I want to give up my career, and that's what happens to women in my field. They meet some guy, fall in love, get married, and then they leave the life. Sure, they stay in the agency and work a desk job. Become a handler, like Mandi did, and for what? Some asshole who will probably cheat on her. No, thanks.

"Marcus, the world could never handle us together." I play on his name since he keeps screwing up mine. Not that he knows what my real name is.

ten

LUCKILY, THE MOTEL HAS a room in the location we want. It has a view of the street, and it gives us an escape out the window in case we need one. "What was the last contact you had with your guys?" I ask as we set up our gear.

Mark brought a bunch of stuff. It's all small and folds down, but it's still a lot. I'm not used to having so much tech stuff on assignment. Usually, I'd have Mandi run the intel I needed, and then she'd relay what she found so I could stay as off the grid as much as possible. This will be my first time working without her.

"This location is where they should've ended up. That's why I'm here. Maybe they went silent for a reason. They could've realized they were being tracked or targeted and decided to cut off communication. I've done it before."

"What's the company protocol?"

He looks at me with a grin. "None of us dictate protocol to our field guys. They're all highly trained and able to make decisions on their own. I'm not here to babysit. I'm here to support them with the best equipment and training possible."

I take a seat on the edge of the bed. "Okay, so basically they have carte blanche?"

"No, they have permission to do what's necessary to carry out the mission. One thing both Jackson and I hated about the

Navy was worrying about politics. These guys know what to do. They're keen, loyal, and can decide right from wrong. Jackson set up parameters and these guys respect him. They wouldn't fuck that up."

I raise my hands in surrender. "I'm not accusing."

Mark sits next to me with a reassuring smile. "I know. I just get a little defensive about my men."

"Understandable. I feel the same about my work."

He nods. "Yeah, tell me about the mission where you found Aaron." His request somehow seems like a demand.

I'm not accustomed to speaking freely. While I've debriefed the agency on everything, Mark doesn't hold the clearance for all of this—at least I don't think he does. However, there's a part of me that doesn't care about that. The agency took that from me when they gave the case to Vanessa. They took away years of my life. So I decide to give a tiny bit and go over the info I'm sure Aaron has already disclosed to him.

"I was on assignment to gather information about a terrorist who is dealing arms. I was very deep and in that camp for a long time gaining their trust. I'm very persuasive."

He laughs. "I'm sure of that. I don't know many men who would look at your dark hair and blue eyes and tell you no."

I smirk. "I don't know any either."

"Now who's cocky?"

"Anyway," I continue with my story. "I'm sure this part won't make you happy, but I was there for a while before I could relay that Aaron was alive." I wait for his disapproval.

"I knew this. I don't like it because he's my friend and his wife suffered greatly because we thought he was dead, but I get it. The mission comes first. Sometimes in life, especially our line of work, others suffer for the choices we make." Mark grabs a protein bar, opens it, and bites into it as if he couldn't care less.

It's so confusing to me. I would slit someone's throat if

they kept my brother from me for a year. Yeah, I offered Aaron what little protection I could, but I couldn't destroy all the work I'd done. He suffered because I had to keep my mouth shut. Sometimes I could hear the screams from his beatings, and it was horrible. I knew he had a wife and child, yet I pretended. These were the parts of my job that sometimes kept me awake at night.

"It's not something I took lightly."

Mark's green eyes deepen as she shifts forward. "Did you and Aaron get a chance to really talk?"

"Here and there. We were monitored, so I had to be careful. He told me about Natalie and their baby. He wondered if she was okay, what the baby looked like, if anyone knew he was alive. I couldn't give him too much information because I wasn't willing to put the assignment at risk. It was the first time I ever truly hated my job," I admit frankly. Mark sits in rapt attention as I offer a little of my truth to him. "Aaron told me, though, at the end of all of this, he wanted those to suffer for what they were doing. He knew he would get us both killed if he did anything. So he shut his mouth, took it like a man, and hoped I would be able to keep my promise."

Sometime during my speech, Mark covers my hand with his. I could pull back from him, but his touch comforts me. "What information did you give him?"

"I told him . . ." I feel a pang of guilt and stop. It was the first time I ever wished to blow my cover. Aaron was broken. He confessed his life to me not knowing I was a CIA operative. I was so deep into being Fahima that I forgot who I really was. Aaron snapped me out of that.

"Charlie?"

"I told him lies, Mark. I didn't tell him who I was until about two months before I contacted my handler. Then I lied and told him I had my team working on extracting him. I lied because I'm a liar. I'm a liar who cared more about myself than him or his family."

Mark pulls me close. I don't know how the bastard knew it was something I needed, but he did. I sink into his embrace. I blame the drugs even though they're far out of my system.

"You got him home."

I huff. "What did he go home to? We still talk, you know?"

"He told me." Mark keeps me against his side.

"I know his wife married his best friend. They now have a kid. It's kinda fucked up, no?"

Mark releases me. His eyes study mine before he speaks. "Natalie made her choices based on the information she had. If he told you anything, he wasn't exactly a model husband. Liam is a good guy, and he loves her. He stepped in and raised Aarabelle when Aaron couldn't. And when Natalie's world fell apart, he never left her side. I don't agree with the choices Aaron made, but it's not my place to judge him."

I nod and mull over what he said. I know all about Aaron's pisspoor decisions. As a woman—and his only friend at that time—I let him know just how I felt about it, too. "I think he more than paid for his sins."

"Maybe." Mark pauses. "I think Aaron had PTSD, but no one was willing to step up. He was injured in the mission when we lost our friends. We all fucked up by ignoring it."

I know how he feels. I've been there. At least Mark wasn't too late.

"I know an operative who killed herself after her intel got in the wrong hands. She was so broken over it, but none of us knew what to say. We all just kind of swept it under the rug. She talked to me about it once." I pause as I remember the look in her eyes. "She told me how she thought she was being watched but didn't trust herself anymore. I'll never forget the way she begged me with her eyes to reassure her. I laughed her off, thinking she was just being paranoid. When they found her, I knew it was because the paranoia was too much."

Mark's hand grips mine. "It's not an easy life we live."

"No, it's definitely not. A lot can't handle the guilt that comes along with things we all do."

"Taking a life isn't something most are okay with," he admits. "Is it fucked up that it doesn't haunt me?"

My hand squeezes his. "I don't think so. It's kill or be killed in our circumstances. I've never set out to take a life that wasn't trying to take mine, have you?"

"Fuck no. I was protecting my own life or the lives of my guys."

"Exactly. We're not monsters, Mark."

"No," he says hesitantly. "But we're not saints, either. I sometimes wonder what I'll answer to when I go. Will I be viewed the same as someone who murders?"

I understand his question, but I never delved that deep into it. I'm not walking around picking people off. "I really think it's different."

"Maybe. Maybe not."

We both pause, giving ourselves a minute to mull over what was said. I've never had problems killing someone. I know that doesn't make me the typical woman. I'll do what I have to do in order to get home safe. It's the way the job is. Of course, I'd bet my body count is way lower than his.

Mark stands and walks toward the window. "Can I ask you something?"

"Does my answer really matter?"

He laughs, "No. Probably not."

"Then ask."

"Are you happy?"

I look at him with my mouth slightly agape. "What does that mean?"

"Exactly what I asked."

"I'm doing just fine."

"So that's a no."

"No, that's a . . . I don't have to answer your questions."

"Defensive much?"

"Invasive much?" I retort.

Mark just chuckles, pulling the curtain closed. "I thought so. You and I are the same, Charlie. We both have jobs that force us to be strong. We face death, corruption, and fucked up shit. We live alone."

"I have Dominic and my mother. I'm just fine."

He nods but doesn't appear to believe me. "Like I said, we're the same. We both have used our careers to mask any loneliness." He heads into the bathroom, and I think over our bizarre conversation.

Am I happy? I don't know. Is anyone ever really happy? We're selfish creatures. We always want more, bigger, better, and then when we get it . . . we want again. I wanted to be in the CIA. When I finally got in, I wanted to be an operative. When I finally moved up enough to be placed on assignment, I wanted the most dangerous one. It was never enough.

He exits wearing a distracted expression.

I wait for a minute before I finally crack. "What is it?"

"Tomorrow we'll do a sightseeing tour. My asset will be in touch then."

"How did he know how to get in touch?"

"You have your secrets, Charlie, I have mine. I'm not about to divulge everything."

Such a bastard. Just when I start to like him, he goes and says something that reminds me why I need to keep my distance.

"Here I thought we were finally becoming partners." I shrug. "But I guess I was wrong. You don't have to be such an asshole."

Mark shakes his head and lets out a groan. "Un-fucking-real."

"I need to do a little recon tomorrow before we head out. I also don't think we should stay here too long. Mazir isn't in Egypt, and he's where the target is. I'll share my plans, since you insist on being an asshole."

Mark steps so close I have to look up. He leans forward so our noses nearly touch. "I have to be an asshole to you. If I don't keep pushing you away, I'm going to end up pushing myself on you. I could be your partner, but you're hell bent on reminding me that'll never happen." I gasp. "So know this, when I'm an asshole or a dick to you . . . it's so I don't rip your clothes off and fuck you until neither of us can walk. It's because you make my blood boil to the point I'm going to lose it. And I never lose it." He keeps his face this close for a beat before he turns his back on me.

I sit there completely stunned. I could lie and say there isn't a part of me hoping for option one. That my stomach isn't clenched at the idea of Mark and I going at it, but that shouldn't happen. It's dangerous and completely reckless. We have a job to do, and I've already screwed up this mission once.

He returns to the bathroom, slamming the door behind him. I think there's something more behind his words, but I don't know him well enough to truly tell. So instead, I sit and plot our next move, study the map, and wish my father were here. He'd know what to do. He'd have a clear plan that would enable us to get in and out without any issues.

I miss him.

He was my sounding board when things got tough. He's the reason I'm the agent I am.

Someone set him up to die.

Someone knew he had that file.

Someone made sure it was never leaked.

Now I pray that same someone doesn't know I have a copy of it.

eleven

I FLOP BACK ON the bed feeling exhausted and frustrated. Not having Mandi feeding me small bits of information is different. It's like flying blind. On the other hand, I have a real-life handler of sorts in the form of a six-foot-one man-child. This was supposed to be easier with Mark not harder.

With my eyes closed, I think back to the mission in Afghanistan. It was by far my hardest assignment. It helps that I have naturally olive skin, almost black hair, and an exotic look. It allows me to blend in almost any region of the world. I can play up my attributes depending on the assignment. My father used to joke that I was the ultimate chameleon. It's more than looking the part; it's knowing the job. I don't always have to look the part, but I need to play the part.

"I can not help you once you are in the compound," my asset reminds me again. He's worried about leading me into a situation I can't handle. It's almost cute. However, at this point there's no turning back. I have strict orders to get any information on whom Mazir is working with and his location. Losing someone isn't a situation the agency takes lightly. I need to reassure him and then move forward.

"Just remember the story, Khalil. It will be fine."

He sighs and looks down. "I don't like this. I'm putting my family in grave danger. If you are caught, it will not go well."

My hand rests on his arm. "No one will find out. Not if we stick to the story." I pause and wait for him to acknowledge. We've spent months fabricating the details to align. He nods in agreement.

My cover is uncomplicated. "I'm your niece who's been studying in Europe. I'm home because I couldn't stand to be away any longer, but that left me as a burden since my parents have died. You get them to take me in to pay off the debts I owe, and I'll get what I need before anything can happen to your family."

"They won't hesitate to kill you."

"I'm not scared." And I'm not. It's a chance I take every time I go on assignment. There are times I've seriously wondered if I would make it out alive, but that's when my training comes in. That's when I strip down the situation and let my instincts take over.

Khalil has been feeding me small bits of information for six months. I realize he's reached the maximum of what he can discover. Someone must go inside to learn more. He's not willing to do what needs to be done—and I don't blame him. If he's caught, he'll lose his life. I have no plans to blow my cover.

"They will want you to cook and clean . . . I can't protect you."

"Trust me," I implore. "I know how to be careful. I'm Fahima Salib, and it's time for me to help the family the only way I can."

Khalil nods as we walk down the street toward Mazir's last known location.

The heat is absolutely ridiculous. I'm sweating like a pig. I open my eyes to see why the air has stopped working only to find something—someone—has me pinned against the mattress. My heart accelerates when I realize it's Mark's arms. The moonlight shines through the window and across his face.

He's peaceful, calm, and for once—quiet. His arms encircle me as he lies on his side. I twist cautiously in his heavy embrace until I face him. I hate being spooned or being cuddled. I don't like to feel trapped, but it's different in his arms. I'm careful not to wake him as the desire to touch him mounts. My hand lifts and I gently push the hair off his face with my fingertips. The silky strands glide back and his arms tighten. I smile and wish things could be different for us.

In another life, I'd date him. We could stroll down the street, hold hands, and laugh. But I have a red target on my back. I'll forever be watched, possibly even hunted. I can't bring someone else into this mess. Not until I feel safe.

The pads of my fingers brush the stubble on his chin. "I wish," I whisper. "I wish I could let myself get lost in you." I continue to touch him. I allow myself a minute of normalcy. A few seconds where I'm just a woman and he's just a man. It would be nice to believe that is the case, but our lives are complicated. There can be no dating because at any moment, when I go back to work, I might need to disappear. "If only you knew just how much I wish it could be."

I lie this way, looking at him, hoping that maybe I can find love. Hoping that some day I'll be able to put my past behind me and sleep in my husband's arms, unafraid of what tomorrow will bring. I close my eyes and pretend that someday is today as I drift back to sleep.

"Charlie." Mark's voice seems far off. "Don't fake sleep just to get a kiss."

My eyes flutter open, and I scan the room. "What? What time is it?"

"We gotta move," he says as he leans back off the bed. "Now."

I bolt upright as I take in Mark's alert demeanor. "What happened?"

"Erik got a location on the team. I don't have time explain." He throws some stuff in a bag. "He was able to get their tracker working and thinks they're hunkered down in a safe house. We have to move quickly." He races around like a tornado but leaves nothing in his path. Mark stills and eyes me with confusion. "Are you coming or are you staying here?"

I scramble from the bed. "I just need a minute." I grab my bag and head into the bathroom.

I spend a few minutes cleaning myself up and reflect on last night. I'm confused and unbalanced. Everything with Mark is so damn complicated. I've never allowed myself even a little bit of freedom with this kind of thing. Sure, I've had superficial relationships, but with him, it feels like . . . more.

"Charlotte!" Mark bangs on the door. He has the best timing. There goes my 'more.' "Let's go! Either you're out in thirty seconds or I'm leaving you."

I throw open the door with my eyes narrowed. What I wouldn't give to kick his ass. "I'm coming!"

"You can bet on that," he mutters under his breath.

"What?"

He smirks. "I said I'd like to beat you with a bat."

"Uh huh."

We finish packing up the room faster than I imagined possible. Instead of taking the front exit, Mark chooses the side. The energy around him is different. It's as if he's wound tight, ready for battle, and part of me feeds off it while the other is nervous. He's always so calm and collected; whatever information he received has him rattled.

Once we're in the car, I decide to ask. "What was the information?"

He sighs and his fingers tighten on the steering wheel. "They think they're dark for a reason, but my office heard chatter of the safe house they chose. I can't confirm it with him because if they are there, it could be a trap." He faces me, and I nod.

My hand slides across the center console and grips his forearm. He relaxes slightly and shocks me by grabbing my hand. "Your guys are trained. It's only been a few days. I'm sure they've survived worse."

"The safe houses in the regions are stocked. If they're there . . . they're fine."

His fingers lace with mine, and he keeps hold of me. "Mark," I start but I don't quite know what to say. Do I tell him how good it felt in his arms? How maybe when this is all over we could talk?

"You know, one day you'll realize just how perfect we are for each other. You're going to look back and see how much fun we could've had."

Damn him. "Do you have to ruin any moment we have together?"

"I'm just pointing out the obvious that you've failed to realize."

"I don't know why I'm asking, but what's the obvious?"

He smiles without answering.

I wait.

And wait.

"Mark!"

"That you're falling for me. I can't blame you." He pauses. I'm sure he's waiting for some smartass remark from me. I'm going to keep him on his toes. "I'm prime real estate, princess."

"Yet you're not even under contract."

"Simply waiting for the right buyer."

"I assure you, I'm not interested in your property."

He laughs. "Keep lying to yourself."

I roll my eyes and look out the window. I try to pull my hand back, but he tightens his grips. Since taking his hand, he's back to the same guy. The warmth and humor I've come to know is in place. We're both reeling from our pasts. He's lost friends while I've lost my father due to our careers.

We spend the next thirty minutes driving in silence. It's nice to have someone who doesn't need to fill the air with noise. He's comfortable just being. Mark starts to slow the car and lets go of my hand.

He surveys the area. "I'm going in first."

"The hell you are. We're partners. Let's think about this rationally." He looks over while I start to form a plan. "If we go together we can play the part of a married couple lost in the area. Hell, we can be missionaries for all I care, but having a story gives us an out. Your guys will know it's you."

"They have cameras at the perimeter. They won't hesitate to shoot if they think you're a threat."

I smile. "I'm not worried. If they're in there, wouldn't they have used a secure line to call you?"

He rubs his hands down his face. "They wouldn't risk it. Not with who they have in their protection."

My mind starts to race. Who the hell is the company protecting that would require no contact? Of course, a lot of private government contractors do high asset transports. It's common not to want to alert anyone, so they hire outside people. It gives them the secrecy they want, but whoever it is must be a lot higher than I originally assumed.

"So, what do you want to do?" I surprise myself by asking. I don't normally sit on the sidelines, but this is his part of the trip.

"I need them to see me first, then they'll know. So you need to look madly in love with me. Hang on me. We'll get close enough to the camera, and then we'll be in."

"Why did I agree to this?" I ask myself more than anything.

"Because you wanted to be close to me."

"Whatever helps you sleep at night."

His eyes flash but he recovers so quickly I'm not sure I really saw it.

We exit the car and start to walk the area. It's a larger city, filled with people. There's no cover. No place to hide, except in plain sight. Kids run around outside and the streets are lined with cars. This means we'll be able to blend in easier. I lift my scarf over my hair and walk beside Mark. We move around easily and unnoticed. I stay close to his side, and keep my eyes lowered. Once we get closer to the safe house, Mark's hand grips my arm.

"Stay close," he warns.

We pass through two small alleyways while my mind flashes to the last time we were in an alley. Once again, we're playing the part of lovers. I wonder how much of this act is his way of getting to kiss me.

Mark stops and turns to me. He pulls the scarf down, cups my cheeks, and leans in close. "Behind you is the camera." His hands tilt my face to the side as he peers up at it. "I'm going to turn you so they see your face." I nod.

He turns me back to face him and presses his lips to mine. I grip his wrists as he holds me there. Suddenly, he breaks the kiss.

"Mark," I say. My breathing is shallow. "We can't stay here."

"I know. Let's move."

We head upstairs to the apartment and the door opens. The man on the inside of the doorway is tall, dark, and appears ready to kill anyone in his way. There's a gash on the side of his cheek, and he has a bandage around his leg.

"What the fuck is going on with these missions, Dixon?" One of the guys asks as soon as we come into view.

Mark visibly relaxes as his gaze lands on everyone present, but continues to search. "Where's the ambassador?"

What? I gape at Mark, and he returns my stare as if waiting for me to say something.

"He's fine and in the back room. He has his meeting tonight so we're completely silent until that's over. Then we can get him the fuck out of there."

Mark looks around before he finally asks the leader, "What happened?"

The guys all settle around and describe how the mission went down. When things started to feel off, they decided for the safety of the ambassador to go into hiding. The team had set up to take him a roundabout way through Egypt so he wouldn't be detected.

I listen in and form my own suspicions. It seems unlikely that there was someone seeking out the ambassador, even though he's been in hot water regarding a bombing that happened a few years ago. Mark watches me while they talk; I observe the questions that churn in his own mind. Why them? Why would this small, covert mission be targeted? It still doesn't make sense. There's something behind all this. Someone is repaying a debt they never collected.

I think it's time someone gets answers from Jackson.

twelve

MARK CALLS IN A private jet again and we leave Egypt once he ensures the ambassador is secure after his meeting. Instead of heading to the Middle East, we go back to the States. There are some things that need to be handled right away. I also need to check in with the agency, since I'm pretty sure they know I disappeared. Plus, it's time for me to do some digging to determine exactly what Mazir's last known location is. We agree there's no point in heading somewhere already ten steps behind.

The flight so far has been uncomfortable. Mark is withdrawn and seems lost in thought. We don't say much to each other, each of us working through whatever is rolling around in our head.

I head back to the bedroom to change. I've slept like shit since getting drugged. The only time I really rested was last night in his arms. It pisses me off. Stupid boy. I don't have time for this; I have a terrorist to find, but the notion of how safe I felt doesn't evade me. I'm in so much trouble.

Removing my clothes, I contemplate how easy it could be once all of this shit is behind us. We could have something—maybe? Once everything is done, I can determine if there's more than friendship between us. I mean, he's known me more than a year, and he's still interested—as am I.

Someone is after them, and Mark isn't immune to the possibility that he's next. Jackson's been shot, Aaron's been kidnapped. It would only make sense that Mark is the next target.

I'm down to my bra and underwear when I hear the click of the door. I quickly use my shirt to cover myself. Mark's eyes stay locked on mine. "What are you doing in here?"

"I'm not sure."

He looks a little lost. I know the feeling well. "You should've knocked."

He takes a step closer but keeps his gaze firmly on me. "I knew you'd tell me to wait."

"Mark," I say cautiously. He's standing so close my chest touches his. Our breaths mingle and the energy around us is electric. "We can't do this."

"You're so beautiful." His eyes close. "Every time I look at you, it literally takes my breath away." When he returns his gaze to me again, I melt. Every part of me becomes liquefied, and I want nothing more than for him to take me in his arms. I'm falling for him. Against my will. "I see you, Charlie. I see it all."

I don't doubt he does. He seems to have a way of breaking me down and seeing who I really am. Right now, I'm worried about him. I also feel vulnerable at the prospect of what's to come, and for once, I want to forget. "And what do you see?"

"I see a woman who has had to fight for everything." His hand pushes my hair back. "I see how strong you are, even when most would be weak. I see the fucking sexiest woman in the world." He steps forward, and I take a step back. My knees hit the bed. "I see how your mind never stops working, but you want someone to make it stop. Let me take it from you, baby." Mark holds my head in his hands, waiting for me to say something. It's the first time he asks for permission.

"And what about you? You don't think you need someone?"

"I'm tough."

"We should talk about what's really going on," I say.

Mark tilts my face and subtly shakes his head. "Not tonight. I need you to let me take it."

I can't answer right away. Part of me is stunned, while the other part of me is scared. I have a feeling Mark needs me to take it away from him, not the other way. He's being hunted, and I'm sure he knows it. This kiss will change everything between us, though. It isn't an act. It isn't part of a mission. This will be just Mark and Charlie. It's me giving him an opening that I'm not sure I should. But when I look in his emerald eyes, all I want to do is say yes.

My fingers rise and touch his face. "Take it tonight, but if you hurt me . . . I'll kill you."

Mark smirks and tightens his hold as he slowly pulls my mouth to his. When our lips touch, I explode. Our mouths mold to each other's as passion erupts. It's weeks of toying around the edges of desire. It's months of wondering what this would feel like. It's a year since I laid eyes on him and believed this could never happen, but it is. He takes, and takes some more. But really . . . I'm giving it up. I free myself of anything but him.

His hands drop, and he grips my ass to pull me tight against him. The lust that has lingered is now in full force. I'm surprised we've lasted this long. Mark's tongue pushes against mine. When he moans, I surrender.

My hands tear at his shirt and pull it up. We break the kiss so I can remove it, and I toss it across the room before we both come back for more. I don't ever want to stop. I know this is reckless, but I'm completely at his will. My fingers descend against his skin, feeling every ridge and valley of his chest. There's not an ounce of fat anywhere. His hand glides up my back as he unhooks my bra then slowly pulls the straps down. Mark steps back and we both devour each other with our eyes. My breath halts for a moment as I get to admire how absolutely perfect he is. His arms are covered in color, his muscles are defined, and his waist tapers in, leaving a very delicious V. What stop me are the tattoos that he's covered in. Each one is intricate and beautiful. His right arm has Poseidon emerging from the water. Around it are vessels as it climbs higher. On his left arm, he's covered in tribal ink surrounding a frog skeleton that I've come to know means he's lost a SEAL brother on a mission.

My eyes travel up his chest until I reach his eyes. I've never been self-conscious, but right now, I'm filled with nerves as his intensity rivals mine. Feeling awkward, I raise my arm to cover myself, but Mark stops me. "Don't think about it. I want to see every inch of you. You're fucking stunning."

I don't reply. I close the gap between us, pull his head down, and kiss him with everything I have.

His hands glide down my back and he grips my thighs. The feel of his rough hands on my skin causes me to burn. He lifts me up and wraps my legs around his waist. I feel him walk forward but I keep my mouth fused to his, enjoying the way his kiss tastes.

Mark holds me effortlessly before he lays me down on the bed. He hovers above me, again giving me an out. I won't take it. There's no way in hell I'm stopping this. I want to forget all the shit that's happened. I want a moment, and as much as he's giving it to me . . . I'm taking it. "Take it, Mark."

"There's no going back, Charlie. Be warned, I'm going to fuck you so hard you'll never think of another man. I'm going to take everything and you're going to give it to me."

"What makes you think I'm not taking something?"

"Oh, I don't doubt you're taking something." He rises up on his knees and unbuckles his belt. I watch as he unbuttons his pants with a gleam in his eyes. I wait, growing wet as he takes his time. "You're going to take it all. Every fucking inch of you will be filled. I'm going to ruin you, princess."

"Why are you still talking and not naked?" I taunt him.

He smirks as he pulls his pants down. The only thing between us is our underwear. As if he can read my thoughts, he looks down to where I'm still covered. His lips twitch as he leans down against my ear. "First, I'm going to fuck you with my mouth."

His tongue glides down my neck, leaving a hot trail as I squirm beneath him. The feather-light touches of his lips, then the heat-searing feel of his breath against my skin sends me into overdrive. I moan when he reaches my breast. His lips wrap around my nipple and he pulls it into his mouth. "Holy shit," I cry out. Mark licks and sucks as I writhe in pleasure.

Mark tortures me in the best way as he moves to the other side to repeat the same motions. His hand moves down and slips into my panties. Slowly he presses his finger lower. "Not sure you're ready yet," he muses as I clearly am. His finger explores me, applying pressure against my clit before he removes it. I nearly cry out. I need more.

"Why are you trying to kill me?" I ask as he does it again.

He sits back up and removes his hand from where I need it most. Ever so slowly, he moves to my hips, and the Neanderthal tears my underwear off. I start to protest but his gaze stops me. His eyes appraise me. "Because I've had to suffer." His voice is thick with want. "I've had to imagine this. Now, I'm going to drown myself in you. Be ready, this is going to be a long fucking night."

I lean up on my forearms and stare him down. "Good. Now shut up and put your money where your mouth is."

Mark's hands push against the backs of my legs and thrust me up on the bed. I gasp at the sudden move, but before I can say a word, his mouth is against my pussy. He doesn't tease me or make me wait. He devours me. "Oh, my God!" My eyes close as he licks and circles my clit. It's been too long since I've had someone go down on me. I almost forgot the amount of plea-sure that comes with it. Mark is playing my body like I'm his own instrument.

The pleasure builds, and I could explode at any second. He hooks his hands under my legs to pull me closer to him. His tongue pushes, circles, and swirls, drawing me near the edge. When his tongue enters me, I detonate. My toes curl while ev-erything around me flashes. It goes on and on. He doesn't let up. I can't breathe. I can't think. It's too much. I fall further than I've ever fallen before. I lie there trying to remember my name.

When I open my eyes, he's above me. My hand snakes around his neck, and I pull him down. He kisses me like he owns me. I flip him on his back; I need to drive him wild.

"No," he protests.

I straddle him before he can say anything more and place my hand on his chest. "I need this, too."

"Tonight is about you."

"It's about us. Don't deny me."

Mark's hand cups my neck, pulling me so we're nose to nose. "I'll never deny you. You've got me all turned out, and for some reason, I can't say no to you."

I briefly press my lips against his. "I feel the same." I want to reiterate that this is a one-time thing. That once we get back, I have a feeling things will change for him. There's so much going on that I don't think he's fully accepted.

"Don't think." His voice is desperate. "Be here. Take what you need, Charlie."

"What if I don't need anything?"

"You're lying," Mark replies. "You need more than you'll ad-mit. You need this. You need me to make you feel good, don't you?" His hand moves down to where I lay open to him. He doesn't waste time, he inserts a finger and my head falls back. "That's it, baby," he coaxes. "You need a man who will put up with your shit. Someone who can handle your need to control, and know you want to be out of control for once." Mark inserts another finger. My back arches, rubbing my breasts against his chest. He removes his fingers suddenly and my eyes fly open. "Now, do you need this?"

"Yes."

"That's it," he says before my lips meet his again. "Now, take what you want."

I break away and move down his body. Our eyes remain on each other as I slide down slowly to pull his boxers and free his cock. He puts his arms behind his head as I look down at his length. I press my lips against his stomach, kissing all the way down.

"I hope you're ready for payback." I smile before I take his length in one pull.

"Holy fuck!" His hand flies to the back of my head.

I bob up and down, twirling my tongue around the tip. I moan, adding vibration, and enjoy each noise he makes in return. Mark's muscles tense as I continue to blow him. Each time his breath hitches, I suck harder and deeper.

"Charlie," he groans. "You gotta stop, baby. I'm gonna fucking lose it."

I give him one more time down before I come up.

Mark doesn't give me a second to recover. He practically throws me on my back, puts a condom on, and is back on top of me. "Tell me your name." He puts the tip of his dick in and waits.

I look at him and wish he could understand, but there's no way. I won't give that part of me to him. "No.".

"No?"

"It's the only thing that's mine."

"I need to know." He presses just a little bit deeper.

I wiggle beneath him. I need more. "Don't stop," I beg.

"Tell me."

"I need more."

Another inch deeper.

"Mark!" I practically scream while I try to push him using my heels against his ass. I fight with myself. It's just a name, but it feels like a complete surrender.

"I can't fuck you if I don't even know your name." He pulls out a little.

I whimper at the retreat. Then I get pissed. Fuck him. How dare he use this moment to extract information? "Wrong way, you son of a bitch!"

"Ahh!" He smiles. "There you are. Not so calm and badass when you want my dick?"

He thinks he's so smart. Well, he's not the only one trained. I slap him across the cheek. I watch the shock flash on his face and know I only have a second before he'll recover. So, I push him on his back and practically impale myself. "Looks like I got what I wanted anyway."

Of course, this is just the beginning. There's no way I'm not going to pay for that. Sure enough, he uses the fact he's double my size and rolls me back. He pushes so deep inside me, I can barely breathe. "You want this?" he growls.

"Yes!"

Mark sets an unrelenting rhythm as he takes everything. We fuck like animals, clawing, grabbing, and pounding into each other. I climb higher and higher as the sweat drips down my face. I dig my nails into his back as I start to build again. I scrape down his back, hold on, and teeter on the verge of another climax. "I'm gonna come," I say through gritted teeth.

"Give it to me." Mark pounds harder. "Squeeze my dick."

My head rolls back as he continues to slam into me. "Mark!" I cry out as I get closer.

"Fuck, baby. I'm close. Look at me. Look at me as I fuck

you."

We lock eyes as he slips his hand between where we're joined and presses against my clit. That's all I need. I fall over the edge, screaming his name and clawing at his back.

Mark thrusts a few more times and follows me to the finish line.

After a few minutes of lying there to catch our breaths, we get up to clean up. I head into the bathroom and look myself over. My hair looks like shit, my make up is smeared, and I'm flushed. I lean back against the door, letting it sink it. I just had sex with Mark. The man who drives me insane and makes me wonder what the hell is wrong with me.

This is bad. This is very, very bad.

I'm a stupid woman. I know better than this. But there was something in his eyes. A part of him I've never seen before that called to me. I wanted to take it away. And now, I don't know what the hell I'm supposed to do.

thirteen

I EXIT THE BATHROOM to find him sitting on the edge of the bed. "Thought you might spend the rest of the flight in there."

"Funny." I smile. I walk over and sit next to him. "I thought about it."

"What changed your mind?"

I shrug. "I figured you'd eventually break the door down."

Mark laughs and grips my thigh. "Look," he says, but I put my hand up.

"Let me go first." He stops talking for the first time—ever. "I need to be clear. That was just what it was."

"And what do you think that was?"

"Sex. That's it."

That's all it can be. I need to focus. I'm going to betray him when I get home. There will be no more partnership. I'm doing this on my own. Working together was a mistake. There's no way I can remain objective. I have to distance myself from this mess, and Mark needs to get a handle on what is going on with him.

He stands and pushes his blonde hair back. "You really know how to kill a mood."

"I'm just being honest."

"I didn't ask you for anything," he counters. "But you're lying to yourself if you think I didn't see through the bullshit you just said. It wasn't just sex. You felt everything that happened between us. You fucking enjoyed every second I was inside you."

"Yeah! The sex!" I yell.

He laughs and mumbles under his breath, "You're so stubborn."

He's right. "And you're being targeted!" I can't talk about us when there's all this other shit. "I'm being targeted! I mean, shit! Do you really think *this* is the best time for us to start something? Because I sure as hell don't."

"I can handle myself," he states with no room for discussion.

Frustratingly stubborn male. I've never doubted he can handle it, but I don't think he really grasps the full picture. "And what about the people around you? Are you handling them?" I stand and move around the room.

"I fully intend to." Mark stands and, begins to walk toward me, but I put my hands up to stop him.

The questions assault me as I allow my mind to work. He has to wonder the same things. It's time to lay it all out. "There's a lot of things that don't add up. Why did the villagers know about the Humvee that was carrying Aaron? Why did they know you and Jackson were in the country? How did anyone know about your mission with the ambassador? What the hell did Jackson do to get anyone associated with his company on their radar?" I fire off my thoughts without pause.

Mark grips my shoulders and turns me to him. He then takes my face in his hands and kisses me. I grip his arms and hold on while he holds me to him. I lose myself so quickly that it terrifies me. He shouldn't be able to unbalance me, yet that's exactly what happens when he touches me. Mark elicits the vulnerable side of me, and I hate him for it.

I pull back and run my fingers through my hair, gripping the sides in frustration. "Stop doing that!"

"Doing what?"

"Kissing me like that!" I shout.

"Wanna tell me it's just sex again?"

I glare at him. "That's exactly what that was. It won't happen again. You need to wake up and see what's happening."

He takes a step closer. "Don't worry about me, babe. I plan to handle it, and then we'll see what you say when this happens again."

"It won't."

"Oh, it will." His voice is ice cold. "You'll be on your knees begging for my dick." He presses his body against mine with his arm hooked around my back. "Only next time I won't be surprised when you slap me. I'll be ready for you. I'll hold back until tears fall from your eyes and you want nothing but me. Then . . ." He pauses when my breath hitches. "I'll fuck you until you're begging to stop."

I want to deny that his words turn me on, but the moisture between my legs proves otherwise. I want to throw him on the bed and screw his brains out. However, I do have some sense of control. There will be none of that. This ends now. "We're done here."

I push away from him and walk out into the main cabin of the plane. Mark Dixon is playing a game that could kill us both. I can't be around him until we know what we're dealing with, and I need to learn who's following me. We have too much at stake to let his happen.

"WHERE THE FUCK ARE we?" I ask as the plane lands, and not in the Washington DC area.

"California," he responds, as if this is to be expected. "We need to talk to someone."

"We? How about you should've asked me!"

Mark smirks and then leans back in his seat. "Listen, I need answers and you're a human lie detector. If Jackson knows anything, you're the best chance at finding this out."

I inwardly groan. I see his point, but this just means I need to spend more time around him. "Fine. You have two days."

We arrive at Jackson's office outside San Diego. Mark and I discuss his plan, but his plan is to wing it, which scares me.

"Muff!" Mark yells as he throws the door open to the tiny room. "You got some 'splainin' to do," he says in his best *I Love Lucy* impression.

"What the fuck? Oh," he says after spotting me behind Mark. "Hey, Charlie."

"Jackson." I smile and put my personal feelings aside. I need to assess his demeanor. He's clearly surprised by our arrival, but I have a feeling Mark lacks finesse in handling this.

"So, who the fuck did you piss off that now we're being hunted?"

I was right.

Jackson, though, was an intelligence officer for the SEALs. We share some of the same training. As much as our visit is unexpected, it seems this question isn't. "I don't know. I've been going over it, and I can't figure it out."

"It's clearly on you, Muff."

"No shit, asshole. I know this is on me. I know *all* of this is on me."

He moves around the desk and sits down. I take a closer look at him. His dark brown hair is messy. The color in his eyes seems dim, as if he's barely hanging on. And the dark circles under his eyes clearly show lack of sleep. I'm not sure if this affirms guilt or shows stress. Whatever it is, it's certain Jackson Cole is not himself.

"Why do you do this shit time and time again?" Mark bursts

out, his arms thrown in the air. "You never fucking learn."

"What the hell are you talking about?"

I sit back and watch the two of them.

"You take it all on yourself. You make it your life's mission to be the goddamn hero. You're either into some shady shit, Muff, or you pissed off someone big."

Jackson surges to his feet and braces his hands on the desk as he glares at Mark. "You think *I'm* behind this?" His voice is laced in acid. "You came here thinking I have some fucking part in this? After all this time, you think I would ever jeopardize my friends? Get the fuck out!" He points to the door.

"No." Mark stands his ground.

"I swear to God, Mark. Get out before I kick your ass from here back to Virginia."

"You can try, but you're going to answer my questions, and then we'll figure out what's going on."

Jackson glares at Mark, "Some fucking friend you are!"

This can't be easy on either of them, but I commend Mark for not beating around the bush. On the other hand, he could've done better at allowing some information to be extracted differently. He'd never last in my department.

"I'm not the one getting us picked off like target practice."

I stand and move toward the other chair, a little more out of the way. While neither of them seems to remember I'm there, I want to stay farther in the shadows. Mark grips my arm before I can slink away. "Stay here."

Jackson huffs. "You've been my friend a long time. You've been through it all. You really think I'm capable of this?"

"You want this shit to stop, Muff? Time to prove it."

Jackson shoves aside some papers and then grabs a folder. "You want to know what I know? Here!" He shoves the folder toward us. I decide I want to see it first. "It's all there."

I open it and start to read through. There are a lot of

surveillance photos—some of Mazir, his men, and my asset, others of the area where Aaron was detained, and a few are satellite photos of the IED right at the explosion site. There're a few notes regarding timeline and a guy named Neil. Nothing of significance, but it's proof he's investigating it himself. "Who's Neil?"

"Catherine's ex," he answers abruptly. He's clearly pissed off, but he can't blame anyone for being suspicious. "He works for a company we deal with frequently."

"Does Catherine know?" Mark asks from beside me.

"Fuck, no. I'm not bringing that low life piece of shit's name up. I'm watching him and having one of our FBI friends monitor him, too. Anything else?" he snaps.

I hand the folder back to him, and Mark pulls me against him. "Jackson," I say, and draw his attention. "I've seen people do unimaginable things, as have you—and Mark. We've all seen people at their absolute worst. It's kind of our mentality to assume that before anything else."

"I get that, but not from him. You don't know me, so fine. But him," he points at Mark. "He knows better."

"Why the fuck do you think I'm here?" Mark bellows. "I know you're not behind this shit, but she doesn't."

I'll kill him. I'll strangle him with my bare hands. "What the hell does that mean?"

I yank my arm away but he tightens his grip and manages to pull me even closer. "It means you're a giant pain in my ass who doesn't believe anything anyone tells you. I knew you needed to see it with your own eyes. I know Muff would never betray his own guys. You'd say I missed something, though. You'd tell me I was biased, but I know him. I'd lay down my gun if he told me to. That kind of trust is unbreakable."

"You couldn't have just given me that exact speech?"

"This was way more fun, and dramatic."

"Are you a ten-year-old girl? You needed the drama."

Mark pulls me flush against him. "You know damn well I'm far from a girl. I'll prove it again if you want to challenge my manhood."

My mind flashes to the many ways he's definitely all male. The way he felt on top of me, beneath me, and inside me. How every inch of his body is molded to fit mine perfectly. Our breaths mingle as heat spreads across my cheeks. I want him. I want him so badly I can hardly think. I close my eyes and inhale all that is Mark.

Jackson breaks the spell by clearing his throat. "Want me to leave you two alone for a while?"

Mark smirks. "I'll take care of her later."

"The hell you will." I push against him and he releases me this time.

"We'll see about that."

fourteen

Mark

"**KITTY!**" I PULL HER close and squeeze until she slaps my back.

"I hate that I missed you." Catherine laughs as she extracts herself. "It's like you're a fungus that grows on people."

"Nah, you're just bored with Mr. Domestic over here." I throw a jab at Muff. He just gives me his normal you're-an-asshole look.

"Must be it." She laughs.

"Catherine, this is Charlie. Charlie, meet Catherine, Jackson's fiancée."

"Hi," Catherine greets her. "You're stunning! Sorry, that was a little forward, but seriously."

"Thank you." Charlie laughs, and just like that, the two walk off into the living room as if they're best friends.

That's the one thing I can say about Cat, she's always good at this crap. Her career in public relations gives her an edge over always knowing the right thing to say.

Jackson claps my shoulder. "Let's grab a beer."

We walk toward the kitchen, and I know what's coming. Our little showdown in the office isn't going to pass without some form of commentary. He can't help himself.

"I have a feeling I'm gonna need more than one." I slap him on the back as we move. "You think they'll be all right?" I nudge my head toward the living room.

"Catherine is all too excited to meet the girl who took your balls from you," he jokes.

"No one took my balls."

"Yet."

"At least I had balls to begin with."

Jackson laughs and pops the top. "She's worth it."

"That's what they want us to think. Then they get you where they want you, and boom!" I make a loud noise with my hands. "They fuck with your head."

Jackson takes a pull from his beer, as do I. "Yeah, well, you really fucked yourself by trying to date a CIA agent."

"Don't I know it." He's right. I picked the most complicated and difficult woman I could find. She's a challenge, though, and I sure as hell love to win. Charlie is already caving. I can see it even if she doesn't. She wants me, not that I can blame her—I'm a catch.

"You'll bring her to the wedding in two weeks?" Jackson asks with a sly grin.

"I'll trick her into it." I laugh and take another swig. Enough bullshit, though. It's time for Jackson to cough it up. "Now, why don't you tell me what was in the papers that you hid from that file."

"Caught that, huh?"

"I know you well."

"I wanted you to see me slide them."

I laugh while I watch his every move. He was subtle, but if I caught it, there's no way Charlie didn't. "You should remember she's no amateur, either. So . . ."

Jackson downs the bottle of beer, grabs two more from the

fridge, and thrusts one at me. "You'll need this. Let's go for a walk."

This can't be good. He doesn't want there to be any chance of her overhearing. He knows something. Something I won't like.

"Catherine, we'll be back. We're gonna head toward the beach so Mark can see what real waves look like," Jackson calls out as he's already opening the door.

"Okay, Charlie and I will just order food and spend your money on pretty things!" She chuckles as we head out.

"She's killing me with this damn wedding," he admits.

I can imagine. It's his second marriage, but it's Cat's first. Between the loss of her father and the fact she can barely stomach her mother, the wedding is being held at a vineyard in Virginia. I'm Jackson's best man, and Ashton, Catherine's best friend and my former conquest, is Catherine's maid of honor. We've become close friends once we realized we should never try to date. I can't wait to see that fiery redhead again. At least I won't have to try to score a bridesmaid if I bring Charlie.

"You should've just eloped. Given her less of a chance to realize what an idiot she is for saying yes."

"Dick."

"My offer still stands to officiate. Lee and Liam were very happy with my services."

Jackson laughs while he shakes his head. "You're a moron. Catherine got a legitimate minister."

"I'm legally a minister."

"Did you want to keep talking about how holy you are or did you want to know what I found?"

I have a feeling the news Jackson is about to deliver won't be good. So, I decide to get the one thing I've been debating for a while out into the open. "Before we get into it—" I pause.

"Yes?"

"I want to make you a deal."

Jackson stops walking and then crosses his arms. "This oughta be good."

He has no clue where this is going. "If we figure out who's behind all this shit—if there even is a real *this*—I'll buy into Cole Security Forces. We'll go half and half and I'll become your partner."

Jackson extends his hand, and I take it. "Deal."

"Now, tell me all the shit you didn't want Charlie to know."

"Just how much do you care about her?" Jackson rebuts, and his tone tells me all I need to know.

This is bad. This is going to fuck everything up.

fifteen

Charlie

"**Y**OU BOYS WERE GONE awhile." My suspicions are ringing loudly. They went for a walk two hours ago. Two hours is a very long time to stare at the waves. It's also a very long time to hear about a wedding.

Don't get me wrong—I like Catherine. She's really nice and was more than accommodating. They weren't just checking out the surfing, though, and I'd have much rather gotten some answers.

"There was a competition," Mark explains with a smile. "Did you miss me?"

"I won't next time." And I don't mean longing-wise. His ass is grass.

"Oh," Catherine says. "That's right, we were planning to watch it today and tomorrow, but I completely forgot."

"That's what happens when you become an old married couple," Mark jokes.

"Whatever, ass." Catherine throws her jab at Mark before turning her attention to Jackson. "Charlie and I were getting hungry and were going to order dinner, but I figured we could take them somewhere by the water."

Jackson smiles, wraps his arms around her waist, and then places his lips on her forehead. It's so intimate I have to look away. "Sounds great, baby," he says as if she's the only woman in the world.

I look back over at them as Catherine rests her head on his chest. "Mark, are you still surfing?"

Mark slowly nods his head. "Yeah, when I'm home. I went not too long ago."

"I didn't know you surf," I say, drawing his attention.

Mark comes so close I have to tip my head back to meet his intense eyes. I draw in a deep breath, inhaling the salt air that clings to him. He always smells like fresh air. "I'll take you out tomorrow."

"Umm . . ." I step back. "No thanks."

"It's fun."

"Have you *seen* the news? People get eaten. They lose limbs. I like my limbs."

His grin grows and his eyes glimmer. "They only eat the tasty ones. So maybe you shouldn't go."

My jaw drops at his innuendo.

"Idiot. I don't do the ocean. I like the beach but not the water."

Mark smirks. "I'll protect you."

I laugh. "Not a chance in hell."

Jackson and Catherine stand off to the side, just watching us argue. Mark can manage to bring me from perfectly calm to ready to shoot someone in no time. Infuriatingly stubborn and maddening man. I want to hate him so much, but he makes that damn near impossible.

"Oh, come on. Sharks are just misunderstood. They want to be friends, cuddle a little, or maybe it just wants a hug." Mark is enjoying this a little too much.

"And maybe it wants an appetizer."

Mark chuckles. "There are more meaty options for them. You'll be with me."

"I'm not going." I stand my ground.

"This is like dinner and a show." Jackson speaks up.

"Right!" Catherine laughs. "They're worse than us."

Jackson replies, "I know, but my money's on Charlie."

"Mine too," Catherine says.

Mark and I both burst out laughing then he pulls me close. I try to shove my way out of his grasp, but his strength doesn't allow it. I need to work out more. Or go back to Jiu Jitsu so I can take his ass down. Jackson and Catherine head out the door and Mark leans in so only I can hear. "I would never let anything hurt you on land or at sea. Trust me." He kisses the side of my head and releases me.

I stand there for a second, unable to move. What do I say to that? Because the truth is . . . I don't think he'd hesitate. He'd protect me with his own life if that's what I need. It's who he is, and I need to realize how special he is before he decides I'm not worth the chance.

The evening goes off seamlessly. I enjoy spending time with Jackson and Catherine. The more time passes, the more I understand that Jackson could never be behind any of the issues at his company. His loyalty and dedication to his men is first and foremost. You can see the emotional strain he's under. However, I catch the look that passes between him and Mark. Their walk wasn't just a stumble upon a surfing contest. I let Mark think he threw me off, but he didn't.

"We're heading back tonight," Mark informs Jackson, which is news to me. He doesn't feel he needs to share his plans.

That's fine. I don't feel I need to inform him of mine either.

"Why don't you guys stay at least tonight?" Catherine asks. "As much as I love California, we never see our friends."

"See, Kitty misses me." Mark wraps his arm around her

shoulder and she groans.

"Not you."

"Admit it," he taunts playfully.

"Nope."

"Fine. I know the truth."

"I feel bad for Charlie. Being stuck with you on a plane for an extended period of time would be enough to make me contemplate jumping."

Mark's eyes dart to mine as a grin spreads across his face. "I think Charlie likes having me as a travel partner."

I hate that I have these moments of weakness when I warm to him. But then he effectively takes care of that by reminding how much I should hate him. "I've had better flights, buddy. You were . . . decent."

His grin falls slightly as he studies me. "I'll be sure to change that word for you this go."

Jackson lets out a loud guffaw. "You're totally fucked, dude."

I decide to keep my mouth closed. If I provoke Mark, it'll only backfire. There won't be another round, though. This time, I'll lock the damn door.

We say our good-byes and head back toward the airport. I will say that flying like this is a hundred times better than commercial. I can see why Jackson keeps a private plane for himself and his staff. Plus, there are times they need to get out quickly and can't wait for a flight—especially with their luck lately.

Throughout the car ride, I try to figure out the tie between Mazir and Cole Security Forces. I spent an absurd amount of time studying him, his family, his links to terrorist organizations—which is vast. How Jackson and his team fit? I can't make the connection. Yet, I know there is one.

"What are you thinking about, beautiful?" Mark asks. It's the first time he's ever called me that.

"I'm contemplating who, other than me, wants to destroy

you and your friends, and why."

He takes my hand in his and pulls it into his lap. "Let me worry about that."

"Isn't this why you called me in the first place?"

"Nah." He smiles. "I just wanted to see you again. It had been too long since I had someone to spar with."

"I don't doubt that, but you and I know that's not the only reason."

Mark mindlessly rubs the top of my hand. "I'll figure it out. I have some ideas." He glances over with an emotion I can't place in his eyes. It's not suspicion, but he's not as clear as he was before. It's as if he's erected a wall inside himself, closing me off to whatever he's thinking. I'm not sure what to make of it.

Before I can dissect it too much, we arrive at our plane. We board easily, thanks to the ease of flying private, and find our seats. The silence between us feels heavy. It's not like earlier when it was comfortable. This feels ominous.

My gut tells me there's something brewing. But he takes my hand again, and it helps anchor me. His touch reminds me of what has transpired between us—also, how quickly it seems to have disappeared.

Could Jackson have said something? I know they're keeping something from me, which pisses me off and raises my red flag. Jackson, on the other hand, doesn't know me. He knows I'm an operative. I'm a professional liar. I can con, talk, and bullshit my way out of almost anything. There's reason to distrust me, if I'm perfectly honest, but Mark has never exhibited a lack of trust. I hate what I'm about to do, but I can't forget my own mission.

Once we're in the air, I decide it's a good time to start talking.

"Mark," I whisper. "What happened on your walk?"

He rolls his head my way. "Nothing happened."

"You're lying."

He sighs and rests his head back against the seat. "No, I'm not."

"Okay, then what was said?"

He opens his eyes but keeps his gaze at the ceiling. "We talked about some of Jackson's concerns about getting married again. He was married before, lost his wife, it's been a lot of shit for him the last few years."

That makes sense, and Catherine confided that he's been especially stressed. Still, there's this nagging part of me that insists that's not the whole story.

"So, nothing about the nature of the company?"

"I agreed to become partner." He finally meets my gaze.

"Oh?"

"He's been up my ass about it for awhile. I told him once we get this shit sorted out, I'll come on as part owner. Why are you asking?"

I lift the arm bar between us so I can get closer. I need all of his attention, and all of his mind focused—elsewhere.

He's about to find out just how manipulative I am.

Mark watches me with narrowed eyes, but he doesn't stop me. I slide closer and release his hand. He glides it around behind me and presses against my back. I'm forced to put my hands on his chest to stop myself from falling. He doesn't let me stop there, though. He leans down and pulls my leg up so I straddle him.

He's making this too easy for me.

Our bodies press together as he keeps me secure. "Mark," I whisper.

"Shut up, Charlie," he says before he grips my neck, pulls me down, and kisses me.

I keep hold of my control because this kiss has to be mine. This one is a means to an end. All of this is. I need information, and I'll fuck it out of him if I have to. I glide my tongue across his lips, but he resists me. My head is being held tight—I'm at his mercy.

I know he feels me fighting him. My hands push against his chest, but he doesn't budge. After a moment, his lips part and allow me in. That's when his hands move. He cups my ass, lifts me, and before I know it, he's standing, carrying me back to the bedroom. I want to cry. For the first time in my life as a spy, I wish I could abandon my mission. I realize, right now, that I would abandon it all for someone like him.

"What are we doing?" I ease the pressure of our kiss to speak against his lips, but return my mouth before he can answer.

Mark keeps me in his arms effortlessly. He kicks the door shut with his foot, walks toward the bed, and gently lays me down, causing my heart to kick into overdrive. I can do this. I have to do this. I will get the information I need at any cost. I've never done this, though. Sure, I've toyed with men, but never like this.

"You underestimate me, beautiful," Mark says while undoing the buttons on his shirt.

"What?"

He stalks toward the bed. "You think I can't see."

"You sure like to tell me what I can see and can't see." I rise up on my elbows.

Mark climbs onto the bed and hovers above me. "Tell me, do you think I'm an idiot?"

I lie back and slip into my mind where nothing can touch me. He can't even get close, because this act is for information, not pleasure. "No," I reply. "I hate how you make me feel. I hate that you make me want you."

His smirk falls as his head descends toward my lips. I think he's going to kiss me, but he shifts his head to the side, his warm breath tickles my ear. "You're going to hate a lot more than that, princess."

Out of now where, he grips my wrists and pins them above my head. At first, I think nothing of it, until I realize it's not sexual. I try to fight him, but he's so much stronger than I am. Without breaking a sweat, he ties his belt around my wrists and rests his weight on my hips so I can't move.

"I'm going to gut you like a fish." I try bucking my hips to move him, but to no avail.

"I like dirty talk." He chuckles.

"I hate you."

"Another lie. See, you tell so many that it's hard to keep up after awhile," he muses. Mark's one hand holds my arms up, while he rests his head leisurely against his other. "Here's what I figure. You like me. I can see it. I know it, you know it. But you're afraid. So you play these mind games with yourself to push me away."

"If I did like you—which I don't—I hate you now."

"As I was saying, you really need to see things between us for what they are."

"Over?"

"Not even close." Mark shifts so I can feel his erection against my core. God help me, it turns me on. "You want me so much right now. I can feel the heat coming off you, see the color in your face change. It's all there. I clearly want to fuck the stupid out of you, but I won't just yet."

"That's called rape."

"You can't rape the willing, baby."

"Untie me!" I push against him.

"Why did you think trying to seduce me would work?" Mark asks. "Did you think you'd find out something you want to know? Did you think I would give it up so easily? We could've been back here while I suck on your tits, eat you out, fuck you until you see stars, but you wanted to play this game. Remember that . . ."

I loathe him. I wish him nothing but to burn in the fiery pits of Hell. Satan can use him for a damn pig roast for all I care. He's ruining me. I'm better than this, better than him. "I swear, you better leave me tied up the duration of the flight, or I'm going to butcher you."

He digs his hips deeper, rubs against my clit. I try to fight the moan. I try to bite it back, but it escapes. "You've tortured people, haven't you, Charlie? You've pulled information out by using any means necessary, huh?"

Mark moves again, and shoots a current through every limb. "Fuck you."

"I thought so, but see, so have I. I've had to use methods against people in order to fulfill my mission. And right now . . ." He leans against my ear. "You're my mission."

He's out of his ever-loving mind if he thinks I'll tell him anything. "For someone so smart, you're awfully dumb. I'll die before I tell you a thing."

"I won't hurt you," he explains as his hand travels down to my breast. "I'll pull every ounce of pleasure your body can handle. I'll show you why I'm right for you. Why you want me so much that you hate yourself. Why you think about me, because we both need answers, and we're going to get them now."

His words, his heat, his touch makes me want to sob. I want him more than ever. I'm soaking wet, turned on, and pissed off. It's not a good combination. "Mark," I pull his attention to me.

"You lied to me—again. I can't fucking handle it. Because here I am, thinking you're going to start treating me the way I treat you. That you respect me even half an inch, but no, you leave shit out of your half-truths."

I twist and turn to get him off me. "What did I lie about?"

"Tell me about the mission." He holds me so I can't move.

"What makes you think I'll tell you anything right now? You tied me up!"

"Because you're a liar! You lie," he says through gritted teeth. He leans down and traces his tongue down my throat. "You lie to me. And now to think this . . ." He shakes his head and lets his words trail off. His words are cut off altogether as he pulls my shirt down to expose my breast. The warmth as his lips just barely touches me. I try to rub my legs together. It feels so good. "Do you like that? Tell me," he says before he licks my nipple. "How loud do you think I can get you to scream?"

His blonde hair falls in his eyes and shields his gaze from me as he sucks my breast. One arm holds mine as he tortures me.

"Stop! Not like this," I cry out. This isn't how it was supposed to go.

I have no idea what he knows, but it's bad. Right now, there's a good chance this is the end of everything between us. My stomach drops at the idea of whatever Jackson may have told him.

His eyes latch back on mine. "This is your last chance. No lies. Is there anything I need to know?"

"I need you to untie me." Tears form in my eyes and before one can drop, he releases his hand from my arms.

"Fuck!" he yells, and pulls me up. "Fuck! Don't cry. I would never."

"I know. I'm sorry. I shouldn't have tried to do the same to you," I admit. "We need to trust each other if we're ever going to work together."

"Charlie, look at me," he implores. "I never want to hurt you. Clearly, I have feelings for you." I move my hands to my chest. Now that he doesn't have complete control, I can breathe.

He runs his hands through his hair. I see the regret in his eyes. "Why wouldn't you just ask me what I know?" Anger seeps through his words.

Is his short-term memory broken? I only went to the means I did because he wouldn't talk. "I did ask you. I asked what you talked about. And this is what I do! I get information. I don't ask because people are never honest. So I did what I know."

Mark looks away with shame. "I needed some time to get my head in the right place. I planned to talk to you on the plane, but I can't think straight when I look at you."

I can understand that. He has the same effect on me.

"What did Jackson say?" I need to bring this conversation back to our issue.

His eyes bore into me. "He has photos of you."

"*Me?*"

He nods. "Around the time of Aaron's IED. You were on the road. Then again when Jackson was shot. There's surveillance of you in the village." Mark leans back and pulls me upright with me. "How the fuck am I supposed to process that?"

"I was there, but I wasn't a part of it." The words taste like poison. I've done awful things. Things I would never wish on others, but I never hurt any of them.

"I need more than that, Charlie."

Seeing Mark right now . . . breaks me. His smile is gone. The affection he had in even the simplest gaze isn't present. And I realize just how much they mean to me. How he makes me feel. He makes me want to be a better woman. Mark accepts me for the faults I have, he doesn't try to fix me. He just lets me be. They all deserve the truth, but with that might come the end, and I have to be okay with that.

"My mission was to infiltrate. I was ordered to get Mazir's location, get any pertinent information, and get home. We thought it would take six months, tops. It turned into two years. It was bad, Mark. I forgot who I was—until I saw what was happening to Aaron. As much as I might have been responsible for finding him, it was the other way around. I was lost. Sometimes I think I'm still lost." I look away with tears in my eyes. Crying isn't something I do around anyone. I don't allow myself that weakness.

Mark tilts my face toward him as a drop falls down my cheek. "Don't hide that you're human from me."

His words stun me, and then another tear falls. This time for the words I'm about to say and the man I never had but am about to lose. "I was there, Mark! I knew they were going to set that bomb. I knew they were going after a team of men to get their weapons. I knew! I knew and I couldn't stop them. I knew and I couldn't blow my cover, so it happened." Tears fall like rain for the first time in years. I don't care that he sees it. It's not an act. It's true emotion. "But all I wanted were my answers. I needed to know how to get to my father's killer."

"You knew?"

I wipe my eye with my wrists still bound. "I was their house-wife. My job was to live in the shadows. So I heard them talk about the Americans coming. How they needed to be handled. At first, I thought they meant me."

He waits, weighing my words for what feels like forever.

"Say something."

He doesn't say a word. He just let's me go.

"Mark." I wait until he looks back up. "I was a glorified maid. I cooked, cleaned, washed their damn clothes, and listened to every fucking word they said. I didn't have a voice in that house, because that's how it was meant to be."

There's never been a time in my life I would take back, but looking at his face makes me wish. I would go back, shoot them all in the head, and walk away tossing a match behind me. The disappointment in his eyes hurts more than I can comprehend. He's the first man I've let anywhere close to my heart since my father.

I scoot closer to him, take his hand in mine, and wait for him to say anything. "Do you know why the fuck they're after us?"

"No." I shake my head. "The men I was around were just militants. They didn't have any kind of power. They just carried out orders. My mission was to gain access to Mazir, because he calls the shots. Mazir wants you guys dead. Or Jackson . . . I don't know."

He releases my hand and pulls the belt off my wrists. "And what's in this for you?"

If I tell him this, I'll be entrusting him. He'll know more than any other human alive. No one but me knows what's in that file. My father kept it from everyone, except me. There's a reason, I just don't know what he was trying to tell me. "My father was investigating him," is all I can get out. "I'm sorry, Mark. I'm sorry I didn't stop them. I'm sorry I hurt you, but I couldn't tell you."

His bright green eyes shimmer. His features soften and give me hope. "You kept Aaron alive. You got him home, and Jackson's a tough motherfucker. He lived. You know what I kept thinking when he showed me all of that?"

I shake my head.

"That this was it. That I would lose whatever this was. I can't stop thinking about you. The minute I saw you, I knew I had to have you."

"That's crazy," I say. I wipe my eyes.

"So are we. I'm crazy about you, Charlie. I can't explain it. It's ridiculous, because half the time I don't even like you."

I laugh and so does he.

Tenderly, Mark takes my head between his palms. His thumb wipes a lingering tear. "I understand doing a job that sometimes causes you to question your morals. I don't like it. I don't appreciate knowing my friends were hurt and you were a part of it, but I get it. I want us to try."

I let go of my training. I let the wall crumble and become ash. My heart is what I'm listening to this time, and my heart wants Mark Dixon.

"I want that too, but this won't be easy."

"Nothing worth anything is ever easy."

He leans in and places his lips to mine ever so gently. I melt into him. This time will be different. I'm giving myself to him. A part of me will be vulnerable to Mark, and as much as it scares me, it also gives me hope. This is something no other man will have ever had. I just hope he understands how much I'm offering.

sixteen

MARK'S LIPS PRESS AGAINST mine. We move together, both of us releasing all that just happened. My heart feels light, free, and hopeful. I know that if I let go completely, I'll fall in love with him.

His tongue and mine collide, and all the tenderness is gone. It's the way I need him. It's the way we are . . . a battle. He pulls his lips away, and the feel of his rough fingertips against my lips elicits my mind to float. His hand slides slowly downward. I savor his touch. I pull his mouth back to mine—it's a needed distraction from how good this feels. His other hand grips my hair and he pulls my head to the side. The bite of pain from my scalp only turns me on.

"I'm going to drive you to the brink," he warns. His lips brush against my ear lobe before he pulls it in his mouth. Then his tongue glides across my neck down to my shoulder. He repeats the motion, but this time kisses and sucks along the way.

My legs move. They need the friction. "Mark . . ." I moan his name as his teeth scrape against my shoulder. He bites down, and my back bows off the bed. "Oh, my God!"

"I want to hear you, Charlie." Mark demands as his hand squeezes my breast. "I want to hear every fucking sound you try to hold back." He pulls my top and bra down and then runs his tongue around my breast. "You and I, we're fire, baby. And I'm about to burn you to the ground."

I don't have words. All I feel is heat from his mouth. He sucks, squeezes, and massages my breast before he moves to the other. I'm bound by my own shirt. His lips never leave my skin as I liquefy beneath him. Every cell in my body is screaming his name. I've felt passion. I've had unbelievable sex. But this . . . this is something else. This is life. This is air. This is heaven, and I never want to go back to Earth.

"Take me," I beg. I actually *beg*.

"Not yet." He moves lower, pushing my shirt up. I help him by removing it.

The desire to touch him overwhelms me. I want to lose myself in him as well. "I want to feel your skin."

"We're partners, beautiful. Everything about this time is equal."

I don't know how to do equal. I've always been in charge, but I suspect the same is true for him. We're both in uncharted territory. It's a new country. A new language for both of us.

"Then let me participate."

Mark leans up on his knees. He removes his shirt, exposing every perfect inch of his chest. I allow my fingertips to touch him, to remind me that he's real. We're real. His arms cage me in even as he keeps his weight off me. "By all means, participate."

I push him onto his side and straddle him. The penetrating way he gazes at me makes my stomach clench. His eyes burn with heat, his lips part, and his breath comes in shorter bursts. "How bad do you want me?" I ask. This could be fun. "Do you want to touch me?"

"Are you sure you want to play this game?"

I lean down and allow my nipples to brush against his chest. "I think we're done playing, don't you?" I lick the shell of his ear. "Besides, we know I always win."

Mark lets out a throaty chuckle. "Beautiful . . ." He grips my hair and pulls my head back. "You were never playing in the same league." He flips me back so fast my head spins. "Now it's time you get in some practice."

"Is that so?" I love that we can argue during sex. He pushes me as much I push him. "Then, by all means . . ." I get comfortable.

"First, you have to warm up." He smirks as he unbuttons my shorts. "I wouldn't want you to get injured."

"Of course not."

His eyes remain trained on mine as he pulls them off. I lie at his mercy, unafraid of giving him a little control.

"I need to look you over, get the lay of the land." His brow rises.

I giggle. I fucking giggle. I wasn't even sure I knew how to giggle.

Mark seems to take notice. "Cute."

"Shut up and kiss me."

His eyes turn intense as the green deepens. "Where would you like me to kiss you?"

I lean up on my elbows as a challenge. "I think you should start at my breasts."

"You have perfect tits," he acknowledges before his mouth is otherwise occupied.

My head falls back as Mark licks around my nipple. He takes it between his teeth and pulls back. The jolt shoots straight to my core. "Fuck!" I cry out. I'm unable to keep quiet.

Mark's mouth stops and his eyes lock on mine. "What now? Tell me what you want me to do to you."

That he's giving me any control this time says it all. We're equals. There's no surrendering, just giving. "Touch me."

"Where, Charlie?"

"My clit."

He slides my shorts and underwear off without pause. Everything about him right now is downright sexy. The way he moves, the things he says, the way his eyes darken when he looks at me. The funny thing about becoming invisible is that sometimes I worry I'll disappear. That no one would even notice I'm gone. I go through periods of time when I could be gone, and only two people would actually know. When I'm with Mark, I'm not in the shadows. It's as though he sees nothing but me.

With care, Mark pulls my legs apart. He hoists each one over his shoulders. "Mark," I say.

His lips turn up. "You didn't tell me how to touch you, so I'm using my judgment."

Before I can reply his tongue gives a long hard swipe. "Oh, God."

He repeats it again, and my eyes roll back. His hands under my ass lift me closer as he delves in over and over again. I burn. A sheen of sweat forms across my body as I pulse and tense. He circles my clit over and over, applying pressure before he lightens it when I get close.

Mark inserts a finger as he sucks and then gently bites down on the bundle of nerves. I want to cry, scream, explode, but he keeps me hovering over the breaking point.

"Please," I beg. I need release.

His finger curls as he sucks harder, and I detonate. Every part of my body goes tense before it finally relaxes. I cry out his name as he continues to pump his finger and gently lick me.

"You," I pant. "Are fucking amazing."

He leans up and takes my face in his hands. "You . . ." He pauses. "Own me."

Neither of us says a word. I'm not sure if he meant to admit that to me, but the truth is that he owns me as well. I'm not ready to say it, though. I'm not even ready to think about it. It's all too much and way too fast.

He leans over to grab a condom and returns to his position.

Before he can go forward, I have to warn him. "We can't go too far. This can't get serious."

"We've already passed that point, babe. You just weren't paying attention." He slides inside with no warning.

I groan, and my eyes close as he fills me. It's sweet and tender, so not like our last time.

He doesn't move, but I feel his gaze on me. "Open your eyes," he commands. "Look at me."

My eyes flutter open as he watches me from above. "I can't fall for you."

His hips rock, my breath hitches, and Mark's lids never blink as he takes me. "Too bad."

"You can't fall for me," I plead as pleasure courses through my body.

The fact is that I'm a liar. I may want him. I may want to try some kind of normal, but I'm not sure I'm capable. My entire life has been set into motion since I was a child. I was groomed to be a spy, to live this life, but now everything is changing. I'm battling things I never knew I wanted. I want to be honest, I want to love, and I want to want for more.

Mark rests on his elbows with our noses touching. It's so intimate, as though he's able to look right through me. See the ugly, but see the beautiful too. "Too late."

"No," I whisper.

"Shhh," he murmurs. His lips press down on mine. "You can keep fighting as much as you want, but so will I. And I fight to the end."

"Why me?" I ask as he pushes deeper than before.

"Because no one else sees through your lies. No one has ever tried. You're worth everything hiding behind those blue eyes."

Why can't he say it's because I have nice tits? Instead, he has to say something profound and freak me the fuck out. When I said I would try, I mean *try* . . . not fall in love with him. I'll try to let him in a small amount, not blow the damn door off.

"Stop talking."

"Tell me," he insists. He's still not moving. His muscles tense—it's killing him to stay as still as he is. The need to move is something he's battling.

I'm not telling him what he wants to know.

"Move!"

His smirk grows as we prepare to stand off. "Tell me."

"For once, don't push me," I warn him.

He leans down, allowing our lips to touch as he finally starts to move. Seconds. Minutes. Hours pass and I could not care less. We get lost in each other, completely unaware of the ground soaring beneath us. For once, my mind isn't on the next step. I don't have some plan in place to get information. I'm just free. Freedom is something I never realized I didn't have. I always believed freedom was what I fought to keep, not fought away. This though, this is what free feels like, and I never want to lose it.

MARK'S HOUSE IS EXACTLY as I envisioned. The ultimate bachelor pad. It's covered in dark wood, metal countertops, and every possible video game system you can imagine. We landed about an hour ago—in Virginia Beach, which was a shock—and headed straight here. I've been looking around, taking in his chosen décor. It's clear a woman has never touched this place.

"So, were you going for industrial?" I ask.

"I was going for cheap. The last few years are really the only time I've spent any time in the house."

"How long have you owned it?"

Mark gazes off to the side as he thinks. It's cute. And annoying. "I think about ten years. I got it before the area really got overdeveloped. It's worth at least ten times what I paid for it."

"So, sell."

He walks forward with a torn look. He grips my hands with his and the conviction in his tone causes my heart to sputter. "You don't just get rid of things because something else is more valuable. You cherish it. I'm not a man who easily throws things away. Even when this house is falling apart, I'll find a way to fix her."

"Her?"

The intensity in his eyes softens, "I've learned women are usually the ones that give me the most headaches. This house definitely fits the bill. So, she's a chick. A giant pain in the ass woman who drives me bat shit crazy, yet makes me need her at the same time. Sound familiar?"

I burst out laughing. "I don't know what the hell I see in you."

"Humor, good looks, sex appeal, the fact that I have a big dick probably helps. I mean, really, the choices are endless."

My eyes widen as I listen to his self-proclaimed attributes. "Perhaps the big dick helps."

"Yeah." He wraps his arms around my waist and pulls me flush against him. "Feel free to tell me how much you love my ginormous dick anytime." He kisses my lips. "You . . ." Another kiss. "Want."

I shake my head with a smile. "I didn't say ginormous. It's average."

His hands drop. "You'll pay for that. Now, go change for the party."

"Are you sure they'll be okay with me showing up?" I feel like an outsider.

"For someone who knows how to blend, it's entertaining to see you nervous." Mark informed me on the way to his house that we are invited to Natalie and Liam's for a barbeque. They're celebrating Liam's birthday. I haven't seen Liam since the rescue, nor Aaron for a few months. A lot has changed in that time, and I'm not sure I should be around them.

"I'm not nervous. I just don't know that I'm everyone's favorite person."

"Listen, if Aaron is coming to his former-wife's-new-husband-who-happens-to-be-his-former-best-friend's   birthday, you're fine. You and Aaron still talk, so relax."

Aaron and I e-mail, but that's easy to push away and ignore. The last one he sent was almost like a farewell. I'd done what I could to fill in some of the blanks for him. It's hard to be around him too much. We spent a long time in close quarters, and he's able to get a read on me.

"I haven't seen him in bit."

He lets out a deep breath and grips my hands again. "Do you need me to hold your hand? Are you scared?"

"No, but you should be." Annoyance surfaces. I'm not scared. I'm trying to be in a relationship with an idiot who happens to be a part of my very fucked up past.

Mark smiles and kisses the top of my hand. He'd better knock that shit off. "You want to slap me, huh?"

I smile sweetly. "More than anything."

"You didn't mind me being sweet a few hours ago," he reminds me.

I roll my eyes as I pull my hand back. "That's because you were giving me my third orgasm. I would've let you recite sonnets as long as you kept doing that shit with your tongue."

"Good to know."

"You infuriate me."

He shrugs and then slaps my ass. "You've got two minutes or I'm tying you up and carrying you out."

I think tonight Mr. Dixon will see what happens when you mess with the bull. He's about to have the horns rammed right in his ass.

seventeen

Mark

"HEY LOOK! IT'S THE Fudge Packer!" I yell as I see Liam in the backyard. Of course, he likes the Green Bay Packers. He's even got my goddaughter wearing that crap and yelling things about it. It's fine, soon she'll realize all the talent is with my G-Men.

"There are kids at this party, asshole. Watch your mouth." Liam walks forward to greet me. We clap hands and hug.

"You should talk."

"Who sent him an invitation?" he asks as Lee appears at his side.

She slaps his chest and peers up at me with a smile. "Hey! I wasn't sure you'd make it back." I wrap my arms around her and engulf her. She's so freaking tiny, I'm afraid I'll break her. "Maybe next time you'll show up on time." Even though her attitude is anything but little.

"Lee . . ." I step to the side as Charlie walks forward. "Meet Charlie. Charlie, this is Natalie Gil—, I mean Dempsey." I still fuck that up.

"Nice to meet you, Charlie. I have a lot to thank you for." Lee takes Charlie in for a hug, surprising us both. Even though

I shouldn't be shocked, that girl would hug a leper. "Sorry, I'm a hugger."

Charlie smiles. "It's really nice to meet you. Sorry Mark brought me along without an invite."

She waves her hand, "Oh, please. You're more than welcome. You know my husband, Liam, right?"

"Good to see you, Charlie." Liam shakes her hand. I need to ease the tension clear in Charlie's body language.

"Now!" I clap my hands loudly. "Where are the kids? Because really, they're the fun ones here!"

"I'm glad you came," Natalie says as we walk farther into the party area. "Aara has been asking for you."

"I couldn't miss our only child's stepfather's birthday. She's my sparkly baby."

Natalie shakes her head with a smile. "I swear to God."

"Don't do that. I command you to say some Hail Marys and shit."

Liam laughs as his wife's face colors. She wears her emotions so well. "I regret ever letting you talk me into marrying us."

"Now you're admitting you wanted to marry me too? Sorry, babe. The brother husband phenomenon isn't really my thing. No guy should subject himself to having another cock in the hen house," I joke and she slaps me.

"Oh, how you know all my secrets," she deadpans. I love the easy sarcasm around this group. We're all equal assholes and love nothing more than to make fun of each other. If Jackson were here, this would be complete. But with him coming into Virginia for his wedding in two weeks, he had to miss it.

I didn't realize how much I've missed my friends until now. All of us are bonded and are more family to each other than our real families. I was there for Natalie when Liam couldn't be. Hell, I'm the one who had to tell Lee that Aaron was dead. Aaron was there for me after we lost our three other teammates.

While I didn't mourn or have an emotional episode like the others . . . it wasn't easy on me, either. I was close with Devon and Brian. Sometimes I think my friendship with those two was tighter than Aaron and Jackson at the time. Devon lived with me when his wife left him. We surfed every day. Losing him was a fucked up time in my life.

"Untle Mark!" Aarabelle runs with her arms open.

"Aara!"

I lift her in my arms and squeeze her tight. This little angel kept this broken, screwed-up bunch afloat and she doesn't even realize it. We were all saved by her life. She brought us back to center and reminded us that we needed to band together. She also saved Aaron after he lost it all.

"Charlie, this is Aarabelle." Charlie smiles and takes Aara's hand.

"Nice you meet you, Aarabelle."

"Meet you, too!" she squeaks.

Charlie laughs. "I like your dress."

"Tanks! I like pinkt."

"Me, too!"

"Athair!" Aara yells at Liam. "Chartie likes my pwetty dwess."

Liam laughs, as do I. "I'm sure she does. Why don't you go make sure Shane is still sleeping?" Liam suggests.

She squirms down and rushes toward her brother who sits in his swing. Life goes by so fast, and if you blink, you'll miss it. These kids are talking, walking, and soon they'll be grown before we even have a chance to enjoy them. And here I am, in my thirties, unmarried and childless. It sure as fuck isn't where I thought I'd be.

"One day." Quinn Miller comes up behind me and places a beer in my hand.

"Quinn." I nod. Dude's on my shit list.

"One day I'll understand why the hell he thought getting married was a good idea."

"One day you will. Until then, you'll keep being a dumbass who walks away from a girl who was willing to even consider looking at your ugly mug." I take a swig and let him take that in. While Ashton and I never became anything, what he did to her is completely fucked up. He's lucky I don't lay him out right here, but I respect Liam too much. So Quinn gets to live another day. Until I no longer feel charitable.

He huffs, "If you only knew."

"I know more than you think." This guy is something else. Ashton called me a few weeks ago in tears. She fell for Quinn, dated the stupid fucker, and then he just dumped her.

"Yeah." He shakes his head. "You know what Ash told you. I'm sure she didn't fill you in on what the fuck caused it all."

I lock our gazes so he understands I mean what I'm about to say. "Girls like that don't come around daily. Girls who are willing to accept you for the dick you are, deal with deployments, and know that you may not come home again aren't a dime a dozen. I've been through my share of women figuring this out. I've fucked my way through Hot Tuna—and a host of the other bars in Virginia Beach—but those chicks are all after one thing, man, and it ain't your heart."

These young SEALs don't understand it, and they need to learn. When we're gone, we can't worry about life at home. Our minds are focused on the job. There are some women who can take it, a lot who can't. Ashton needs to cut off his balls.

"Whatever, man." He turns his attention to Charlie. "Nice to see you again, Agent Awesome."

She starts to chuckle. "I don't even want to know, do I?"

I wrap my arm around her waist, clearly letting Quinn know she's here with me. And *with me* as in more than just a guest. "It's just our name for what we think your ass looks like," I explain.

Charlie's eyes widen. "Oh, so you talk about my ass? Is it part of your company meetings?"

Not a bad idea. *Hmmm.* I may have to add that to the agenda. On the other hand, I don't want anyone talking about her ass. "No." Fuck that.

She smirks as if she knows why I'm so adamant. "How long are you guys home for?" she asks Quinn.

Natalie was approaching, but she stops in her tracks. Quinn notices and just nods. "Not sure."

That's bullshit. They're leaving soon, and Lee knows it. She's just having a hard time accepting the idea of it. Part of me wants to tell her to buck up because this is what she gets being married to a SEAL again. There's a part of us that goes insane being home too long. Sure, it's a great break, but we live for the field. Being home keeps us human while the field keeps us animalistic. I miss that feeling.

"You can say it, Quinn." She thaws out. "I know you're all leaving."

"I won't be responsible for you throwing shit."

"I only throw things at you." Lee gives him a condescending look. "Because you're an idiot."

I huff, open my mouth to say something in support of his stupidity, but Liam walks in with the food. "Let's eat!" he says. At least he gives us a reason to shut up and not get in a fight. Quinn and I *will* have words, though.

Liam must be aware of the energy in the room. Natalie places her arms around him. He's a lucky dude. He has the woman he loves, kids, friends, and still gets to kick everyone's ass.

I'm getting there. I just need to get Charlie fully on board with actually dating and not this trying shit. I don't need marriage and all that yet. But we've been friends for a year, and I know there's potential.

Everyone digs in while I sit back and just observe.

Surrounded by the people who matter, I think about how easily Charlie fits in. She's one of us. She knows everyone here, and all of us are in that same field. We understand leaving, coming home, and never really having a place. We live on the outskirts of relationships.

I glance at Liam and he tilts his head toward the house. I nod. He's got information I requested.

"Mark," he says. "Can you help me with the keg?"

"Sure thing."

We both get up, but he takes an extra minute because, of course, he has to kiss his wife. I swear they make me sick with how much they love each other. Their honeymoon period is never going to end.

"Do you even have a keg?" I laugh as we walk toward the kitchen.

"Of course I do. It was cheaper than cans between you, Quinn, and Aaron."

"Is he showing up?"

Liam shrugs. "He said he was."

Aaron says a lot of things regarding Lee and Liam. I know he's trying, but a man can only take so much. While they're all really sensitive around him, it's still hard to miss their glances and shit. It's kind of like watching a movie you weren't invited to.

"So?" I'm unwilling to talk about anything other than what he might know. "I assume you really didn't need my help with beer."

Liam checks behind us before he begins. "I made a few calls." His voice is barely audible. Which is good considering Charlie is a spy and all. "One of my buddies up there is a private investigator. He was on our team a while back, good guy, great at intelligence and scouting. You may want to think about hiring him, since he seems to be good."

Is he serious? "Liam," I prompt.

"Anyway," he gets back on topic. "He said there was one guy who apparently left early. That waiter though, he doesn't exist. Kind of like Charlie, if you get what I mean."

"You think the guy is CIA?" I ask. That makes no sense.

"Based on the little information you gave me, the fact she was tailed before, and then she was drugged at a function . . ."

"Why would they drug her?"

"The question you should be asking is: what were they planning to do with her once they had her knocked out?" Liam grabs the keg, leaving me to mull over his question.

If the CIA is after Charlie, what the hell does she know that puts her on their list? Since they were unsuccessful, they're sure as hell going to try again.

Charlie

TWO WEEKS PASS AND as much as I hate to admit it, I've enjoyed being around Mark. We connect on so many levels. Today we're going shooting, then he somehow coerced me into going to Jackson and Catherine's wedding. It also could've been that Catherine almost demanded it. It's weird, having friends . . . that are girls.

"Ready?" Mark comes out of the bedroom wearing his camouflage pants and brown tee that clings to every delicious dip and ridge of his chest. My mouth waters while I stare at him. His hair hangs long enough he could pull it back. I really hope he doesn't or we'll never make it out of here. I've become insatiable when it comes to him.

Could be the fact that he gives multiples. A lot.

"You ready to have a girl show you how to shoot?"

He rolls his eyes as he grabs the guns. "I was a sniper."

I shrug. "I think we should wager."

"You really think that's a good idea? You and I are competitive enough without adding on top of it."

I slide up next to him in his Jeep and push his hair back. "I'll make it worth your while," I say in my sexiest voice.

"You love my dick. I don't need to bet to get you naked."

"Smug asshole."

"You know what? I like winning, so sure, I'll bet you. Make it good because you can bet your fine ass that I'll counter."

Mark and I seem unable to stop ourselves when it comes to one upping the other. I don't doubt he's a good shot, but he has no clue how good I am. I won every award for shooting during the academy. When I was young, it was the only sport my father would allow me to compete in. He'd say, "A woman who can shoot cannot be taken down. Remember that, Charisma."

"Hmmm," I pretend to need a minute. "I mean, you're a sniper and all, so I should get a handicap."

"Ha!" He laughs in my face. His arms wrap around my hips as he tugs me close. "You're out of your damn mind. How about this . . . If I win, you tell me your name, and if you win, tell me your name."

"Or not."

His lips touch the tip of my nose. "You'll cave soon. I can see it."

"So, if I win, I want something good. I'm thinking a full day of anything I want." I wiggle my brows and he smirks.

"Anything?"

"Anything."

"I don't know about that."

My fingers slide up his chest. I relish in feeling his muscles tense at my touch. "I give you my name, you give me anything I want for a day." I continue my path until my fingers tangle in his hair that just touches the back of his neck. "I think it's a fair trade."

Mark stares into my eyes, and seems to weigh the offer. "I don't think this is a good idea, beautiful. You wouldn't offer up your name unless you thought you had a good chance of winning."

I hate him sometimes. "Or I just really want to tell you already and need some incentive."

"Liar."

"Maybe."

"You know what? I have no doubt I'll outshoot your ass, so I'll take your bet."

I smile deep within, but on the outside, I look a little scared. This is going to be so much fun. Of course, there's a chance I could lose to him, but I'll take that risk. He might play down to me, and I will be sure to get in his head a little.

We arrive at the range, which is on the outskirts of Virginia Beach. You can tell it's a Special Operations type range. There's a host of barriers and targets. It gives a wide variety of positions and angles to shoot from. Remaining shielded will be a challenge, but I learned how to shoot on the move. I think I actually have better scores when I'm forced to be mobile, since that's how most shooting is done anyway.

It's not very often that we fire our weapon from behind cover and have time to take a clear shot. I know all about adapting and still making a good shot. However, there's no way to lie to myself that this isn't Mark's course. He has the advantage, so I really do need to be on point.

"Okay, do we want to just say best scores?"

"I think that's the most fair. Three points for any center mass shot, two for body, and one for head?"

Mark scratches his head, "I won't even ask how you know the Navy's scoring."

I grin. "I know my stuff, shiny vampire boy."

"Oh . . ." He nods his head with a smile. "Now you want to trash talk on top of this?" Mark leans back and crosses his arms over his chest.

"I figure we should keep it authentic."

"Fair game then, Charletta."

"What?" I laugh.

"I'm running out of names."

"Come on, let's go see your stellar skills."

We grab the ammo, get our stations set up, and his friend behind the counter comes out to make it fair. He seems easy enough to sway my way. I give him my best smile, bend a little to show some cleavage, and make sure he's watching.

"Not happening." Mark looks over with a no nonsense smirk. "Why don't you just go over the rules, Pugh." He gives him a look that I can only imagine makes the poor guy want to crap himself.

"Don't be mean," I scold Mark.

"Don't show him your tits."

"I wasn't."

He steps forward, grips my face, and kisses me breathless. I try to fight off the desire that builds, but I'm lost to him. I kiss him back, uncaring that anyone is around us. That this is supposed to be a competition, and I'm supposed to be messing with his head. All I care about is his lips against mine. The way he possesses me completely when he holds me like this. Butterflies flutter in my belly as I envision him making his claim in front of everyone. The testosterone he exudes makes me want him more. I'm so fucked.

"Now . . ." He turns me around and slaps my ass. "Let's see how much you cry when you lose."

And all the turmoil is gone. Just like that, he pisses me off and calls to my dominant side. "Yeah, let's see who is the bigger girl."

Mark grabs the nine, loads it, and holsters it. I close my eyes to avoid the throbbing taking place between my legs. He's so fucking sexy right now. Armed, in uniform—but I lose it when I open my lids to see him pulling his hair back. Now, I'm unable to stop myself.

I yank the tie out of his hand, fist my fingers in his hair, and practically climb him. My mouth adheres to his, and I can't imagine doing anything other than this. He's hot, and right now, he's mine.

His hands hold the backs of my legs while I kiss the life out of him. I need this. I need to feel him, and I'm slightly hoping this catches him off balance—but this is want and I'm deluding myself.

After God only knows how long, I pull back. "Hi." I'm a little out of breath.

"Hell-fucking-o."

"You can put your hair up like that later."

"I think you like me."

I groan. "I think you're hot."

"And you like me."

"Just your dick."

"And me too. You can say it."

He releases me, gives me a peck, and a smirk. "I don't!"

"Whatever you say, Charlie."

"Good! Because I say I don't like you. Just the sex."

Pugh stands to the side watching us. I forgot he was there. "You guys should make movies." He shifts and adjusts himself. Gross.

Mark's protective side seems to explode as he pushes the guy back so he hits the wooden pole between us. "Keep your fucking comments to yourself. Got it?"

"Relax, Dixon. Just saying that was hot." He seems to be unimpressed with Mark's hostility. "Let's get to the game, eh?"

I stand back, leaning against the pole to watch the interaction. Mark seems to cool off as fast as he got heated, but really, Pugh just did my job for me. He'll be slightly distracted.

We go over the rules, and thanks to a coin toss, Mark goes first. It allows me to see the course first hand, get the lay of the land, and prepare. It'll give me a chance to almost run it with him in my mind.

"Okay, blindfold her," he tells Pugh. He hands him a rag.

"What?" I squeak.

"No way in hell am I giving you any advantage here."

"No way in hell are you going to blindfold me!"

"Charlie." Mark's exasperated. "Put the fucking thing on. You're not watching this. I would expect the same if you went first."

No, no, no. I'm not doing it. During our night training, I was once blindfolded and left for hours. I refuse to experience that again. And I'm not telling him my name. Yet, I always honor my bets. Damn him.

Okay, I can do this. I can find the confidence. I can beat him because I'm Charisma Erickson. I'm a badass female who can outshoot any man I've shot against before.

"Fine!" I allow my anger to flow through me. "Give it to me, you giant pussy. You're sooo good that you need to blindfold me? Big, bad Navy SEAL is afraid of a girl."

He grins. "I love it when you get all mouthy. Makes me think of new ways to shut you up."

"Suck my dick!" I yell at him as I throw on the blindfold.

"How very G.I. Jane of you."

"If you even think of touching me—I'll bite it off." I warn him as I slide down to the ground.

"Okay," Pugh says and pulls Mark's attention away. "Highest score wins." He reviews the course with Mark, and because I've lost my vision, my hearing is heightened.

I listen to everything I can. Standing, prone, kneeling, and then back to standing. I at least know the first four obstacles. If for some reason we tie, the fastest time will be the breaker.

"Ready?" Pugh asks.

"Oh, yeah," Mark affirms, and I can imagine his face. That

smug smile, the side eyes on me, before he runs his fingers through his hair.

Shooting is a high. Shooting allows you power that you can't explain. It's a thrill of handing something so deadly with so much precision.

I hear the gunfire pop off fast. The bullets bang as they hit the metal targets one after the other. *Bing, bing, bing.* After a few more seconds, all goes quiet. I'm practically bouncing in my skin.

The sound of their boots crunching grows closer. "Ready, princess?"

So, we're back to that nickname. I pull the fabric down from my eyes and his face comes into view and toss it at him. His eyes are alight with joy. I can see how much fun it was for him. The enjoyment oozes from his entire face.

"Only thing I'm ready to do is hand you the tissues."

"Tissues?"

"For all the crying you're about to do." I pat his cheek and jump up.

His head falls back as he laughs. "God, how much I love you—" He locks his gaze with mine "Talking shit to me." He tries to play it off as though he was finishing a sentence.

There's that awkward moment between us, but I laugh it off. "Good thing I'm really good at it."

I turn away and let out a heavy breath. There's no way he loves me. It was just a slip. A stupid slip, like when you accidentally say it hanging up the phone. Instinct. That's it.

"Happy shooting!" he says to my back.

I turn and glare. "Put the blindfold on, glimmer stick boy."

"I already shot."

"I don't want you to see shit!"

"I can't get an advantage."

I stalk forward, rip the blindfold from his hand, and tie it on. "You also can't distract me this way. Now sit down, shut up, and be a good little boy."

"You'll pay for that."

"I'm so sure." I roll my eyes and prepare to kick his pomp-ous ass.

Pugh explains the course, same as he did for Mark. We get back, I crack my neck and find my center.

Here we go.

I fly through the course, hitting my mark better than I could've imagined. I don't concentrate on the bet, the targets, or anything except me and my breathing. Everyone presumes the key to shooting is aiming, but it's actually about timing your breaths. That's what's instrumental in making sure you don't pull the round. When you're at that perfect release, you can hit anything perfectly. So I time myself, counting my in and out. I shoot better than I have in a long time. His ass is grass.

Once we're done, Pugh tallies my score. If Mark beat me, it'll be by a hair.

"Feel confident?" Mark asks. He wraps his arm around my waist. I swear he's always touching me.

"Did I mention I won a target competition at age ten?" I boast. I haven't mentioned a word of it.

"Okay." Pugh gives his hands a loud clap. "Ready to hear who won?"

"Sorry, Charlie." Mark says stretching his arms overhead. "I'm so ready to know what to scream out tonight."

I slap his unprotected stomach. "Let's hear it."

Pugh looks down at his paper. "Okay. The winner is . . ."

nineteen

"**I** KNEW IT!" I scream out while I dance around. I shake my ass and do a little jig. "Ha!" I say in Mark's face as I continue my taunting. "I win. I win. I win, I win, I win."

"There is no fucking way." Mark grabs the paper from him and looks it over. "By that much?"

"The targets are there. You can count for yourself," Pugh offers.

"Oh, the things you will do!" I practically squeal.

Mark growls as he stomps off to check the course.

He returns with a scowl. Clearly, I won. He couldn't even lie to himself. This is a glorious day. "Thank you, Daddy," I whisper to the sky.

"There need to be boundaries to this," Mark grumbles.

This is going to be so much fun. I mean, he said he would do anything. Stupid, overconfident man. "This is what happens when men like you get cocky. You say words like anything and always. It bites you in the ass, but I'll be happy to be the one to take advantage of this."

He saddles up next to me in his Jeep. "Will do you your ass shaking dance again?"

"For you, maybe." I grin, and lean back.

"Don't drown in your victory."

"Don't worry about me. I would start preparing for the Day of Charlie."

"You're naming your day?"

I huff. "Of course. Now to decide when to cash it in."

"I'm sure it'll be the most inconvenient of days."

"Duh!"

When we pull into the driveway, Mark surprises me by taking my hand. He shifts his body toward me and his green eyes bore into mine. I wait for him to say something, but he just sits with our fingers intertwined. "We need to leave in a few hours for Jackson and Catherine's wedding."

"Okaaay." I'm confused by the tone in his voice.

"We don't have long."

"Mark?" My brow tightens. "You okay?"

"Never better."

This reminds me of the time he got all weird on the plane because of the conversation he had with Jackson and what he thought he knew about me. We've spent almost all of our time together, so I don't think it's that, but he's acting really odd right now. I turn my mind back to when he almost said those three little words, but . . . I don't know.

"Let's shower," I offer. Maybe his mood will switch.

"You just want me naked."

Of course that snaps him out of it.

"You know me oh, so well." My playful tone makes him smile.

After our long and very dirty shower, we pack an overnight bag and head off to the vineyard. Mark and I make small talk and laugh about stories of old missions. I wish I could tell him more, but I can't. Instead, I'm vague, but he doesn't push. It's a nice thing about our relationship, that there's an understanding that work sometimes can't be shared.

"Wow!" I exclaim as we turn into Keswick Vineyards in

northern Virginia. "This place is breathtaking."

The driveway is a little dirt road that hugs the vines. We travel until a huge white house comes into view. It has grand pillars and a gorgeous fountain in front. The dirt road circles around it, giving a magnificent picture. Everything is crisp. The greens are deep and rich. The white of the house is stark, and makes everything feel elegant. I can see why they'd pick this place. It's perfect.

We park off to the side and Catherine rushes to the car. "Charlie! You came!" Her smile is luminous. She's the image of a blushing bride. Catherine is so happy, so hopeful, so full of life.

"After phone call number eight, I knew I couldn't say no," I tease her.

"This is my best friend, Ashton." A gorgeous redhead comes forward. Her blue eyes are stunning. No wonder Mark had a thing for her. Thankfully, he told me their story and how they never really dated. It was more of a, we could, but we won't situation. Neither of them were willing to make an effort, but remained good friends.

"So, you're the girl who tamed the idiot." She smiles and embraces me. "It's so nice to meet you."

"I've heard a lot about you," I reply.

I'm not a jealous person. But I can't help but hold a slight bit of curiosity about her. I know she had been seeing their friend, Quinn, but still. Mark is a hundred times better catch—at least in my opinion.

She laughs. "Believe nothing you've heard. Especially if it's from him." She lets go of me and walks over to Mark. She punches him in the arm playfully then they hug. "It's good to see you, Twinkles."

"Quinn here?" He asks with an edge to him.

"No."

"Asshole."

"Let's not ruin today with talk of the douchebag." Ashton

smiles before turning to Catherine. "It's not every day I get to see my Biffle get married."

"Biffle?"

"Best friend for life," Catherine explains. "Ashton has her own language. It's ever growing with her made up words."

"Whatever!" she says with her hand up as she saunters away.

I'll need to drink to keep up with this group. It's funny how Mark is so integral to so many people. He fulfills a different role for each of them. For Natalie, he's her support in some ways, only more brotherly. With Catherine, he's more playful and again brotherly, but more annoying. With Jackson, he's his rock. He stands beside him, will fight for him, and he has this serious-ness around him. Then, when he's with me, there's a side no one else gets to witness—something just between us. Then again, he sees something with me that I've never shared.

Catherine giggles. "Come on, we're having wine and hors d'oeuvres over in the picnic area."

Mark takes my hand and we follow her over. When we ar-rive, Jackson immediately stands, kisses my cheek, and hugs Mark. When he sits down, Catherine perches herself on his lap. God, they're so in love.

Ashton makes a choking sound when they start to kiss. "You two need to just get this over with so we can all stomach food."

"Oh, shut up."

Mark laughs. "She's not kidding. You'd figure by now it would've worn off."

Jackson regards Catherine and then brushes her hair back. "It'll never wear off. When it's right, it's forever."

I'm not sure whether to laugh or swoon.

Mark grabs his drink and downs it. We spend the evening this way, drinking wine and eating until the sun sets. The lights from the fountain set off a glow. The night is so beautiful, it makes me wonder how I would feel if I were the bride.

"Okay, people." Catherine slaps her legs and stands. "We've got a big day tomorrow." She gazes at Jackson as he pulls her in his arms. "A day I feel we've waited for forever."

Jackson holds her close. "I'll see you tomorrow."

"I'll be there."

"I've been waiting for this day for a long time. Tomorrow you'll be Mrs. Cole."

My heart swells. This is what true love looks like. It reminds me of my parents. My father used to say the sweetest things to my mother. If they were fighting, my dad would just tell her some beautiful line and she was putty in his hands. They loved each other with every part of their being, and I see that in Jackson and Catherine.

"Awww," Mark says sarcastically. "You're going to be Mrs. Muffin."

She glares at him. "You're such a tool."

Mark shrugs. "I've been told that a time or two. But it's better than being the nickname for a pussy."

"Ignore him, baby." Jackson cups Catherine's face. The adoring way they look at each other sends shivers down my spine. "Tomorrow we'll be married. You're already mine, and I'm already yours, but tomorrow . . . I'll show the world."

"Hallmark has nothing on you two. Maybe you should debate a career change to gynecologist since you apparently like being a vagina." Mark busts out laughing, and Ashton slaps the back of his head.

Does he do this with everyone? "Mark," I say, to diffuse another bickering match and the fact he ruined such a beautiful moment. "Let's head back to the room. You have to be nice tomorrow, and I'm sure that requires sleep."

"Again with needing me in bed."

"Let's go, Romeo."

We both are a little drunk from the wine. I slip into Mark's

T-shirt and climb under the covers. His arms open, and I climb in. I've never been a spooning type girl, but something about letting him hold me is appealing. We fit together, in so many ways.

"Tell me about the last mission," he says against my neck.

"What about it?"

"Why did they take it from you?" I tense, and being that his arms are around me, he has to notice. "Sometimes, after we came home from a mission . . . our group would talk it out. Things we did wrong, things we did right, the things we wanted to do differently. It was a time to kind of air it out. See things from everyone's eyes. Jackson would view something in a way I didn't and vice versa. It can help."

I understand his logic, but that's what a debrief is—in a way. "I've already laid it out."

"No, you had to give details. You had to talk about the way it went down, not paint a picture. There's a difference. Paint me the entire scene. How you felt, what you saw, where you went."

Mark throws his leg over mine, traps me, and then shifts so he's on top.

"Hi?"

"We're not having sex."

"Well, that's a disappointment."

He laughs. "Tell me. Let me see it through your eyes."

I don't want to do this, but maybe he's right. There's a chance Mark can pick up on something I missed or help me to see it through his eyes. At this point, it's worth a shot. We're not any closer to finding either of our targets.

IF I THOUGHT THE grounds were beautiful yesterday, it had nothing on today. I spent the morning with Catherine and Ashton. We had a small breakfast and talked a little about how they grew up together.

Around midafternoon, Natalie and Catherine's other friend from New Jersey, Gretchen, showed up.

Ashton and Gretchen kept both me and Natalie a part of everything. All these women are so different from the ones I've known. They're sweet, considerate, and truly—nice.

Natalie and I decide to sneak off for some wine while the girls are getting their hair done. "I never had a chance to really talk to you," she says with nerves clear in her voice. "I hope you don't mind."

"I'm sure you have a lot of questions."

"I do. I mean . . . I did. Aaron has answered a lot of them. Liam has helped fill in the gaps of what he thinks went down. It's a really weird place for me when it comes to all of this." Natalie pushes her blonde hair behind her ear. "I mean, on one hand I should hate you. You kept my husband at the time hostage. One the other hand, if that hadn't happened I'd be living a very different life."

I know what she means. It's the guilt of almost being happy that it turned out the way it did. Had Aaron come home, she wouldn't be married to Liam. She may have never known all the secrets that Aaron kept. It's a really hard place to be.

"I think things turned out the way they should've. Don't you?"

She nods and fills our wine glasses. "To fate."

I lift my glass and clink it with hers. "To fate."

"You should really be happy that Mark is the best man."

"Oh?" I wonder what else he would be.

"Oh, yeah. I'm sure he tried to convince Jackson to let him officiate their wedding. Catherine is a much stronger force than I am. I was an idiot and let him."

"Wait!" I'm stunned. "Mark is a minister? *My* Mark?"

Well, I guess he's my Mark now. That slipped out a little too effortlessly.

She laughs. "Yup. The one and only Father Dixon. Let's not get too carried away, though. He got that damn thing online, and he's taken it to a whole new level."

"Why doesn't that surprise me?"

Lee looks at her phone "We should head back," She says. "It's almost time."

Catherine insisted that Natalie and I get ready in their room. My dress was absconded so I had no out. It's funny that I can take down heads of mafia rings, terrorists, and monsters far scarier than most will see, but I can't fight off a bunch of girls.

I knock on the door and Ashton opens it when she sees it's me. She's beautiful. Her pale purple one-shouldered dress fits her like a glove. "Hey, come in. Catherine is finishing up her hair."

"Thanks." I smile. The room overlooks the vineyard. There's nothing but green as far as the eye can see. As I turn the corner, Catherine comes into view. "Wow," I say as I get my first look at her. Her long brown hair is pulled low but has intricate braids crossing the back of her head. Her makeup is soft but still dramatic. She looks like a movie star. "You look gorgeous."

"Wait till you see the dress." Ashton grins. "She's going to give Jackson a heart attack."

"Stop!" Catherine's eyes roll. "I'm so glad you could be here. I might need someone to take down Ashton if she tries any of her shenanigans."

I laugh. "I'll protect you."

They finish up and she heads into the dressing area to put on her dress. I gasp when she emerges. She's absolutely breathtaking. Her dress has a long, tulip-shaped bodice. Lace adorns the entire thing down to her hands, revealing her skin beneath. The tiny beading along the edges literally makes her sparkle.

"Do you think he'll like it?" she asks.

Natalie steps forward. "Catherine, you are positively radiant. There's not a man in the world who wouldn't be proud to have you on his arm. And Jackson, well, I've got a hundred bucks that says he's sobbing before you reach the end of the aisle. You're perfect."

Catherine's tears fall and mine start to form.

"It's just . . . this isn't his first time . . ." she trails off.

Again, Natalie comforts her. "Madelyn is his past. You are everything he ever wanted. Loving someone before doesn't make you love the next person any less. That's the beauty of love. It's ever growing. You and Jackson have something so few ever have known. He loves you, he would die for you, move to the ends of the Earth. His previous marriage isn't even in this place, trust me." she smiles as she wipes her own eyes.

Natalie, of anyone, would know.

"I'm being silly." She shakes her head. "I've loved him so much, and I'm always afraid the other shoe is going to drop. He's everything that matters in this world to me."

My heart cracks at her words. My mother used to say the same thing. This is what I've always wished for. A love where the idea of it disappearing would ruin you, but fear has kept a piece of me from ever letting it happen.

I wipe a tear from my cheek. "Charlie?"

"Sorry, you just look so beautiful. Jackson loves you when you're not looking. That's true love. It's when your back is turned—and I've only ever seen that a handful of times."

"Jackson and I almost lost each other because of pride and stubbornness, and secrets almost tore us apart. I wasn't sure today would ever come. But you're right, he and I have something unique and perfect. It's time to move forward." Catherine lets out a deep breath. "I'm ready."

The girls squeal a little and hug. "You're getting married!"

"I'm getting married!"

"We're going to head down and get our seats," Natalie says. She takes Catherine's hands in hers and pulls her close. "I'm so happy for you."

They smile and Catherine steps toward me. "Thank you. You'll never know how much Mark means to all of us. Having you around him gives all of us hope."

He gives me hope. Instead of saying anything, I just nod with a smile.

twenty

WE'RE USHERED TO OUR seats by the groomsmen. Aaron seats me, which makes me laugh. I spot the guys from Cole Security Forces. They all wave with a smile. I look around for Mark, but Lee sits next to me before I catch him.

"You look beautiful, by the way. I didn't get to tell you that when we were upstairs."

Thankfully, I happen to be a fantastic shopper and found a dress to die for. It's burgundy red with a low, scoop back. I already had gold heels from the gala, which worked perfectly. "So do you." I smile. Natalie has her blonde hair twisted in the back so she is showing off the low back of her pink tea-length dress. It's pretty, with a little fuller skirt and a high neckline.

Liam slides in next to her and takes her hand. "Hey."

"Hey, you're not in the bridal party?" I ask.

"Nah, these guys have been friends since the beginning. They kept it small, which works for me." He pulls at his tie. "Just means I can loosen this sooner and drink more."

I smile and Natalie shakes her head. "He'll be asleep before the last song plays. Don't let him fool you. This is the first time we've been without kids in a while. He's excited about napping."

Before he can respond, the music pipes up. I take a moment to soak it all in. The sun is just starting to set behind the orchard.

There are white chairs that line both sides of a makeshift aisle, their backs wrapped with lavender bows. The trees behind the pergola are filled with tiny white twinkling lights. Every detail was thought out, but before I can get too deep, Jackson and Mark emerge at the front.

I can't see anything but him. It's as if the entire wedding fades and all I can focus on is Mark. His long blonde hair is pushed back, his green eyes bear into mine. No one exists but us. Mark's broad shoulders fill out every inch of his tuxedo. The jacket tapers at his waist to show off his trim frame. He's positively sinful. The grin that paints his face tells me he can read my thoughts. He winks as the music switches to Pachelbel's Canon in D.

This is the moment I love most about weddings. The bride entering and seeing the man she loves. I may not have been the Barbie and princess little girl, but a wedding I dreamt of. I imagined it in my head. My parents were the epitome of love and devotion, always kissing, touching, and telling each other how much they loved one another. Dominic and I thought they were gross, but now I appreciate the gift they gave us. I won't settle for less.

I realize the emotions stirring in me are dangerous. For me to want this, to wish it were me. Even to entertain the notion of gazing at Mark with anything close to what I feel now is scary. Maybe I could trust him. Maybe we could find ourselves in this same situation.

Catherine continues down the aisle. She doesn't look at anything other than Jackson. Mark's eyes meet mine, and hope blooms deep in my heart.

The ceremony is just as I imagined—timeless. They say their vows, tears flow, and you can see the love they share. The sunset casts its blessing in pinks, oranges, and reds throughout the sky overhead. We move into the huge white tent set up on the other side of the vineyard. The tables are decorated with centerpieces of various glass candlestick holders surrounding tall vine-wrapped willow branches.

Being the date of the best man puts me at the wedding party table. However, thanks to Catherine's thoughtfulness, I know everyone. Ashton, Gretchen, and Aaron all make me feel like a lifelong friend. Not that I'm not fine in uncomfortable situations, but it's nice not feeling out of place.

Mark is with the bride and groom taking pictures, so I head to the bar.

"A glass of chardonnay please." I smile as Jackson and Catherine enter the tent. Their smiles are electric. Their love is palpable.

"Having a good time?" Mark bumps my hip and hands me a flute. "Don't worry, it's safe to drink the champagne here."

"How do I know you didn't slip me something?"

"I don't have to drug you to sleep with me. You know you love my dick."

"Is that so?"

"I rev your engine, baby. I speak your language. I'm your weapon of choice."

"Oh, Jesus. You need a shrink." I laugh and take a sip.

I lean against him. The urge to be close is stronger than I can fight. He makes me happy just to be around him.

"They're really happy together," he muses.

"You mentioned they didn't have it easy." I never pressed for more answers. It kind of seems fitting to talk about them now.

Mark takes a swig of his beer. Only he would drink beer at a vineyard. "Yeah, Jackson has a history of keeping shit to himself. He's a weird guy. We've been friends for a long time, but even I don't understand his thought process. The thing about secrets," he pauses to cast me a look. "is they eventually become uncovered. No matter how hard we try, they don't stay buried forever."

My heart races at his words. My life is a stack of carefully constructed secrets. If one were to get pulled out, everything would fall. People—colleagues, friends, loved ones—would all be in danger. I would literally have to disappear, because I would be killed. The more time I spend around Mark, the more I exposed I become.

"Hopefully, people don't dig. Sometimes it's the thirst for knowledge that ends up making things worse." I plead in my own way that he'll understand.

Mark mulls over my words, but the intensity doesn't ebb. "The truth, though, can't be denied."

"Sometimes the lie is safer than the truth."

"I'll protect you. Do you believe that?"

"Mark." I can barely speak. I know he wants to think he can, but there are some things even he can't stop. Instead of letting me finish, he takes me into his arms.

"I can live with your lies, Charlie. As long as you don't lie to me."

"I won't always have a choice. If I go back to the agency, my life isn't always my own."

This has always been the struggle I've faced. Loving some-one, letting them into my life, doesn't provide them with any promises. I'll do whatever my country needs me to do. I'll go where I have to go and use those around me to get informa-tion—at any cost.

Mark takes my drink and sets it down. "Your life is always your own. It's what you choose that makes it someone else's. Come." He puts his hand out. "We have people to make jealous." His smile is inviting, and my hand slips right into his. "Right after

I give my speech. You read for epic?"

"I'm scared more than anything."

He laughs. "Jackson should be too."

twenty-one

Mark

I'VE THOUGHT ABOUT ALL the things to say to my best
friends. The stories I have that would make him turn colors,
but I promised his mother I would behave. Then again, behaving
for me is probably a running joke for her.

"Did you write it down?" Charlie asks as we make our way
to the head table.

"I got everything I need here."

"What was he thinking, making you the best man?"

I shrug. "No clue." The deejay calls for everyone to take a
seat. "That's my cue."

I rush over toward Jackson and Catherine. She gives me a
look. Aww, Kitty has the claws out. Jackson, of course is doing
just as I expected, scowling. *Yeah, be scared, Muff.* I go around behind them so their faces have to remain smiling.

"Welcome, everyone. I'm so happy to be here to celebrate
the marriage of two people I love dearly. Catherine and Jackson
have come a long way. Most of you know that I've had the priv-
ilege of serving with Muffin here." I clasp his shoulder. "We've
worked together as civilians since then. He's one of best guys
I know, and somehow he managed to convince Catherine to

marry him." He laughs, and Catherine grits her teeth in a fake smile. "She's the best. She's so much smarter than he is. Clearly better looking." I turn to Jackson. "Sorry, Muffin but let's be real here. She beats you." Everyone laughs. To think they were worried. "But to be serious, there are no two people in this world that deserve to be happier than these two. And I would know, because I'm ordained. So, with the power vested in me, I bless this marriage. May my holy power wrap Kitty and Muffin in its arms and hold them close. To Jackson and Catherine!"

I lean down as the clapping continues, along with a lot of laughing. I drop the mic and kiss them both on the cheek.

"You're dead." Jackson's voice is barely audible.

"Your threats don't bother me."

Catherine stands, wraps her arms around me, and laughs. "I expected nothing less. I love you, Mark. Don't screw up with her. This could be you in a year."

I rear back as she smirks. She has a streak in her people forget about because of her little smile, but she knew. "Nice one."

Jackson wraps his arms around her and kisses her cheek. "You scared him, baby."

"Nah . . ." She leans back into him. "Just maybe opened his eyes a little."

"Aww, group hug." I laugh and pull them both into my arms. "Just because you're married now, doesn't mean you can't still lust after me."

Catherine, in true form, just huffs without saying a word and heads out to the dance floor.

Jackson and I stand while he watches her. "I'm happy for you, man." He deserves it.

"Thanks."

"I'm probably going to head back out. I've been following a lead that I think might be worth a look."

Charlie and I found something in a new file that came in

about a bid. It could be nothing, but it was enough that we both paused. Jackson was right to pencil down Neil's name. I would've never had it on my radar, but the bid came across my desk with his name on it. Seems after he was fired from his job in marketing, he got hired with a firm that does contract work. They get a request from a company, source out the work, and then decide based on the offers that come in. Lo and behold, his name was on the contract for the ambassador.

"Anything I should be aware of?"

"Nope. It could be nothing, but I'm crossing every possibility off the list. Now, go dance with your wife." I shove him forward and he stalks after her.

We spend the next hour dancing, laughing, and telling old stories. Ashton tells me very little about her fight with Quinn, but the anger is evident on her face. If he tries to talk to her, she's gonna rip his balls off. That ginger, she's a feisty one.

The night wears on, and I learn that Charlie is a sexy-ass dancer. I'd really like to find one damn thing that she sucks at—well, I know she's good at sucking. I still can't believe she beat me at shooting. I'm just going to claim it's because I haven't been to the range in a while.

Charlie and I slow dance, and the feel of her body against mine makes it hard to think. Her honey scent filters through the air. All I can do is think about how sweet she tastes, and how I can't wait to get my next hit. She's like a drug that after you've had it once, you're fucked forever.

"I'm glad you agreed to come as my date." I sway her to the music.

Her blue eyes connect with mine. "I am too. I had a really good time."

"The night is still not over."

She presses her head against my chest and melts into me. "I had no intention of it ending."

I rub my hands up and down her bare back, making patterns against her skin. "Charlie," I say as she lifts her head.

"Yes?"

"Stay for a while."

I don't know why I said it because the idea of her going back to DC makes me want to punch holes in the wall. Having her around . . . it gives me something I didn't know I was missing. It's like seeing things in a different way. The shit she has thrown all over my bathroom comforts me. The fact she comes to work with me, reads through old files, and helps me has me wishing it could be like that for longer. Plus, knowing she's close and that I can protect her is driving me insane. I don't want her back there alone. She has no clue what the hell could be waiting for her.

Put all that aside, though. I'm falling hard for this girl. I want her in my life, and I think if I can keep her around longer, she'll see she wants it too.

Knowing her ever-stubborn self, she'll continue to tell herself differently, but I see it. The way she watches me when she thinks I'm not paying attention. How her entire demeanor shifts when I come around. Her body relaxes, and she looks at me a little longer than she used to. She's starting to trust me. Even though she wants to believe she's a ferocious tiger, she's more like a pussycat lately. Sure, we fight, because that's what we do, but it's different.

"I have to go back. I need to finish what I've been doing."

"I'm not asking."

She stares over my shoulder without responding. I'm sure she wishes she could punch me, but that's kind of frowned upon at a wedding. Fuck this. I grip her chin, and force her to look at me.

"I'm telling you to stay. I'm telling you I want you to stay. I'm not saying forever, just until we get some things settled. Take it, Charlie. Take what I'm offering you."

Her shoulders sag. "Okay."

"Okay?"

"Yes, you insistent ass. I'll stay for a while."

My hand cups the back of her neck. I realize the slip I had earlier wasn't a mistake. I'm falling in love with her. Fuck me sideways. I'm in love with Charlie. I pull her to me. I need to feel her lips. I kiss her differently—not like we're not always explosive, but this has more of a build. It's a promise of all that's to come tonight, because this time . . . I'm going to make her mine and steal her heart.

twenty-two

Charlie

IT'S NOT AS IF we've never slept together. This is dumb, being nervous over spending a night with Mark. But between the wedding and the wine, the emotions are different. He's different. The way he looked at me, just . . . everything. I'm being dumb, but we're still not safe. We still don't know who's doing things, and Mark is still a target.

If I were to let him in my heart . . . who am I kidding? He's already there. I told myself not to allow it, but here I am.

Screwed.

I feel like that virgin on prom night, questioning everything. Do I take my clothes off? Do I slip under the covers naked? Never mind the fact that I've joined the mile high club with him. Had shower sex, wall sex, sex in his bed . . . I mean, we've done it. Just tonight . . . isn't about sex. God, I'm being such a girl.

Fuck this.

"Mark!" I bang on the bathroom door. "Mark! Open up! Now!"

He flings it open, scanning the room. "What's wrong?" His chest heaves as he searches for the danger I must've made him certain was here.

The only danger is my emerging feelings. That needs to stop. I'll prove that there's nothing more than great sex. "This!" I grasp the back of his head and jerk him down.

Our lips collide. He's clearly surprised by my sudden attack, but he kisses me back. I hold on tight, trying to get him to thaw out a little. I need this. I have to be able to feel nothing but sexual chemistry.

"Charlie," he mumbles against my lips, trying to pull back. "Stop, beautiful. Stop." He pushes me back.

My lips throb from the force of our kiss. "Kiss me, damn it!" I rush toward him, but he puts his hands on my shoulders.

"What the hell has gotten into you?"

"Hopefully, you."

"What's the rush?" he asks as he lets his hands slide down my arms. His voice is smooth like silk. "We have all night."

I can't speak. One part of me just wants to beg him to fuck me because I don't want us to have this. The other part wants to love him. I want to be the one, and I want him to give me this. I know though, in the end, this is a mistake. It puts us both at risk. When you love someone, you're vulnerable. I would prey on that weakness. Use someone's loved ones against them. It gives an edge that I've never allowed anyone to have.

Mark's hand glides back up. It leaves a stream of bumps in his wake. Slowly his fingers hook under the strap of my dress. I stand, statuesque as his fingers slide the fabric down. "All night, beautiful. I'm going to take every second to show you." I shiver as his lips touch the sensitive spot where my neck meets my shoulder. "Every inch of you will be touched," he promises. "Every part of you will be mine."

My head rolls back as the other strap falls. The dress, being made of nothing, pools at my feet. As much as I may not have wanted this, I knew it would be different. I stand before him with no bra, and commando.

"You're the most beautiful woman in the world. Everything pales compared to you."

Why can't he just shut up? He's hell bent on making me fall. "Stop talking."

"You need to hear it." His lips return to my skin.

Every touch between us right now is intentional. He wants me to feel him touching me. I want him to feel me giving myself to him, and yet, I want to hold myself back.

Mark's lips touch mine, slowly, softly, purposefully. His fingers touch the side of my neck as he guides the kiss. Our tongues slide against each other, and I feel it all the way in my core. My heart pounds in my chest because there's no way I can shut myself down. I can't fight him; he's too strong for me. I can taste the determination in the air. We'll surrender every pretense, we'll love, and we'll no longer be able to pretend.

"This will change everything," I whisper as his mouth moves to my neck.

"Good," he says while he walks me backward. "It's time all the games stop. I can't play anymore. Just us, beautiful. No more bullshit."

My fingers press against his face. "I'm gonna hate myself tomorrow."

"Then let's have tonight."

His stubble pricks the pads of my fingers as I fight my answer.

"Say it, Charlie. Say you want me to love you tonight."

Every part of my body is pulled taut. I want him. There's always someone in our lives that ruin us for all others—it seems he's mine. He's the Achilles heel that will bring me to my knees. God, how I want it. I want it all, but I'm so scared. I don't want to be hurt. I can't live through losing someone else. Part of the fun has been that this wasn't serious. This was just sex. That's a lie. I'm in love with him, and I'm safe with him, well, as safe as

I'll ever be. The beauty in this night causes my emotions to over-load. "Love me, Mark. Love me for tonight," I say as a tear falls.

"I'll love you for much longer than that." His lips brush mine. Our breaths mingle as we stand wrapped around each oth-er. My chest heaves, as does his. We are both fighting to gain our footing. Finally, Mark's lips press against mine.

We lose ourselves, joining together into the unknown. The darkness surrounds us, but the light shines through the window and illuminates us. This is how falling feels. It's weightless, easy, terrifying, and magical all at the same time. He hoists me up in his arms and carries me to the bed.

He lays me down and spreads my dark hair across his white sheets. I reach up, tangling my fingers in his hair. "Don't let me fall."

"What if I promise to catch you?"

I smile. "I'll be the one who will have to catch you."

We both let out a chuckle. He rises up and removes his shirt. The moonlight spotlights the bright ink on his arms. It shows all the stories he doesn't speak, but rather shows through art. "I knew you liked being on the bottom."

"Shut up and kiss me," I demand.

"Yes, ma'am." He smirks and all my fear dissipates. This is the Mark and Charlie I know. Quick witted, smart mouthed, and a little foul at times.

Mark makes his mouth busy by dragging his tongue down my neck to my breasts. His hands cup them and rub my nipples until they harden. The warmth of his breath against them and then the pinch from his thumb causes me to squirm. He repeats this over and over until I grab at his head to get him to put it in his mouth. "Mark," I practically whine. "Please."

Instead of doing what I plead, his hand presses against my stomach, moving painfully slowly to my core. I need him to touch me, ground me before I float away. He doesn't, though.

He skirts the area I need him most.

"I'm gonna make you feel good. I just need you desperate."

My eyes lock on his. "I need you."

"You have me," he says as his mouth wraps around my breast and his finger presses against my clit.

"Oh, my god," I cry out as his teeth pinch down.

He does it again, but this time he slips his fingers inside my pussy. The pleasure spikes like a drug through my veins. It's heaven and hell, pleasure and pain, victory and loss at the same time. He continues until my back bows off the bed. I'm so close.

Instead of going further, he stops, throws my legs over his shoulders and his tongue swipes against me. "I could die here. I want you to come in my mouth. I want to taste every drop of what I do to you. I'm going to love you with my tongue as you show me how much you like it."

I never thought talking during sex was hot until he just said that. "You have a dirty mouth, Mr. Dixon. And I like it."

"Well, let's see how dirty I can get." He smiles before he pushes his tongue inside me.

"Fuck!" I grip his hair and pull him harder into me. I don't care what the hell happens as long he doesn't stop. He doesn't disappoint. Mark drives inside me with his tongue and then makes circles around my clit.

The electricity currents through me. My orgasm is on the brink. "I'm so close," I pant while sweat beads down my face. "So, so close." Each breath is laborious as I try to hold off a little longer.

Mark's hand finds my nipple, squeezes, and he sucks my clit. I fracture into a million pieces, all of them tied to him. I struggle to find my lungs. He just rocked my entire world and left me in the wake of his flood.

"Look at me," he commands.

Eyes closed, I shake my head.

"Look in my eyes, baby."

Slowly, I open them. His green eyes hover above me. "I want to feel all of you, nothing between us. I'm clean and I get checked. Are you okay with that?"

I don't know if I am. This is so much more. My chest tightens as I look in his eyes. If I give him this, it will be the last barrier. But I know how I feel. I know I love him. I know I want him to share this with me.

I nod. "I'm clean and get the shot."

The look in his eyes tells me that he understands the meaning behind this. Mark's arms flex as he presses his lips against mine. His erection sits at my opening. "Just us, Charlie. Just us." He rears up and lines his dick up with my core.

I look down as Mark glides into me. I try to keep my eyes open, but it's too much. The connection, the words, the promises, the relinquishing of the fight is overwhelming. There's nothing else here but us. Nothing that matters but him. I don't tell him I've never allowed a man to not use a condom. I don't admit that he's the first. I don't let him know that I've never even considered not stopping someone, no matter where we were—that he's the only person I've trusted.

Unable to fool myself any longer, I open my eyes and watch him. We make love. No other words are spoken between us, because none are powerful enough for what's being said with our eyes.

Mark and I lose ourselves throughout the night. I take him, just as much as he takes me. I fall asleep in his arms and then he wakes me to do it again. Just for tonight, we live in a world where there are no monsters, nothing haunting, and nothing that can break us. Because when the sun comes up, that world will fade and reality will return.

twenty-three

"LEE!" MARK YELLS FOR Natalie as we sit in his office. After we returned from the vineyard, we agreed to get back to determining the source of Cole Security Force's issues. I really like Jackson and Catherine and don't want to see something happen. When she doesn't come quickly enough—which, let's face it, is two seconds—he calls her again. "Sparkles!"

"Are you sure you weren't dropped on your head as a child?" I ask from beside him. "I know you have a phone intercom."

He shrugs. "This is so much more fun."

"What?" Natalie glares at him from outside the door. I like her so much.

"Thanks for coming so fast."

Her lips purse as she continues to shoot him dirty looks. "I was summoned. What do you need? I'm up to my eyeballs in bids."

That's a good thing. At least, given their issues, they're not losing contracts. "I want to check in with all the employees. Get a sense of what's going on."

Natalie's head tilts to the side as she studies him. And since it's Mark, it's like a secret language. "I'm not catching what you're throwing."

I laugh under my breath. "Just send Erik in."

She steps toward the door with aggression rolling off her. "Use the damn phone and call him. I swear you only do this to me." Natalie turns on her heel and stomps off.

"I love you. Let's make more sparkly babies!" he yells after her and then turns to me. "I don't really, beautiful. Don't get jealous."

"I hate you!" I hear Natalie's faint response.

"I'm far from jealous. She and I might just team up and form a club."

He's so full of himself it's a wonder he can manage to hold his head up. But then again, I know it's all a front. Mark isn't really self-centered. In some ways, he's almost selfless. He'll give up anything for anyone he loves. He'll take a bullet for a friend or go to the ends of the world to find out who's causing havoc in someone's life.

Erik knocks on the door a moment later. "Lee said you wanted to see me?"

"Come in," Mark says to him before he returns his attention to me. "See, she really does love me."

"Whatever you need to tell yourself." I return to the file I've been studying for the last hour. It has a lot of unimportant information, but it also has this photo. I swear I've seen it before.

Erik sits, and they start bullshitting. I try to tune them out and focus on the photo, but I'm only growing frustrated. This is one time I wish I could call Mandi and have her run it. I consider the idea, because she would help me. At least I think she would. Of course, it would put her at risk, but she might be able to do it without alerting anyone.

I decide to press it a little and see if she bites. Instead of texting her on her regular number, I use the phone that only she and I know about. If she responds, it means she's willing to talk.

Me: Hey, sorry how we left things.

I send the text and then wait.

"Did you and Garrett hang this weekend or do anything fun?" Mark asks. The two babble on and on about whatever. I try not to listen and not to let my nerves go haywire as I wait for Mandi to respond.

"You know your brother." Erik laughs. "Always up for doing something stupid."

"I figured I'd see him more now than I did when he was in New York, but I actually see him less." Mark turns to me. "Erik lives with my younger douchebag brother."

"Ahh," I comment, feigning interest.

My indifference must show, because Erik laughs at the expression on my face, and then he continues his conversation. "I really never see him, which makes him the perfect roommate."

"He should've just moved in with Annika."

Mandi: I've been worried about you.

Me: I wasn't sure you'd respond.

It's true. There was a good chance she wouldn't. If I'm honest, she shouldn't have. But this is good. This is something to hold on to. With her help, we could really do this.

Mandi: I wasn't sure I should, but you wouldn't be texting if it weren't important.

"Are you two done being girls?" I ask. I need this conversation to stop. "I'd like to get back to DC sometime today. I'm tired of being your hostage, so the sooner you get this done, the sooner I can head home."

The grin on his face forewarns me that I'm going to pay for that. "You'll go home when I'm ready for you to go home."

I glare at him as he's sure as hell going to pay for that.

Erik laughs. "We see who wears the pants in this

relationship."

"Shut up. You're dismissed. Send in the next of my royal subjects." Mark stands with his arms spread open.

"Mark, we should talk," I say as the next minion approaches the doorway.

"Or better yet, we'll do this again when I'm in the mood."

A few people laugh from the corridor, and Mark shuts his door in the guy's face. "What's going on?"

"We have hope. We have Mandi in our corner."

Mark scowls. "Isn't this the same girl who sold you out at your debrief?"

"Yes, but she's answering on the line only she and I know about."

"And you think this is a good idea?"

"I think it's our best shot."

His eyes drift as he seems to weigh his thoughts. "You trust her?"

"I trusted her with my life. I don't think she'd double-cross me. And the info I'd send her wouldn't be crucial."

He shakes his head, "I don't want to involve the agency."

"We're not."

"We are." He puts his hands down on the desk. "I say no. I don't want you to do it. I think we can find information another way. I don't want the CIA involved."

"Mark."

"No, I don't trust them." His eyes close and he lets out a deep breath. "Look, I think they're behind who drugged you."

No. I mean, it's not impossible, but it's highly improbable. I'm not a risk. It makes no sense that they'd drug me. Plus, where the hell would he come up with this idea? He has no proof.

"I think you're wrong."

He crosses his arms. "I'm not. I'm telling you, there's something going on, and I'm not going to let you risk it."

"Mark," Lee says over the intercom and interrupts our argument. "Sorry to bother you, but there's an issue with the bid. Can you look at this?"

"Sure." He stands but turns to me before he goes. "We'll finish this when I get back, but my answer is no. I don't want anyone from there tangled up in this. We'll handle it. Just us."

Mark exits the room, and I start to pace. *Let me?* Let me risk it. I hear the words over and over, but I don't agree with him. I think he's not seeing the information I can get if Mandi comes on board with this.

I know it's a stretch, but if we can get her to gather info that I can't get, then I can dig deeper. It'll take less time, less energy, and there will be less of a chance of being found out. There are a lot of cards laid out, but if we can use the resources of the agency, then it'll be okay. If we can just have everyone not disappear, get shot, or be taken hostage then we can get our answers. He's not calling the shots on this one. It's my handler, and I trust her. I grab my phone.

Me: I need your help, but I need to trust you.

Mandi: I never betrayed you, Charlie. I never would.

"I SWEAR TO GOD, if I get bitten by anything, you better hope it kills me," I threaten Mark for the tenth time. I can't believe I let him talk me into this.

"I told you, sharks need to eat too."

"It's a wonder that you've been single this long."

He smirks. "I was just waiting for you, princess."

"Sure you were."

It's been a week, and Mandi and I have been communicating regularly. I hate keeping it from Mark, but we disagree, and I'd rather ask for forgiveness than permission.

However, he kept his promise, and I kept mine. That night in the vineyard was an anomaly. No more talk of making love, even though I do a shit job of not looking at him. I catch myself frequently, but for the most part . . . we're back to Charlie and Mark—the hostile, sex-craved, sarcastic assholes who want to be on top of the world. It works better this way, even though I'm hopelessly in love with the jackass.

His eyes roll as he lays the surfboards down. "Whatever you say, Chartreuse."

"That's the worst one yet."

"If you'd just tell me, I would stop having to guess. Unless your name really is Charlie?" I shake my head with a smile.

We spent some time with Aaron last night. It wasn't as awkward as I thought it would be. He's doing really well, and he actually had some information that might help me find Mazir. Seems I wasn't the only one listening to everything.

"If I told you, I'd have to kill you." I smile over my shoulder as I go to put my toes in the water. I really hate this. There's not much I'm afraid of, but sea creatures are one. I hate not being able to see what's beneath me. It's a vulnerability that doesn't sit well with me. I understand, considering the amount of time Mark's spent in the water, how this feels like home to him. I, however, do not feel the same. The only reason I agreed to this is that he promised to take me home soon. I've been gone long enough, and all this mushy shit between us has me spooked.

My toes dip in the cold water and I suppress a shiver. There's no way I'm going in. It's ice cold, and as much as I don't do the swimming thing, I sure as hell don't do cold. I head back up toward the beach, but I've barely turned before strong arms wrap around my middle, lifting me off the ground. *Oh, hell no!* "Mark!" I scream as he hoists me over his shoulder. "No!"

"The best way to overcome your fears is to face them head

first."

"I'm not kidding! If you do this, I'll smother you in your sleep!" I promise as I slap his back and flail my legs. "Don't!"

"It's really important to know your surroundings. Here, I thought you were a spy," he chides. "You should never let your guard down, babe. You never know when a predator is around." His taunting is not cute.

We're now clearly *in* the water. Mark seems to be completely fine with the temperature. He acts like he's forging into bathwater. Stupid man.

"I hope your balls shrink into your throat. Maybe then I won't be able to find them to rip them off!" He spins me around as water splashes up around me. I slap his ass, which causes him to do it again. "Goddammit, Mark! Put me down!"

Mark lets out a chuckle, but his forward motion doesn't stop. "Be careful what you ask for," he warns.

He keeps walking deeper into the ocean as if the loud slapping against his skin is a featherlight touch. I start punching. Maybe that will deter him. "Don't do it!" I threaten.

Instead of heeding my warning, the son of a bitch drops down into a sitting position, submerging us both.

We come up for air. I glare. He glares back. Then I lunge for him. "You asshole!"

He laughs and splashes me as I try to catch him. "Gotta catch me if you're going to kill me." This is truly his advantage. He submerges, which is when I know I'm truly in trouble. I start to move as fast as I can toward shore, but his hands wrap around my ankles. As he yanks back, I fall forward and go under.

When I come up, he's laughing hysterically. He moves slowly as I stand with my arms crossed over my chest.

"I hate you!" I spew the words.

"You don't."

"I do."

"Not believing you," he says. He's standing close enough that I have to tip my head back to see his eyes. "You're so beautiful."

I fight the smile that begins to form. "You're in so much trouble."

His arms wrap around me and bring me flush against him. "I knew you would back out. This was me vetting my opponent."

"Dead."

"I'll take the risk."

He dips his head down and then his lips brush against mine. I breathe him in, trying to memorize this moment. As angry as I want to be, I've never had so much fun. Felt so carefree and . . . safe. He brings out the playful side of me but always seems to be watching what's going on. Mark is so much more than what he lets people see.

I stand here in his arms with our lips just touching. The sun is behind me, casting its beautiful glow on both of us. Mark's eyes are warm, his heart is large, and for some reason, he's trying with me. I'm far from an easy person to love. I'm not warm and fuzzy or open and honest. I'm stubborn, manipulative, cunning, and ready to crush anyone who stands in my way, because I've had to be. This though, is terrifying. It's allowing someone into a heart I didn't know I had.

Neither of us speaks. The motion of the waves shifts us closer together. His lips press harder, and my arms wrap around his neck. Time drifts by us, just like the tide. I'm no longer cold, angry, or even upset. He warms me from the inside. I allow my fears to follow the current out into the great unknown. I have no more control over my heart than I do of the moon.

Mark's lips touch the tip of my nose. "What have you done to me?"

I search his eyes. "I could ask you the same thing. You make me feel like I'm drifting."

"I'll keep you secure. I won't let you float away." Mark spins me so my back is to his chest. "See that out there?" he asks. I stare out at nothing.

"See what?"

His arms wrap around me while he rests his chin on my shoulder. "It's a clean slate. There're no rules right here. We're not defined by our jobs. It's just us, open. You're anyone you want to be."

I lean back in his embrace. "Sounds like we're going on a mission."

"The only mission is us."

"And what are the risks?"

"That you'll fall in love with me."

"Is that so?"

I laugh as his arms tighten. "Yeah, I'd say the chances are high."

I peer up at him from the side. "I'm not so sure."

"I never fail."

Mark leans down, pressing his lips to mine before I can retort. The kiss is short, but poignant. I feel it deep into my bones. He's right. I'm doomed. I've already fallen in love with him, and that shouldn't have happened. I won't stand idly by and have something catastrophic happen. He'll get shot this time, or worse. I'll have to avenge another death of someone I love. I'll lose the two men I've loved in my life, and realize all too late that I'm the black cloud.

"I worry about this." I admit the abridged version of my thoughts.

He rubs his hands up and down my arms. "I would expect nothing less. Your mind is a scary place, beautiful."

"You know I'm not one of those girls, right?"

His hands drop, and I turn to peer up into his face. I want to read his emotions. "Do tell," he says with arms crossed.

"I don't need—or want—you to call me every day, telling me you miss me. I don't need flowers. Feel free to buy me purses though," I throw in offhandedly. "And I don't care if you fuck other people. This isn't a real relationship. This is fucking. Good fucking. Fantastic even, but I won't love you, you won't love me, and we'll be just fine. Oh . . ." I need to make my last point. "Don't think I have to answer to you, either. I'm no one's lap-dog."

Mark's eyes narrow.

He stares without speaking.

And still nothing.

I throw my hands up. "Speak!"

He doesn't respond verbally. No, he's much too aggressive for simple conversation. He steps forward, grips my arms, and crushes his mouth against mine. His tongue presses forward, pushing against mine. His hands tighten as he pulls me so close that I think I could fade into him. I twist and push against him, but he just controls himself more. Each swipe of his tongue against mine warms me. My breathing becomes erratic as I lose myself in his touch.

I could do nothing but kiss him all day and die happy.

Mark tears his mouth from mine, and I gasp for air. "First, fuck you and your stupid speech. You'll answer my calls, and you'll call me because, contrary to the shit you say, you like me. I'll drive to DC just to fuck you, or because I actually miss your frustrating ass. You'll cuddle the flowers, bears, or whatever stupid shit I send you, because secretly you love it." His lust has turned to anger. "And I would never boss you around because that's not who we are. But each time you try to push me away, Charlie," he pauses as I stand before him stunned, "it's because I scare you. It's because you can imagine yourself falling for me, and you don't know what the fuck to do with that."

"Mark—" His hands cup my face, and his mouth comes

back for more. My fingers fist in his hair. I pull at the wet strands as I leap into his arms and wrap my legs around him. His stupid speech. His stupid mouth that I can't get enough of. Let's not even talk about how turned on I am thinking about him driving up just because he needs me.

Mark's hands grip my ass and hold me against him as he sinks back down and allows the water to cover us. Our tongues slide and push against each other. His fingers slide through my hair as he tilts my head.

I fight for control.

I lose the battle.

"I'm going to fuck you now," he informs me.

"The hell you are."

"Shut up and take it." The deep timbre of his voice sends shivers down my spine. He slips his hand between us and thrusts a finger deep inside. "So hot. You're so fucking hot. You make it impossible to think of anything but getting my dick inside you."

"Oh, God," I moan as he pumps his fingers. He pushes another one in and my head falls back. Mark spins us around so his body blocks the view of any possible onlookers. "I want you so bad."

"I know you do, beautiful."

His head dips down and he bites my nipple through my bikini. I bite my lip to keep quiet as he does it again.

My fingers slip under the water to untie his bathing suit. Thank god for board shorts. I slip them down. Mark pushes my suit to the side. He slowly pushes himself inside me and moves deeper. "Fuck me, Charlie. Ride my dick."

I use the buoyancy of the water to rock easier. He holds my ass in his hands and helps control it. "You feel so good," I say against his lips.

"You feel incredible. You're gonna be the death of me like this. Your tits bouncing in the water. Your pussy gripping my dick. I'll die a thousand deaths if this is how I go."

His fingers dig into the flesh of my thighs as I push faster. My climax is looming, and I can't hold off. I use my hips to rub my clit against him. He supports my back, and my hair dips into the water when I tilt back so he hits the spot. "I'm gonna come." I say. I'm out of breath and ready to explode.

Mark pulls my hair as he sucks on the spot just below my ear, and I fall apart. Everything goes bright while my muscles clench. I fall as he pumps his hips and draws out my orgasm even longer. "Fuck," Mark groans against my neck as he follows me.

We stay like this, entangled in each other's arms as we both catch our breath.

"My name is Charisma," I announce without thinking.

Mark pulls back and his eyes flash. "Really?"

"Yes," I say, and I feel a little self-conscious about the disclosure. I hate the damn name, but now he knows. "So, now you know."

"It fits you, beautiful. It fits you, and you fit me. I'll never betray you, Charisma."

A part of me is now his. A part of me I've never given to anyone. It shows me just how deep I really am. "I hope not." Little does he know I've already done so by texting Mandi.

Mark laughs as he starts to slide out of me, and for once, this secret is killing me. I've been lying to him for a week. This is my thing. I'm a liar, but I can't keep doing this. He's broken me.

"I texted Mandi," I blurt it out and his eyes close.

"You did what?"

"She can help."

He huffs and turns away. "I can't even look at you. How could you do this? How could you fucking text her?" Mark spins back to glare at me, and he's screaming. "Do you want to get killed? Do you need me to lose my fucking mind because something happens to you?"

I've never seen him like this. It's as if I just destroyed him.

"Goddammit, Charlie! Did you think I was lying to you? That I was making this shit up for fun? The CIA is behind what happened to you." He steps close. Every emotion plays across his face. He's angry, that's clear, but more than that . . . he's hurt. "I can't believe you."

I need to explain this, because it makes sense. "Look, Mandi isn't behind this. She would've never responded on that phone. There's a bond between a handler and an operative. Something similar to what you and Jackson have! Why can't you trust that I know what I'm doing?"

"Because you're fucking blind!" Mark adjusts himself and stalks off. "You know, I thought we were finally past this shit. I thought we were a team. It changed for us that night. I saw it in your eyes, but then you ask me, I say no, and you do it anyway? Fuck you!"

"No, fuck you!"

"Pretty sure you just fucked us both, babe." My anger boils.

"Did you hit your head? Eat lead paint off the crib?" I ask with sarcasm laced through my words. "You keep putting your foot in your mouth."

He runs his hands down his face. "You confuse the fuck out of me!"

"And you piss me off!"

"Right back at you, babe!"

I start to head out of the water. I'm not about to let him scream at me. His hand grips my shoulder and he turns me. "You're leaving?"

"I'm done arguing with you. I'm not going to justify myself. I've been doing this a long time. I know you feel one way, but I disagree."

"You disagree?" he scoffs. "You disagree that you were drugged in DC at a function? Or maybe that *only* you were targeted? That the waiter doesn't exist on any paperwork, and the other waiter who was supposed to attend is nowhere to be found? I'm not making this shit up! I've been investigating it, and all roads lead to one place."

My mouth falls slightly agape. Okay, but that proves nothing. "And you think Mandi is involved?"

Mark groans and lifts his gaze skyward. "I think every person in your agency from your handler to your boss is a suspect. I'm pretty sure your brain is working overtime here, but you're so fucking stubborn you refuse to admit that you betrayed me. *Me!* The person who has been nothing but honest with you. Take all the other bullshit aside and see what you've done to me."

"Do you think I want this right now? No! I don't!" I inform him. "I don't want anything to happen to either of us. But you're out of your damn mind if you think I entered this carelessly. You dragged me on a plane to California to prove that Jackson was loyal."

His jaw clenches. Fury radiates from him. "You—" He stops. "I—" He stops again.

"Sucks not being in control for once, huh?"

He steps forward but stops when we're eye to eye. I wait for his typical mode of shutting me up, but he just stands here. His nostrils flare and a storm rages in his eyes. I can see how angry he is.

"This isn't about control. This is about you and me. This is about how you went behind my back for how long? How many other times have you lied to me?"

I open my mouth to speak but close it before I say something I can't take back.

"How many times have you told me something but it was just some twisted version of your truth?"

"Are you fucking serious? I've been honest with you."

"How many?" he yells.

I glare at him, ready to rip his throat out. "So much for not betraying me. You stupid idiot! I trusted you. I gave you something no one else has ever had. I gave you my name! If that isn't a sign of how much I trusted you, I don't know what is. Then, you treat me like I've been lying about everything? Fuck you!" Instead of allowing him to answer, I turn and leave him standing there.

"Don't fucking walk away from me!" he yells.

Instead of responding, I lift my middle finger in the air and walk away.

Once I reach the shoreline, I turn back. He hasn't followed. No, Mark turned away, faced the vast ocean, and let me walk. It hurts me, more than I care to admit. Knowing that he's so upset—so ridiculous about me doing my job—breaks me apart.

I won't let him hurt me. I won't allow anyone to tear me down until I'm one of those girls. He won't penetrate the remainder of my heart. Except . . . he already has. If he hadn't, I wouldn't be this upset.

When I lean down to grab my clothes, a tear falls. I hate that he's now made me cry twice. No more. I wrap a towel around my wet body and trudge back to his house without looking back.

I check my phone and notice a new text.

> Mandi: You need to come back to DC. I have something. Text me when you are in a safe place.

I call a cab, pack the rest of my things, and wait. He doesn't return before I'm done, thank God, but that also says more to me. If I were worth anything, he'd have followed. I thought things were different between us. I truly thought he loved me. Steel cages surround me and protect me from the pain. I won't allow myself to feel it. Instead, I focus on what's in store for me. I have a man to hunt down, and by doing so, I'll hopefully save

Mark. That can be my parting gift to him.

The driver grabs my bag and tosses it in the trunk. I open the back door and gaze out at the water once more.

"Good-bye, Mark." I blow a kiss toward the water.

It's time to go home and get back to work.

twenty-four

Mark

O F ALL THE STUPID, irresponsible shit she could've done, this takes the cake. To go to the one person I told her could be behind this is beyond words. My anger toward her is beyond anything I've ever felt before.

Then she has the balls to tell me I'm wrong, and of course, she told me her name without me asking. *Fuck*. If she only knew how close I was to telling her the three little words I never thought I'd say. She'd never believe me, because even I don't understand it. It's too soon, she's too frustrating, and we barely tolerate each other.

I could almost get past even that. I should've known Charlie would go behind my back. It's my job to protect her, and then she fucks it all up. She's like a fucking maniac. Her mind never stops. She thinks she has it all figured out, even when half the time she doesn't. She pushes me, and I shove her right back through the wall she erected.

I stand out in the water, trying to piece together all the shit that keeps going on between us and the damn job. It's a wonder I haven't lost my mind already. Friends dead, friends shot, friends abducted—and then, of course, I've been messed up. Not to the extent of those bastards, but I had dark times.

How the hell does a woman like Charlie make her way into my world, and why do I let her? This is the woman who apparently is aware we were all supposed to die. She kept my friend practically hostage. She lies all the time, about everything, yet I fucking love her—a lot. I need therapy.

After a while, I start to get cold. I make my way back to the shore and notice she's gone. Of course she is. She wasn't happy about being in the water to begin with. It's fine. I'll just try to thaw her frozen heart when I get to the house. I continue my trek and hear someone call my name.

"Mark!" I turn as my brother Garrett jogs over.

"What the hell are you doing out here?"

He's never out this way. Annika, his girlfriend, lives about fifteen minutes from me, but I can count on one hand how many times he's dropped by.

"I stopped up at the house. No one answered so I figured you were at the beach. Catch any waves?"

We both look out at the water where the waves are calm and crap for surfing. "Umm, no."

He lets out a low laugh. "How've you been?"

"Good," I answer apprehensively. I'm not really sure what the hell the point of him being here is. "What's up?"

Garrett rolls his head to the side and then lets out a deep sigh. "I've been thinking about my life. Things obviously sucked in New York. I never should've married Emily, but I thought she was the one."

"I hated her."

"You hate everyone."

"This is true."

We both laugh. "Anyway, when I moved down here, I thought shit would be different. I love where I work. Annika is great. But Erik mentioned he talked to you, then Mom asked me this morning why we don't talk."

"Doesn't she always?" This doesn't really surprise me. Mom learned early on I wasn't a big sharer. She's the world's nosiest person, which means she has the world's biggest mouth—my brother—to tell her what she needs to know. I didn't realize my brother was a traitor, so I told him a lot, which meant my mom knew I had porn in my closet. That was the day Garrett got cut off. Don't fuck with a man's porn.

"Yeah, but she knows you and I don't talk like that."

"Your doing."

He huffs. "I think you remember shit a little differently."

I look up at the house thinking now isn't really the perfect time to get into this with him, but at the same time, Garrett doesn't usually come down for a heart to heart. "I'm not trying to cut you off, but what did you come down here for? Not that I don't want to see you, I'm just curious."

Garrett sits down in the sand. So much for trying to talk through this mess with Charlie. "I want to know why we're like this. What the hell did I ever do to you?"

"You got my Playboy mags taken."

He looks at me as if I just sprouted a second head. "Are you serious?"

"Dude, I had Pamela Anderson's shit in my face to look at. Then you went and told Mom about it, and I had to try to remember it."

"You're fucking kidding me."

"Did you or did you not tell her?"

Garrett shakes his head. "I was eight! She offered me cookies to tell where you kept your magazines."

"Traitor."

"You broke my bike that day. I think that was payback."

"Pffft," I roll my eyes. "Tits or a bike?"

"This is the most insane conversation I've ever had."

I slap him on the back. "That's because you're a pussy and have pussy friends. You prefer a bike over some fun bags. But seriously, it's more than that. We just were never close. I don't know if it's because we have a few years difference or you were smarter than me and would rather study. I was more focused on ways to convince Claire Attar to suck my dick."

"She never did."

"No, but she let me touch her tits once."

He laughs and smacks my chest. "She let me, too."

"God, she was a slut."

"Yup." Garrett gets up and brushes the sand off. "Let's do this again. Maybe with less shit between us."

I get to my feet and extend my hand. "Say you're sorry and that you'll replace my porn."

Garrett laughs. "I'm pretty sure Mom smoked weed around you. There's no other explanation."

I shrug. "Do we have a deal?"

"Fine, Mark. I'll give you twenty bucks to replace the porn I apparently cost you."

"Good. Nice to have you back in the family. Now, I have a sexy woman waiting for me, and I can only imagine how hostile she's gonna be. It's been nice chatting, but I'm going for round two today."

"Whatever floats your boat."

We say good-bye and I head up to the house. I'm ready for knives flying or even a gun. I wouldn't put it past her to shoot me. She doesn't get why this upsets me so much. I'm always thinking of the next step. I plan, prepare, check the plans, and I control the situation. The fact that I never even paused to consider when she'd eventually do this scares the shit out of me.

"Honey, I'm home!" I throw the door open and start to look around.

The bag that was sitting on the couch with some extra girly

shit is gone. I stride back into my bedroom and notice her suitcase is gone. "Son of a fucking bitch!" I yell as I throw on a shirt and shorts. "Nice play, princess, but I have the rule book."

I grab my keys and head out the door. She's about to witness what happens when she runs away.

twenty-five

Charlie

A CHILL RUNS THROUGH my body as I arrive at my apartment door. I look around but there's no one here. My mind starts to spin as I think back to what seemed off in the cab. There was a black SUV parked on 17th Street, but this is DC, there are black SUVs on every street. When I climbed the stairs, someone shifted, but it was subtle. If there is someone here, they know what they're doing.

I've been trained to trust my instincts. If something *seems* off, it probably is. The fact is that I was drugged a few weeks ago. So clearly, I'm on someone's radar. Although, according to Mark, it's the people I work for.

What if he's right?

I was so focused on being angry with him and what he was saying, I never thought about it. But it makes sense. Anything is possible, but it still doesn't fit for me.

Instead of being unprepared, I take my keys out of my purse, grab the knife that's hidden there, and slip it up my sleeve. My eyes shift again, seeking the danger I can sense.

I debate what to do. I'm not sure what is waiting for me, or where. It could either be in my apartment or be behind me.

Releasing a deep breath, I turn the key and open the door.

I glance around, but nothing seems out of place. My heart settles a little as I turn the lock behind me. Once I set my bag down, I turn around and come face to face with what was waiting.

"Hello, Charlie."

I gasp but recover quickly. "Director Asher."

"Let's be frank here, you weren't surprised." He chuckles from his post against the counter.

"No, but I didn't expect it to be you."

He nods. "I see you were away."

I've known Christopher Asher since I was twelve. He worked hand in hand with my father for years. He doesn't make house calls; he summons. His visit means either something happened or is happening. That he was able to penetrate my fortress is enough to let me know this is big. Lying to him is my first instinct, but something holds me back. I recall the last text from Mandi. I needed to get back to her, and then he happens to appear in my apartment. Mark was right. I'll kill her.

"I was. I informed the agency when I submitted my leave paperwork."

"May I?" he asks. He holds his hand out to indicate the table.

"Of course." I pull out my own chair.

We sit in silence for a second, each of us measuring the other. "I'm here about your leave."

"Oh?"

"You're not sunning it up in Barbados, and I know you very well. Hell, I trained you myself. I'm offering you help, Charlie."

I weigh his words to decipher the meaning behind them. This doesn't make sense. The CIA is not on board with rogue agents. They don't allow us to stay off the grid for long, which is why I'm sure I'm being tailed.

"I'll be honest with you, sir. I don't understand what help

you're offering."

"Your father's death was far more in-depth than even you know."

Doubtful.

He leans to the side and pulls a file from inside of his jacket. It falls with a slap on the wood. My hand itches to pick it up, but I have to play this cool. I can't seem too eager or he'll think I'm impulsive. So I wait with my reactions controlled. I slip even further into my training and become stoic. He'll never see anything but what I allow.

Director Asher smirks as if he can read my thoughts. "Go ahead, Charlie. Open it and see."

"Before I do . . ." I pause. "What I'm about to see in this, I'm pretty sure is not something I'm supposed to see. Otherwise, you wouldn't be here alone."

"That's correct."

"Then why read me in?"

"Because I can't trust anyone else with this. You'll need to act on your own. You'll have no help from *anyone* within the agency. I will personally feed you the information I can to help you, but there can't be anything official. If you open that file, you're in. If you choose not to, then this meeting never happened."

"And I'm dead," I conclude. Because it's the truth.

"Of course not. Let's not be dramatic."

He knows I'll open it. There's no way he can dangle a carrot like this in front of me about my father, my mentor, my world, and expect me to walk away. He's using me, though. I'm not his friend. I'm an agent of the Central Intelligence Agency. I'm a vessel to his ultimate goal. Christopher Asher didn't rise to the Director position by being stupid. He's cunning, cutthroat, smart, and has the mind of a politician. I need to be all of that and more. I can't fall into a trap or I'll be the next one in the ground.

I need to stall him.

"I need to think."

"I respect that, but I'm afraid this is a one-time only offer."

"Sir," I say on a sigh. "I'm asking for an hour."

He sighs and pulls the file back. "I can't do that. You need to decide now if you're with me or not."

Fucker. I can't say yes right away, but I can't say no either. I need to know what's in that damn file.

Suddenly, there's banging at the door.

"Expecting someone?" Director Asher asks.

"No, they'll go away." I answer while maintaining eye contact.

Bang, bang, bang.

"Charlie!" Mark yells through the door. "I know you're in there. You need to open up."

Unreal.

"New boyfriend," I explain with a smile.

"Goddammit, Charlie!" Mark screams again. "I can hear you! Open the fucking door or I'll kick it down.

"Yes, we know all about Mark Dixon."

My smile fades. What the hell does that mean? "I need to answer it. Can you?"

"Hide?" The condescension in his tone doesn't elude me.

I shrug.

I need to protect Mark what little I can. If the CIA is aware of our—whatever this is—then I need to end it. I can't work on something that will hurt anyone else. They know about him, and that I left the country. The only thing I'm certain of is that they didn't know where we were. Having the pilot get us out and not alerting anyone of our location was the best thing we could've done.

They could still track us and everyone we were with in California and Virginia. I can't let anyone get hurt. I won't put those people through what I know they're capable of. What the hell have I gotten myself into? I knew this was a bad idea. I knew better, and I caved. I fell in love with him, and now everyone is at risk.

Christopher gets up without a word and heads to the back room.

I throw open the door and allow anger to be the only emotion Mark sees.

"What are you doing here? And could you be any louder? I'm not sure the people in Virginia Beach heard you."

"You're fucking mad at me?"

"No." I lean against the door. "I'm not mad. I'm just done with you."

He pushes his way through the door and slams it behind him.

"Goddammit!" I yell. I push at him. "Keep it down."

Mark scans the room, but he'll find nothing. It appears as if I just came in two seconds before he arrived. He grabs my arms and pushes me back against the door. His lips brush my ear. "Who's here?"

"No one." I shrug out of his grip. "What the hell are you doing here? Was my walking out not enough of a clue to what my thoughts were? It's done."

"Something is going on, Charlie. You and I have a small fight and you take off? Not a note? Not a text? I don't believe you packed your shit and left after you fucked up."

I turn to face the counter and smash down everything I feel. He chased me. He was worried, and he came after me. Now I have to get rid of him. "You fucked up. You can't control me. I won't let you, so this was fun . . ." I spin around and steel myself with rage. "But I'm not really that into you."

Mark scoffs. "Liar. You're a liar, and you suck at it. How's that? You love me. I see it in your eyes. But you know what? I could get over all your stupid petty shit. I could get past the fact you're unhinged because I happen to like you. But then I get in my car and find this hidden in my glove box." He flings something at me, and I catch it. A bug. "Unhinged I can handle, but you doing this? No. Are you seriously not going to trust me? *Me?*"

He's being tracked. He's smart enough to know. I just hope he'll be dumb enough to believe every bitter lie I'm about to spew.

"Yes." It's the easiest answer to get rid of him. "I don't trust you. I don't believe anything you say to me. You and I are nothing anymore."

"You're fucking kidding me."

"No, I'm not. I did what I had to do, and now we're done."

"You're who bugged my car? You're who put a tracking device on me?"

I knew I would betray him. I just didn't realize it would be like this. "Yes. I should've turned it on so I could've been gone before you got here. My bad."

Mark's eyes narrow, but he says nothing. Rage churns behind those emerald eyes. I hate that I'm so willing to do this to him, but that file holds the answers. I won't turn away from finding out who destroyed my family. Not for anyone.

"Okay, then," he finally says.

"That's it?"

He turns and stalks forward as I retreat. Mark doesn't stop, though. He keeps plowing toward me, forcing my back against the wall. "Is that *it*? You have the balls to ask me that? I thought there was something here. I thought you and I had a goddamn moment. You told me your name, for fuck's sake. I was willing to do anything to get you to see what you mean to me."

"What do I mean to you?" I can't help but torture myself further. I have a feeling this moment right here will be what I hold on to. It'll be what I remember when I'm alone and wishing

I wasn't so selfish.

"I almost loved you, Charisma. Or at least I could have. I would've let you be the cold bitch you pretend to be." He steps closer, but I stand my ground. Mark's hand touches my cheek. "I would've pushed you to let me in further. I would've protected you, but you're incapable of loving anyone but yourself. I deluded myself into thinking I saw something in you. It's fine. I'll find someone else to wash away your memory."

My chest is heavy with guilt and pain. If there was ever anyone I could love, it's him. I wish he could see the lies I'm telling. I do trust him. I trust him more than any man I've ever known. I gave him my name. But I'm willing to give him up because my life is one big question mark. If the CIA thinks Mark is a liability, they'll eliminate him.

"Leave," is the only word I can get out. I push against his chest, shoving him out the door. "Go!" I fight back the tears that want to make their way out. I won't cry, though. Not now, not with Christopher Asher God only knows where. "Get out!" I use my anger from this entire situation.

If Mazir had never killed my father, I wouldn't have this fight. If I hadn't failed in my mission, I wouldn't be breaking myself apart. If I weren't so stupid, I would've stayed in Virginia Beach and worked it out with Mark. But my life has consisted of choices, and those choices have consequences.

"When I walk out this door, don't come to me when you need anything. We're done. We're fucking done."

I step forward and put the final nail in our coffin. "We never were, so we were done from the start. Good luck finding out who's after you."

Mark grips my arms and pulls me tight. "I'm not the only one who has someone after them. Remember that, Charlie. Remember what happened at your mother's party."

"You should go," I say. I need him to stop talking.

He releases me and opens the door, but then he hesitates. I want to rush into his arms and tell him I'm sorry. If only this were the movies. His shoulders rise and fall as he grips the door-frame. "You should know something." His green eyes lock with mine. "We were something. We were everything. We could've had it all, but you're too scared. I hope you think about this when you're alone. I hope you remember just how good we were. I hope it fucking hurts your stone heart."

My lips part. I want to say something in return, but Mark's hands fall and he closes the door behind him. He's taking away a piece of my heart—and the promise of something that could've been fantastic.

I slump in the chair, close my eyes, and wait for the master of manipulation to emerge. When I open them again, I'll be done with my hurt. Well, as far as anyone can see. Inside is another story.

Inside my heart, I'm broken. I've just died, and I don't think I'll ever recover. I love him so much that I'm willing to break myself. I'll hold on to the notion that I just did the most selfless thing I could. I saved him.

Christopher's chair scrapes against the floor. I open my eyes as the file magically reappears.

My fingers slide across the rough file folder. "I'm in."

"I knew you wouldn't resist. Go ahead. Open it."

Without another thought, I flip it open, and ready myself for a mission that will probably be the end of either my career or my life.

twenty-six

E MPTY.

The fucking file is empty.

I meet Christopher's gaze and attempt to hide the fury that's building inside. He tricked me. He forced my hand to push Mark away, and the fucking folder has nothing inside. If I weren't a hundred percent sure that he has eyes, ears, and God only knows what waiting for me to react, I'd break his neck.

"Well played, Charlie. You surprise me."

"What do you want?" I fold my hands in my lap. I try to appear as though I knew this was his plan all along. Even though I have no idea why he's surprised, I'm the one with a blank file.

He crosses his leg over his knee and leans back. Smug prick. "I want what should be in that file."

My eyes widen as though I'm genuinely shocked. There's no way I can ever let them know what I have. "And that would be?"

"Let's not play games. You and I both know your father would've passed the information to the only person he trusted—you."

"Sir," I say. I'm still trying to ensure I display the appropriate reactions. Confusion is the one I'm working with now. "If I knew anything that my father knew, wouldn't I have already gotten Mazir?"

He studies me, watching for a tip that I'm lying. They know my tells. They know my every move. They created it, but they don't understand how far I'm willing to go for this. "Unless that was part of your plan."

"What plan?" Now I work on anger. "How dare you question my loyalty to this agency! I've worked my entire life in service of this country. I lost a parent, a friend. I've had countless bruises and beatings, and I've spent years of my life on missions, all for the CIA. Now, you come in my home and do this?"

Damn. That was good.

"Cut the crap, Charlie. I trained you, and I know you better than this."

"You apparently don't."

"I knew your father. He would've told either you or me. He would've never left any chance for the investigation to derail."

I *humpf* and mull over that piece of information. "Well, Chris, if he didn't share with me, maybe you've known it all along. Maybe you want to push me into thinking there's more than I actually know. I don't know your intentions, but whatever my father had—I do not know what it is or where he left it. Besides, you and I both know you're not here for the reasons you claim. You've already proven that."

His hand slams down on the table. "I'll give you one week. One week to fill this file with everything you know. Everything he told you. Or I'll start picking off your family members one by one. Should we start with Pricilla . . . or Dominic? Maybe your new boy toy would like a visit?"

He really doesn't know anything, but he's right about my father. He would've told Chris. They were friends, partners in a lot of ways, and shared a lot of knowledge. Which means my father lost his trust in him somewhere. There's no way in hell I'm telling him a damn thing. I also don't believe him about any timeline. I have no time. No one ever tips their hand like that. I'll die tonight if he doesn't think I have what he wants, or I'll die tonight if he thinks I'm hiding it. So, I have to fight. When I first found the file there was a handwritten note inside that warned me to trust no one.

I shake my head and huff. "I can't tell you what I don't know, sir. Unless you'd like me to fabricate something?"

I alternate between addressing him by his name and title. I want to see if he notes it, responds to it, or reacts. I've known him since I was a kid. There may not be any advantages for me, but I know his kind. I was raised by his clone. I try to imagine what my father would do. He'd threaten me and force me to feel at his mercy. He might alternate from good guy who wants to help to bad guy, keeping me on my toes. Good thing I'm light on my feet, and him threatening my family or Mark just makes me furious. I'll kill him and everyone he's ever known if he touches a hair on their heads. Bloodlust paints my vision, but I keep it in check.

"Don't play coy with me, little girl. You're way out of your pay grade."

I stand because he's out of his damn mind if he thinks he can talk to me like this. "You want information I don't have. I want the information you think I have. So, how does this even make sense? If I knew anything, I'd be in country right now. I'd have Mazir's head in my hands. But I don't. I don't know where he is, what he's up to, or anything more than I gave in my debrief, *sir*. If I already knew what my father was up to, I never would've opened that file."

Director Asher stands so we're eye to eye. "Say what you want, Charlie. This isn't over. Not by a long shot. You have one week to get me what should've been in that file. One week before I start taking matters into my own hands."

He swipes the file off the table and is out the door before I can draw a breath. I scan the room, trying to wrap my mind around all that has happened. I'm sure that they've bugged my house, searched through any possible space they could find. The only solace I have right now is that if they had found the file in my office, that meeting would've never happened.

My mind spins with questions. Do I search for the devices that I know are here or leave them and go to my safe house? I don't even know if it's safe anymore, but no one knows where it is. It's really the only place I can go. But what about his threat? Do I call Mark? Call my mother?

I can't stay here. I can't say or do anything I don't want to be tracked. Notifying anyone is completely out. They need to be left in the dark. It's safer for them.

I quickly change my clothes into something non-descript. My jeans and white shirt will blend easily. There are bound to be a few people out in similar clothing. I throw on my gray hoodie and grab my purse. There are no easy choices here. Either I will end up dead or someone I love will. Once out the door, I lock everything as if I'm just heading to the store. The feeling of being watched is heightened. If Christopher wants me to be seen, I'll have multiple tails. This will have to be timed perfectly.

I walk down toward the National Mall area where tourism is always at a peak. The foot traffic around the monuments will help me blend and disappear. There's really only one place that's safe for me to go. In all my years here in DC, it's the one place I've visited frequently. If things were hard or I needed time to think, I'd go there. Perspective is often found around someone worth immortalizing. My father came here with me when I was little, and it quickly became my spot. The agency knows this, so coming here wouldn't seem abnormal.

"Honest Abe," I say up to the sky as I stand before the Lincoln Memorial. "I think you and I need to talk," I mumble to myself. A sea of bodies mills about, but disappearing will be damn near impossible. I have to go, though. I have to get away.

I stand for about twenty minutes, going over everything in my mind. I think about my father and how he would tell me it's time to do what I know. Our family isn't unprepared for this. Trust isn't something you're afforded in our line of work. It's not given freely, and it takes next to nothing to lose it.

There's an elevator off to the left that descends to the bathrooms and leads to a second entrance. It would probably be the easiest escape, but also the most predictable. However, I know for a fact I can't use the stairs. My speed alone will be a dead give-away. The elevator is my only option.

Walking in that direction, I get in line behind a woman who looks a little like me. She has her black hair up, and she's wearing jeans. It's more than I could've hoped for. I have a glimmer of hope this might actually work. Cameras are everywhere, though, and if I were Christopher, they're all monitored. However, I can't do a damn thing about it. It's now or never.

Once in the elevator, I remove my hoodie and hope they don't catch the quick change. The car descends as my nerves rise. If I'm caught . . . I'm dead. They'll know I'm running. I'll lie, but he'll perceive it as trying to keep my secrets. I can't ever touch that file again. I've never been more grateful for my security system. Even if they lucked on some of my equipment, there's no way they could've found that file. It's in the safest place possible, and all the information in it is in my head.

The ding alerts us that it's time to go. I decide to head toward the bathroom just in case. It would be a plausible lie if I get busted. Luckily, the woman is headed there as well. I follow her in and head into a stall. Once I hear her exit, I follow suit. I throw my hair up to match hers, and head toward the sink.

"Miss?" I ask.

"Yes?"

"I'm so sorry to bother you." I make my breathing appear labored. "I don't know what to do. You're just . . . well . . . my last hope." I look away as if I can't believe I'm about to ask her this.

"Are you okay?" she asks. I hide my face.

"No. I'm not, but I can't ask you this . . ."

"You look like you're about to be sick." Worry paints her face.

It's like taking candy from a baby.

"I am. I'm so scared," I tear up for dramatic effect. "My husband, well, he's abusive, and I'm trying so hard to get away, but I think he's following me. I saw him upstairs, so I got away as fast as I could. He'll kill me if he catches me." The tears fall, my chest heaves, and I clutch my stomach.

She glances around before she grabs me a tissue. "Are you okay? Should I call the cops?"

"No, no." I wave my hands. "I was just hoping you'd switch phones with me? He has mine GPS tracked, and I need him to think I'm moving. You can toss mine once you get somewhere away from here."

The woman doesn't hesitate. She takes her phone out and hands it to me. "Here, I'll leave it on for the day so you can call for help if you need it."

I hoped she'd be amiable. I suspected she would once the tears flowed. Women are naturally sympathetic and usually the first I would approach for something like this. "Thank you," I gush. "Thank you so much."

This sweet lady will never know how much this changes the game for me. "Be careful." Concern is clear in her voice.

"I will. Thank you. Can you give me a twenty-second head start? Go to the left if you can, I'm going right."

I decide it would be best to head out first. It gives me ample chances for lies and changes.

Most of us were trained to go right. I don't know why, but that's the dominant side. I think they would expect me to defect my training. I do what they expect me not to do.

Her hand grips my arm. "Go. I'll think of you."

I don't trust my voice, so I nod. I've deceived her, and I hate that. While it's not my husband after me, it is a man. A man who will kill me if he catches me. So, in a way, it's just a stretch of the truth. The man I love would never hurt me. He would've stood in my kitchen and fought for me, but I pushed him away. To save him.

Straightening my back, I walk out wearing an outfit similar to the woman who might have just saved my life and the lives of my loved ones. The area across the street is crowded with cabs, buses, bikes, and people. If I can get over there, I'll grab a bike and go. I can't risk getting in a cab, they could be there as a decoy, and I'm not giving anyone control over where I go.

Luck is on my side. I'm able to get to the bike share. Someone is about to return one, but she takes a fifty dollar bill for the bike.

"Please, let this work," I say aloud as I start to ride down the Reflecting Pool toward the center of town. My safe house is the only place I can go. The only place I can hide until I get more supplies.

My pace is a little over leisurely but surely not racing. I need to blend. As I ride, Mark's face flashes in my view. He was so angry when he left. The things he said. I remember how much love and trust was there before. How he and I shared so much in a brief time. I know that I'll never see him again. He's not the kind of man who will forgive what I said so easily, and I won't exist after today.

I ride up a little farther to the closest Metro station. I need to get underground. I try not to look around, because someone who wasn't trying to run wouldn't. I could still have a tail. It might not have worked, but I can't risk it. My feet move me forward.

Fuck. The train isn't here. I don't want to wait, but I don't want to move, either. I let out a heavy breath. If I were an agent tracking another agent, I would approach before I stepped on the train. It makes the most sense since you can't really risk the shuffle exchange. I assure myself that if I can just get on board, I have a good a shot.

The Metro starts to make its way. This is it.

Don't draw any attention to yourself, Charlie. Look casual.

The doors slide open and passengers disembark. I step forward, praying this works. Two more steps.

One more step and I'm on my way.

I start to pass through the doors and someone grips my arm.

Fuck. I'm caught.

twenty-seven

Mark

"FUCK HER," I SAY to Natalie for the tenth time. "And just stop. She left, okay? I'm not going back up there with my nuts in a jar."

Her eyes soften and she bites her lip. Then the little terrorist turns angry. "What's wrong with you? Are you dumb? Blind? In need of someone to slap you? Because I'll do it!" She huffs around the room, mumbling. "Idiot. I swear to God, I don't know why I talk to any of you. Jackson, Liam, Quinn, and now you!"

"Are you pregnant again? You're awfully hostile."

"I'll show you hostile!" she screams and throws a wad of paper at me.

"That wasn't very nice. Why the hell do you care, anyway?"

Her horns are sprouting. "Why do I care?" she yells, more antagonistic than actually curious.

Since I got back from DC, she's been up my ass. This is what I get for texting people. Lee immediately called me, demanding I "fix this." Telling me how people like Charlie don't come into our lives every day. How when you have something that's worth it, you have to go for it—like I fucking told her and Jackson. I love it when a woman throws shit in your face. It's been a week since I heard from Charlie. Obviously, it's not bothering her that we're over.

"Lee." I close my eyes. "I know you're trying to help, but we're done."

"Because you're an idiot."

"Sure, we can go with that," I placate her.

"Did you tell her you loved her?" she asks from the chair.

I look over at the leather seat by the window. Every day for the last few weeks that's where she was. Going over file after file, writing down notes on things she wanted me to dig deeper on, but she's no longer there.

"Mark?" Lee brings me back.

"Not in so many words."

"Why?"

"Because I won't lie to her."

"But you'll lie to yourself?"

I groan. I need new friends. I need a new life. Jackson and I haven't signed anything. I'm glad I gave myself the out. This way, I can take off and not worry. I can take the trips I've wanted to go on, surf in places I've only dreamed of. Maybe a break from all this shit is what I need.

"Did I care about her? Yes. Did I love her? I could've. But loving someone like Charlie isn't exactly easy." It's more like sticking your hand into a lion's cage and praying it doesn't bite. Which it will, as she so graciously demonstrated.

"You know, if I remember correctly, there was this guy, let's call him Matt."

"Matt?"

"Go with it."

I shrug. It's her story.

"Matt is a great guy. He's funny, charming, caring, would give you the shirt off his back, but Matt is kind of dumb when it comes to women. He's the quintessential bachelor. Lives in this house off the beach, but it's decorated in pizza boxes."

"Matt sounds like my kind of guy."

"Shut up," she says while she gives me the evil eye. "Matt is a moron. Matt does dumb things. Matt doesn't know how to be a grown up. He's doing everything right but missing out at the same time. Sure, he owns a house. Sure, he has a great job. Sure, he has *amazing* friends. To everyone else, it seems he has it all. But Matt is alone. Everything around him is superficial. The times that matter in life are spent with someone who sees through the superficial. They see you for who you are, and love you despite the flaws." Natalie stands, walks over to where I am, and places her hand on my shoulder. "It's time to fight for something worth fighting for. I've known you for a long time. I've seen you screw around and date, and then I saw you with her."

"Thought we were talking about Matt?"

She gives me a blank stare before she goes on. "Don't be Matt. She may not be the easy choice, but she's the right one."

Lee kisses my cheek and walks off, leaving me stunned. The thing is that I don't know that she's the right choice. I don't know if there even *is* a choice. I went after her. She was cold, distant, and to be honest, a bitch. While normally I don't mind her hostile side, what the hell doors did she leave open? None. I'm not going to beg anyone.

She made her bed, now she can lie in it. She's pretty good at lying anyway.

NINE DAYS WITHOUT HER in my house and it feels empty. Nine days where her snoring hasn't woken me up, or I'm eating her hair in the middle of the night because she flips it in my face. I hate that her perfume lingers in the air. If she could just vanish from my house, that would be great.

I wonder about her more than I should. Is she still following her leads? Did she go back to the agency so she could pursue her end goal? She'll never find him on her own, and I honestly think she's being roadblocked. There's no way with her intelligence, training, and the lair of computers in her house, she wouldn't know by now. Someone is pulling the strings behind her. I have it feeling it's her handler.

Charlie described how it went down. How this girl had to have sold her out because no one else knew the information. Then, out of nowhere, she trusts her again? It makes no sense. I know she's desperate, but it made me question her thinking when she suggested it.

My phone rings and Liam's name flashes across the screen.

"Hey, I thought you were on vacation with Lee," I answer. I'm confused as to why he's calling. We all got the verbal slap down from Natalie about how no one was to bother her. That Liam is deploying and she wants a week of just the four of them. If our houses were on fire, we could figure it out without her.

She's a fun one.

"Yeah, I just got a call from my PI buddy up in DC."

"I'm not worried about her anymore."

Liam laughs. "Sure, you're not. The thing is, he's been keeping an eye on her place. Nothing stalker like, but when Lee filled me in on your situation, I thought maybe he could just keep tabs."

I growl at the idea that he did this. Why the fuck can't these people just stay the hell out of it? We're done. I wish her well, but I don't *care* anymore. I sigh and then it sinks in, if Liam is calling me—the guy called him. "What's wrong? Is she okay?"

"I thought you weren't worried."

"Fuck off." I grab my keys not even knowing if I should, but I need to move. If she's in trouble . . . if she needs me . . . God, I'm stupid. Of course I care. "Tell me what you know."

"He said she hasn't been to her house in nine days, and when she left, she went out for a walk, no bags, no nothing, and hasn't returned. He also said there were a bunch of guys tailing her. I'm not saying anything's wrong, but he figured I might want to know."

I need to get up there. She could've taken off on a lead or be with her brother, but I need to know. I have to make sure she's okay. "I'm leaving now."

"I figured."

"Don't sound so smug," I reply and then think about what Liam did for me. "Hey man, thank you."

"Anytime. Be careful. I'll let my buddy know you're on your way, and I'll text you his info. He can help with the lay of the land."

Liam and I became friends through chance, but he's proven time and again what a stand-up guy he is. "I appreciate it. Really."

"I know. I better get back before Lee realizes I'm not there. Keep your eyes open."

"Always. Talk to you soon." I disconnect the call and get into motion. Time is not on my side. It's been over a week, and I've been here licking my wounds. If they touch a hair on her head, I'll put a bullet in each of theirs.

I need a plan. Do I drive or fly? I can get there faster by plane. Every minute is precious, but by the time I get the pilot, the plane, and everything else ready, I could be there. I throw some stuff in a bag and head out the door.

Once in the car I start to really formulate my first step. If she's in trouble I doubt I'll find anything at her house, but it's the only place to start. Maybe she left a clue. Then again, this is Charlie. I grab my phone and call Jackson.

"Hey," he answers on the first ring.

"I'm heading to DC."

"Took you long enough."

"She might be in trouble," I say. I feel broken. It's ridiculous.

This girl left over a stupid argument and then basically told me everything we shared was imagined, but I love her. I love her, and now I'm scared for her. She was drugged, she's been watched, and now she's disappeared.

Jackson goes quiet for a moment. "What do you know?" His entire demeanor has changed. He's now Jackson Cole, Commander of the US Navy SEAL Team Four. I know this voice. I can respond to this voice, because this is who I should be right now.

I shift in the seat, press the pedal down, and stop my bullshit. "She hasn't returned to her apartment in nine days. Liam had a friend watching out for her. He noticed some activity so he must've been watching her place. Liam called, said what I just told you, and I'm going."

"I don't think you should go near her place. If she disappeared intentionally, they're watching. If she did unintentionally, you won't find anything. You run the risk of tipping them off."

"You're wrong. If it was unintentional, something will be off. If she did it intentionally then her place will look the way I left it. Either way, that's the starting point. I hope the motherfuckers are waiting for me. I welcome them."

"Think, Mark. Think for once. Do you want anything to happen to her?"

"Don't insult me."

He sighs. "I'm not. I'm telling you that you have to think strategically. Not based on emotion. I know you love her, but that's all the more reason to lock it down. What about contacting Charlie's handler?"

"No!" I yell and almost veer off the road. "No way. I think she's behind this."

I fill Jackson in on all my concerns, and we discuss the possibilities. The thing is that we have no idea the mess she was involved in. For all I know, she's been using us. We have no clue the depths of her deceit, or even if there is any. Blind trust truly leaves you in the dark.

Liam's friend suggested I meet him at his office. He has some photos and other things he wants me to look at. I pull up to his office on the east side of DC. Definitely not what I pictured, but then again, neither is our office.

I open the door to the suite, and his receptionist walks me right back.

"Hi, Mark Dixon." I extend my hand.

He gives me a firm handshake. "Glad you found the office okay. I'm Frank Baldwin. Sorry we're meeting under these terms."

I wonder if he knows something. "Have you found anything?" I get right to it. I'm already nine days behind the curve. I don't want to panic, but I won't pretend we're not standing in quicksand, either. Charlie is a target.

"No, I wasn't able to get into her house, either. I tried to pick the lock, but I should've known that was impossible."

"Yeah, she has a fortress."

"Look, someone was in her house the day you paid your visit. They came out, and then she followed about twenty minutes later. I've tailed my share of people, but there was enough of an alarm going off that I think something is wrong. She had nothing on her, didn't get in a car, and then she went to a very public place." Frank shows me a few pictures of Charlie walking. I look closely at the one shot of her leaving her house. There's a red car parked two spots down from the angle. "That car." I point to it. "I've seen it. The license plate I mean. I've seen it before, and I remember it."

The night of her mother's party, there was a red car with the same plate. I swear I've seen it because it had my birthday as the plate number. It's stupid and possibly nothing, but it's the same make and model.

"Are you sure?"

"Yes, I'm sure. Can you run it? I need to talk to someone."

"Of course." He starts to type it in. "Okay, it comes back to a Mandi Milostan."

Mother fucking shit. She was at the party and then at Charlie's house that day. There's only one person who might have clues as to Charlie's location. Time to go see Priscilla.

twenty-eight

I PULL UP TO Charlie's mother's house. Unease is all I feel. One of two things will happen here: she either doesn't know that Charlie has vanished and I'll tell her, or she knows and I look like a love struck fool. Either way, I have to be ready for the fallout.

Here goes nothing.

"Mark, right?" Dominic opens the door as my hand reaches for the doorbell.

"Yeah." I shake his hand as he smiles. "Good to see you, Dominic."

"Call me, Dom. Charlie isn't here." He leans against the doorjamb. "If you're looking for her. I haven't heard from her in a few days."

That's not encouraging. "When was the last time you spoke to her?"

"We don't talk often, as you can imagine. It's more of a when she feels like letting me know things." Dominic steps forward after looking over to the right. Something caught his eye. "Why don't you come inside? I'm sure my mother would love to see you."

I nod and step through the doorway.

"Mom!" he yells. "Charlie's friend is here. I'm going to take him down to the game room."

"I'm not much of a video game player. Never took you for one, either." I laugh.

"Pool," he corrects. His finger goes over his lips and I get it now.

"I haven't played in years, but we had a table at the base in Iraq that we played on after missions."

"Charlie and I grew up playing." Dominic talks as we head down toward the basement. "My dad was the master, though. I don't think any of us ever beat him."

We get to a room downstairs and he flips a switch. The lights go on and sure enough, it's a game room. A minute later Priscilla joins us.

"Mark, it's lovely seeing you again." She smiles and walks toward me. Her hands take mine and she pulls me so we're cheek to cheek. She lowers her voice to whisper in my ear, "Give him a minute before you talk."

Dominic is over on the left, opening up some control panels. He turns some lights green and then nods.

"So, how have you been?" She asks with a smile.

"Good." My voice is even, though I feel anything but. They're family members who have lived this life. They're not stupid, and I'm sure Charlie's father prepared them.

"We're fine now," Dominic says.

You can actually see Priscilla's entire demeanor shift. "Where is she?"

"That's what I came to ask you."

"You were the last person she was with. She called me from Virginia Beach. Told me she was with you, and would call me when she got back. Now you're here without her, and Dominic had to trigger the codes?" Priscilla's brown eyes are almost black. She spits each word as I can imagine terror grips her.

I step closer, letting her see through my eyes. "She left my house nine days ago. I followed her to DC, but she was hell bent on getting rid of me. We argued, and as far as I knew, we were done. At the gala you hosted, she was drugged."

"I assume these are connected?" Dominic asks.

"I think so. I don't know, though. The guy who told me about the waiter and the information was keeping tabs on Charlie after I left her that day. He was concerned for her safety."

"Nine days since you last heard from her," Priscilla muses aloud. "But she hasn't contacted any of us. We have one more day to wait. One more day, and I open it."

Again, I'm slightly amazed at the lengths this family has gone to in the matter of what ifs. "Open it?"

Dominic takes Priscilla's hand and walks her toward the couch. "We have to turn it back on. Five minutes is almost up."

Jesus, these people are fucking amazing. I mean they know the amount of time to keep coms down. How to trick the equipment. I should've been raised by them, not my cookie-baking, porn-stealing mother.

"I need to know what you have to open," I press. Time is running out.

Priscilla's eyes glisten a tiny bit before they turn to steel. "We have a protocol. If she goes out of contact, and we think she's been taken, we wait ten days. Then we open the file. If we open it, though, chances are she's dead. The last person we opened it for was . . ." Tears start to form again. "My husband. But we have to act as if this is normal. That she's on a mission. No one can know we're worried."

"Okay."

I'm not a parent so I can't understand her emotions. I've never lost a spouse, so I can't imagine the movies that must be going through her head. But I love Charlie. For some stupid reason, that girl got in my heart. I don't know if we ever had a chance at fighting it off. But if I lose her like this—I'll never recover.

Dominic shuts the lights back to red and nods so we all know. It's no longer safe to speak freely. We have to play the part that she's just off doing whatever and we're not concerned. All the while, we write notes and burn them in the fire. Dominic suspects she went to a safe house. Priscilla throws that notion out because she would've contacted her once she made it.

My thoughts circle round and round. If she went to a safe house, why no contact if they have this timeline set up? It all seems a bit coincidental to me. So, I think. What would I do if it were me? First, if I knew my house was compromised . . . I'd leave. Which we know she did. Next, she went where she could disappear . . .

"I need to go to my hotel. I'm exhausted," I say and get up.

"I should get home, too. I have a busy day tomorrow." Dominic gets up and gives me a look. I'm sure he sees I'm full of shit, but he keeps his mouth shut. I shake my head so he doesn't get any ideas.

This has to be done solo.

"Mark, stop by tomorrow. I'd love to talk more about the charity and what visions you have going forward. It's great that one of Charlie's friends is so involved. I'm sure she truly appreciates it." Priscilla stands and walks both of us to the door. "Call me tomorrow, Dominic. None of your crappy politics when you're working on the hill this week. I want you to do what's best for everyone, not just you!"

"Good night, Mother." Dominic kisses her cheek, and then he walks down to where I stand, smiling. God, she must drive them insane. "I used to worry someone would kidnap her, then I realized they'd give her back after five minutes."

We both laugh. "She's something else."

"You have no idea. That woman would give anyone a run for their money. I feared her as a kid. My dad was the easy one."

"I doubt that."

"Yeah, true. I was raised by two of the most intelligent and cunning people. It's no wonder why my sister and I went into our professions." Dominic smiles.

I like him. He's good people. Even if he's a politician, he has his head on straight. You can see this thing with Charlie has him worried, but he was smart enough to identify it. I know I'm being watched. We have proof of that from Frank. I can't react, though. I have to act normal, which is hilarious because I'm sure they are aware that I'm aware.

"I'm heading back to my hotel. Maybe we can grab a beer tomorrow?" I offer because it feels like the right thing. No matter what, I'm getting Charlie back, and her family will be a part of my life. Because this woman is mine.

Dominic claps me on the shoulder. "I think you and I will get along just fine." He hands me his card. "My cell is on the back. Call me if you need anything, and I'll see you tomorrow."

We head off in different directions. I got a hotel in the National Mall area. That way I would be around the sights. After Frank showed me the photos of Charlie at the Lincoln Memorial, I figured I should be close to that area. I'll head to her apartment tomorrow, but first, I want to take a look where she was last seen.

If only Frank had followed her farther.

The temperature drops during my walk, and I pull my jacket a little tighter around me. The chill in the air is welcome and seems to sharpen my thoughts. Charlie had someone in her apartment when I was there, that's clear from the photos, but why were they there? They were clearly CIA because of the car they got into. Then they were watching the Erickson's house, so clearly this has something to do with her father. I pick up my pace as I spot the lights from the memorial.

Joggers and people on bikes pass by, even though it's almost ten at night. This city is the ultimate chameleon. There's deception and lies blanketed by the illusion of the truth. Every step closer, I think about how she was here and wonder if she's in trouble. I left that day. I walked out when the predator was in her apartment. I knew something was wrong, but she pissed me off so much I didn't think. "Frustrating female," I mutter as I get closer.

I walk up the steps and look around. This the first time I've been here. Every other time I've ever been to the nation's capital, I've had no time. "Why did you come here, Charlie?" I ask Abe. "What did she tell you?" I look around for something that would give me a clue. Maybe she stashed something somewhere. Then again, I'll never find it. If she hid it, there's no chance it's still here.

I try to slip into what she could've been thinking. If I needed to slip away, then I would've found an exit that gave me a chance to blend well. There was no emergency that day, so she didn't cause a diversion. *Think, Mark.*

"Hello, Mr. Dixon." I turn as a man in a navy suit walks toward me. "You don't know me, even though I know a lot about you. But I thought we should officially meet."

If I were a betting man, I would lay money that he's a member of the agency. Instead of going on the defensive, I relax and appear as if I was anticipating this visit. "I figured it wouldn't take you long to show yourself."

He pauses, and I wonder if I made the right decision. I need to trust my gut. You don't show your hand unless your cards are crap. For him to show himself means they need me in some capacity. "Why are you here?"

"Same reason you are."

"I've watched you for a long time. Once you became a part of her life, we learned quite a bit. Such a pity, all the trouble that's happening to your friends."

My fists clench as I fight the urge to smash them into his face. If they're fucking around with us, I don't care who he is.

Then I remember that they could have Charlie. I won't let them hurt her. "It is." I keep it short and calm myself. I recall Jackson's words about checking my emotions.

"You know." He leans against the wall. "I've always loved this place. It's funny that so many find Abraham Lincoln iconic. He built his legacy on honesty and freedom. Yet, so many of us live a life filled with chains and lies. Baffles me how many agents, politicians, and regular people come here for perspective. They find it and then go back to their ways. We spend our lives in the darkness and shadows, and here he sits for the world to see. Funny, isn't it?"

His monologue is boring. The thing about people like him is they don't often say anything without a meaning behind it. When they speak, they have hidden layers. In my training, I really learned to listen. If I had to break his words down, I'd take away that they don't have her. Her old ways would lead her to stay in the darkness. She's trained to hide.

"Interesting speech, Mr. . . ." I trail off and wait for him to fill in the blank.

"Smith."

I laugh. "Of course. How original."

"You shouldn't be worried about who I am, but rather what I know that you must be desperate to know."

"I love a good riddle. Why did the chicken cross the road?" I'm over this guy. I don't think he knows a damn thing.

"I doubt you'll find this funny, Mr. Dixon." He extends an envelope.

I don't want to touch it, but at the same time, I know I will. My main goal is to stay calm. I can't let him rattle me. In the back of my mind, I'm aware that I'm playing into his hand. Charlie would tell me to throw it down and walk away, but if they have her, there isn't anything I wouldn't do to get her back. I open the envelope and pull out a photograph. It's her bound to a chair.

Her arms and legs are tied, and she sits behind a black wall. Nothing descript about anything in this photo except her. She's gagged and blindfolded, but the tiny tattoo on her leg lets me know it's her.

"What do you want?" I ask. I'm about to become his puppet.

"I thought that would change your tune. There's a file. She has it hidden, and we want it. Now, be a good boy and fetch it."

He has no clue how fast I could snap his fucking neck. I have a feeling this guy is high up on the food chain. There's no way he's acting alone, but if I fuck up, she's dead. "What makes you think I can get it? You're all spies, isn't this your forte?"

"You've been in her office."

"And?"

"Let's not play games. I won't hesitate to kill her."

"I want proof she's okay," I demand.

"File first."

"No dice. Let me remind you of my background. I'm not dumb. I'm not new at this. I want proof of life, and I don't mean some photo you could've doctored for all the hell I know. I want to talk to her or video with a date and time stamp. I mean, my memory isn't what it's cracked up to be." I fake being bored with this. The truth is. I can't remember how the fuck she did that security thing. I doubt I'll ever crack it.

"You're in no position to make demands."

"Actually, I am. So proof of life by tomorrow, or I'll find her and kill anyone who stands in my way. Your choice." I head down the stairs without looking back. I just made one hell of a move, but I have no other options.

If I fail, I lose her. If I lose her, I lose me.

twenty-nine

I GRAB THE METRO past my hotel. I'm too keyed up to sleep, and there's no way I'm going to anyone with this. I get off at the Capitol and decide to walk off my nervous energy. I just need to move, think, and plan.

I wish I had someone here that I could trust. I consider Frank, but then I wonder if I'm willing to put him in the middle of this shit.

My brain needs to run through it all and try to recall how the hell she turned that office into her fortress. I'll never remember that fucking code, and even if I do, turning over the file is a mistake.

There's no way in hell I'm going to let them keep her. Plus, who the fuck will believe the CIA has her hostage? This entire situation couldn't be more fucked up if we tried. She's in trouble, and I don't know if I can save her.

The hairs on the back of my neck prick. Great, another mystery visitor. I move a little faster, and the footsteps behind me follow. I'm not armed, I'm in a strange city, and I'm being stalked by my own government. The same one I served and took a bullet for. How's this for irony?

"You can go home now, I'm not going anywhere," I say aloud, probably sounding like a psycho.

I hear a laugh. "I think you could use a friend."

I turn, and find Frank standing there. "You know I could've killed you in a minute."

Frank grins. "I could've fucked you up before you got a punch in. Let's not forget that I went through the same training as you."

"We probably shouldn't talk," I say as he continues to follow me. "It's not safe for you to be around me."

"I'll take my chances." He laughs as if he couldn't give a shit less. "What's our next step?"

No fucking way. He's not getting involved. "I think this should be a solo mission, man."

"They got her, didn't they?"

"I'm serious."

He huffs. "If it were my girl, I'd want a friend. Someone who can access information, find leads, and kill quietly."

I get what he's saying. We're both former SEALs, but there's a line I won't cross. Dragging someone else down doesn't seem like a good idea. I don't know anything about Frank's life. He could be married, a father, and I have a feeling this won't end well. I can't be responsible for ruining his life. Don't I sound like Jackson now?

Fuck that. All I can do is lay this out for him, and then it's on him.

"Look, I'm going to get her back by any means necessary. I can't sit back, and I don't know you, but if you're in . . . you're in. If you can't for any reason do whatever that means, then walk away now."

Frank stops in front of an Irish Pub and extends his hand. "Well, the least you can do is buy me a beer. If I'm willing to go on a suicide mission and all."

I laugh. "Deal."

We grab a table in the back. Both of us sit so we're able to see the door. Rule one: Never turn your back on the enemy or the unknown.

Once we get our drinks, we get into planning.

"I'm assuming this has to do with the incident I was looking in to?" Frank drinks a beer while I sip Scotch.

"Yup."

"How high up do you think this goes?"

"No idea, but considering the visit I had, I'm not thinking it's a low man on the totem pole."

Frank nods. "I didn't think it was, considering the move they made last month. No one just drugs someone at a family function. There's motive behind a move like that. Any chance her family is involved?"

"I don't think so. Her mom lost her husband not too long ago. I doubt she'd want her daughter dead."

He mulls that over, hesitates a few times, and then finally shares what's on his mind. "Look, her brother though, he's pretty intent on the election. There's a lot of shit that goes down. I think we should look at all of them. I don't know that if my sister's life was on the line that I'd be meeting with another op."

My brows lower. "What do you mean, another op?"

Frank pulls out his phone, swipes to a photo and lays it on the table. "That's Mandi Milostan, she's an operative. The one who was tailing her."

"No," I correct him. "Mandi is her handler. And if I find her, she's got a lot to answer for."

"Well, her brother is meeting with them. Do you know what they're after?"

I gulp the liquid and welcome the burn. I can't believe this shit. I let her leave. I should've known. It was my job to protect her, well . . . in my head. They took her right out from under me. I want their heads. Every single motherfucker who touched her is my target.

"Yeah, but they'll never get it. I want them all, Frank. I want each and every one of them. Since you were tailing me, did you get photos of them?" He's good, and if he was watching me, maybe he got their faces.

He grins, pulls a long draw from the bottle. "I'm already running their names. I'll get you the info tomorrow."

"Good, I'm going to her place early tomorrow. Maybe she left me a clue."

We both finish our drinks with a plan to meet in the morning and exchange our new info. I'm also going to have to look into Dominic and Priscilla. Then I'm going to save my girl and make her realize how much she loves me.

FRANK SAID HE COULDN'T get in, but gaining access to Charlie's apartment was easy. Clearly, someone wanted me to be able to enter. They must really think I'm stupid.

Once I go inside, I decide to look for what I wanted to anyway: something she left behind to alert us. Her bags sit in the entry, nothing really different that I can tell. Of course, I haven't been here much, but I pay attention.

I'm sure the file I'm supposed to search for is in her scary ass office, and in all honesty, I do know where. When she went all panic room on me before, she had it hidden in a trap beneath the floor. Unless I pull up floorboards, though, there's no way I'm grabbing it.

I go through her bedroom, but it feels like an intrusion. Still, I need to see if she left me anything. At first glance, there's nothing, but by the garbage there's one scrap of paper. Considering this place is like a museum, it could be something.

In my hand sits a handwritten note that says, "Just us."

My mind flashes to the vineyard and all we had there. The way we made love over and over again, saying it was just us. This has to mean something. Charlie doesn't do anything by accident. That has to be meant for me. It could mean anything, though. I want to scream at her that if she wants me to follow clues I need a little more. Whatever it means, it's a clue that she wants something to be between us.

My phone rings. Perfect, it's Frank.

"Frank, find anything?"

"You need to get out of there."

"What?" I ask as I acquaint myself with her place.

"Mark, I'm telling you, something is wrong. You need to get the fuck out of there. Wherever they have her, we're not going to find it, and this is going to take some serious work to get to her."

I don't care. I hope they come in, because they'll never get the info. I'll keep everything between just us. "Sorry, dude. Giants are about to play."

"Don't be an idiot," he warns.

"Too late." I hang up and turn the phone off.

They've got her, and I'm going to have them bring me to her. It's the only way.

So, I head into the living room, throw my feet up and put the game on.

I give them five minutes.

The door flies open before the next snap happens.

"Did you think we were kidding?"

"Did you forget my requirements? Would you mind grabbing me a beer?" I ask. "No?" I'm pushing every button, but if this fucker puts a hand on me, I'll snap his neck. I get up, walk to the fridge, grab the beer. "You should grab a seat. No proof of life, and I'm not even looking around. Redskins versus the Giants, should be a good game. My money is on the Giants, though." I head back to the couch.

"I underestimated you," Agent Smith says with a hint of

awe. I don't blame him, I surprise myself sometimes.

"Seems to be a CIA flaw." I pop the top.

He heads over to the chair next to me. "You were supposed to make this easy. Get me the file, save me the trouble of destroying everything here, and then you got her back."

"Well, where's my video? Phone call? Besides, if Charlie told you anything, it's that I never make anything easy." I smirk and turn my attention back to the game.

"You don't seem to understand the gravity of the situation. I will beat her within an inch of her life. Then the only proof you'll have is her cold, dead body."

My body reacts on pure instinct. I surge to my feet, ready to pummel this motherfucker. "If you touch her . . . If she comes back to me in a condition less than the last time I laid eyes on her, you'll see just how much you underestimated me. Take me to Charlie."

He looks over toward the window then back to me. "All humans have a flaw. They're naturally imperfect. It's my job to find the flaw and scratch it until it bleeds."

Here we go with this fucking monologue again.

"Do you know your flaw, Mr. Dixon?"

"I'm sure you're dying to tell me." I roll my eyes. This guy is a tool.

Agent Smith walks forward, and I stand prepared. He's about to make his move. I'm ready to ruin his clothes.

"I'm going to enjoy scratching your flaw."

Instead of him grabbing me like I expect, I hear a zing through the air before something pinches my neck.

Everything goes numb, before it goes black.

thirty

"WHERE IS THE FILE?" he yells.

Fuck! My head is pounding. I feel as if I've been sucking on cotton balls, and could someone dim the damn lights? I sit bound to a cold metal chair. One day I'll learn to keep my mouth shut.

Agent Smith, or whatever his name is, sits across the table of this nasty warehouse. "Where did she hide it?"

"That's a fantastic question. Where is Charlie?"

He stands and then moves around so we're face to face. "The file or we kill her."

Like I would tell him even if I knew. "I thought you might say that, but those are my terms. I want Charlie or you get nothing." His fist connects with my jaw and pain shoots through me. "That wasn't very nice." I try to right my jaw. He punches me again. I spit the blood out right at him. Stupid fuck. "How about you untie me and we see who the real man is here?"

"Tell me where she hid it."

I look around to get any bearings, but there are black curtains over the windows so I have no idea if it's day or night. A single light bulb hangs over the table, but the fucked up part is the amount of blood on the floor. This is a place people come to die.

I'm so fucked. All I can hope is that someone notices I'm not in contact, or Frank finds the scrap of paper I left.

Another man steps forward wearing a clear plastic mask. He doesn't say a word as he throws down a black doctor bag.

"You look pretty."

His dark eyes squint and his voice is muffled. "You're about to find out if she'll still love you after you have some cosmetic work."

I smirk. "I always wanted a nose job. Is this a request thing, or a whatever you feel like doing thing?"

"He told us you had a flair for the dramatics."

Who the fuck is he? My eyes widen at the morsel of information. Of course, they see it.

Agent Stupid Arrogant Prick speaks first. "Oh, you'd like to know something? Do you know why you're here, Mark Dixon, Chief Petty Officer Special Warfare? Do you know why all of the men you're friends with suffer and will continue to even though you'll be dead? I bet you'd like to know that." He picks his nails.

The stupid smug bastard sits there with a grin.

"Maybe if you cooperate, I'll exchange the name of the person behind all your misfortunes."

I have to stay alive. I have to think through this entire situation because once they make one tiny mistake, they're done.

"Funny, I don't believe a word you say."

"Have it your way." He huffs as if I'm bothering him. "Lights out."

The clear mask freak jabs something into my thigh, but before I can make a sound, I'm out.

thirty-one

"**A**GAIN!" HE YELLS AS they take turns punching me in the sides. My arms are tied above my head, and I can just rest my weight on my toes if I try.

It's been at least three days, maybe more. I'm dehydrated, weak, and beaten. I'll never let them see me break, though.

"Now, we know you've seen the file. We know she shared it with you, so what was in it."

"Who do I have to blow to get a cheeseburger?" I reply. I saw a page of the file—*one* page—but, the thing is, I'll never tell them anything. They'll have to kill me. I would never betray Charlie. I love her, and if she's willing to die for this, so am I.

He steps forward and hits me himself.

"Fuck!" I scream while I start to cough. My lungs ache from that one. Shit.

"This can all stop, you know. We'll let you go, tell you who is causing all the problems with your friends, and this will become a distant memory."

"What about a milkshake?" I smile through the bloody lip, even though it hurts like a bitch. "French fries?"

Breaking my body, fine. Breaking my smartass ways, not happening.

"I think you could rot for a few days down in the hole."

Yeah, like that's something new.

Another one of the assholes punches my kidneys and the stabbing pain intensifies.

"Show me Charlie, and I'll draw you a fucking map," I lie. But I need to see her. If they're doing this to me, I can't imagine how she's surviving. On the other hand, they need her. That's all I have to hold on to.

Plastic fuckface punches me in the nose, and the snap lets me know it's broken. Blood trickles downward, the metallic taste seeping into my mouth. If I'm bleeding, I'm living. As long as pain remains, I know I'm surviving. So I welcome it.

Agent Smith walks close. "I've seen men cave. I've made people cry for their God and their mothers. We're only beginning, so I hope you're ready for a long and painful road."

"Let's hear it for the good guys." I give him the best smirk I can muster.

"Beat him a little more and then throw him in the hole," he instructs.

I imagine Charlie's face. How she smiled, her blue eyes that shone so brightly. She holds me to this world. Her face is my absolution. Her love is my reprieve. If she's alive, then I will fight. She's worth every bruise, scar, and broken bone. Our love is true and honest, and true love doesn't fail, it triumphs.

"NICE TO SEE YOU again." Agent Smith bites into a cheeseburger.

I hope he chokes on it.

"It's a great day to be alive, huh?" He tosses some fries in his mouth and washes it all down with a milkshake.

I have no concept of time. It could be a day, a week, a month since I was brought here, and I wouldn't know. All I can see is black. No light, no air, just complete confinement, it's like being buried alive. But I saw her. Every time I felt alone, she was with me. Telling me she was okay and that I had to keep going. It's funny, in all my years of training, I never had something to hold on to. Someone or something that I used to get me through. I have that now, and I lost her.

That I'm in this room, not bound, not being beaten, tells me they won. However, they'll never overtake me. I don't give a fuck if they wave that goddamn file in my face, I'll never give up—for her.

When all you have is time with your own thoughts, you realize what's important. You see your life for what it was, how it could've been—the mistakes, and the promises for if you survive. People are important, not things or possessions. I'll be a better man, brother, son, and someday . . . husband. I'll stop fighting everyone and everything. I won't take the little time we have for granted, because this will all end one day. My days are numbered, I see that now. Right now, all I have is faith that I'll get the chance to right my wrongs.

"Why am I here now?"

He takes another bite and my mouth waters. I'm fucking starving. "Hungry?"

"I'm on a diet."

The stupid bastard laughs. "This will be your last chance. Your body is shutting down. There's no fight left in your eyes, Mark. This could all be over. I could get you some food, a shower, clean clothes. All I need is for you to help me."

"I'd rather die. You should know, when I make it through this, I plan to kill each and every last one of you."

"You couldn't fight your way out of a paper bag at this point. But I appreciate your tenacity. You would've made a fantastic operative." He stands and places his gun on the table with his hand hovering over it. "I'm sorry it'll all end like this. I liked you, but my son didn't."

Son? What the ever-loving hell is going on? "Who the hell is your son, and what does any of this have to do with a file or me?" I'm not sure if I'm hallucinating this entire situation, but I find any ounce of strength I have left. I need that gun. I have to end this. Then he'll see how it feels to be at my mercy.

As if the prick can read my thoughts, he leans back.

"I could tell you, but that would ruin the fun." We stare at each other for a beat. "I hope you see your girlfriend in hell, since I killed her in this very chair not even an hour ago. She pleaded for your life, but I think it's only fair you're reunited"

My heart stops. She can't be dead. I can't have failed her.

He lifts the gun.

I've been in this moment before, but this time it's different. The world becomes a little sharper. Nothing slows, but it comes into focus. I see her clear as day. Her blue eyes, her dark brown hair, the way her face always looks as if she's ready to take on the world. My Charisma. I knew she would own my world the minute I laid eyes on her. There was nothing tying us together, but I felt secured. No matter what, she'll be the last name I utter, and the last thing I see when I close my eyes. But that moment isn't now. He ripped her away from me, and I'm going to end him. I'm going to make him pay for ever hurting her.

I fought because I thought she was alive. If she's gone . . . I'll follow her.

Rage fills me.

The need to destroy him overpowers any self-preservation I have left. I won't let them take me like this. I will never surrender.

Before I can think, I'm rushing toward him as though I'm a rabid animal. I'll go down fighting. I'll draw blood because he ruined the reason I exist. She's the air I breathe, the reason my heartbeats, and I never got to tell her.

Shock registers in his eyes before I lunge for the gun. "You son of a bitch!" I shout as my hand connects with the barrel.

My hands move toward his arms. I battle with all I have. Somehow, I manage to get it out of my face. I'm weak and he pushes me off easily. I step back with my arms lifted. "Look, I don't know where the hell the file is. I've been beaten, starved, beaten again. Don't you think by this point you'd have the file?"

"What makes you think she didn't give it up?" His arm raises again as he takes the sight. I'm about to die at the hands of the CIA.

"Then why kill me?" I ask. I need to keep him talking.

I shuffle to the right with my hands still up in the air. We circle as I think of a way to extend this conversation. His arm drops slightly and relief seeps through. No, fuck that. I can't afford relief. This guy will kill me the second he has a chance. My legs keep going, but I'm so fucking tired. I don't know how long I can keep this up.

"Because you know too much. You didn't really think you'd make it out of here, did you? Let's be real. You know what I look like, and you've probably pieced together who I am. But then, you still don't know who is behind all of your misfortunes. Such a shame."

"Since I'm going to die, might as well tell me."

He lets out a short laugh and lifts his arm back up. "Not a chance. You're going to die completely in the dark."

This is it. He's done talking, and so am I. My body tenses as I prepare for my final chance to end this.

I think of Charlie, how she would've fought to the end. I think of Jackson, Natalie, Catherine, Liam, and Aaron . . . I think of my mother, Garrett, and how they'll suffer, but they'll know this won't have been in vain. They'll find Charlie's information because of the tips I left for Frank. Hopefully, he found my note and discovered who these fuckers are.

His left eye closes, and his finger tightens on the trigger. I lunge.

The sound rings through the air, but I keep going. Nothing will stop me.

Blood spills everywhere. All I see is red, but I charge forward. Another pop goes off, but I have nothing left.

My legs go out and I crumble to the ground on top of him.

This is what dying feels like.

Weightless, numb, and calm.

thirty-two

Charlie

"**WAKE UP!**" I SLAP his face. "Mark, baby, you have to get up! We have to get the hell out of here!"

He's almost unrecognizable.

Nothing could've prepared me for this.

There are so many broken bones, so much blood and bruising. Tears threaten to pool, but I don't have time to cry. I need to get him out of here. Bloodstains cover his clothing as I rip it open to see if he was hit.

His entire chest is painted in bruises—every inch is yellow, purple, blue, or black. "What did they do to you?" I choke on the words.

"Charlie, we have maybe three minutes before they light up the place," Mandi yells as she peers down the hall. "There's no time."

"I'm not leaving him!" I grab water, pour it down his throat, and then splash some on his face. "Come on, Mark. Look at me!" My voice isn't my own. I'm near hysterics, but he's not responding. "Get Jackson in here!"

"You did this to him," Christopher Asher taunts.

I turn to him and raise my weapon. "Don't say a word or I'll put a bullet between your eyes before anyone can protect you. I'll end your pathetic excuse for a life, and smile while doing it. But I'll shoot you in about ten other places first. I'll make you cry, suffer, and beg for me to stop."

"Charlie," Mandi warns. "We need him."

"Get Jackson," I say while I lower my gun.

Mandi nods and then rushes from the room as I hold Mark's head in my lap. "I'm so sorry. They hid you so well. It took us a little time, but we figured it out. I'm here for you. Just you. Please, I love you." I let the tears fall this time. I can't stop them. One drops down my face, landing on his cheek. "I love your stupid pain in the ass, and I need you to wake up."

My hands roam his body for a bullet wound. Christopher fired, but we got a shot off first. I still have no idea if he was hit. I'm running on pure fear and adrenaline. I just need to get us out of here.

Mandi and I got in just in time, and then the jackass almost ruined everything by lunging at Christopher. As soon as I saw the light flick in his eyes, I knew I had to move. Mark was done with the charade of talking, and so was Christopher. I've felt that same final burst of spirit enter my eye, the one that means it's time to end it.

We were able to penetrate the warehouse pretty easily. They were cocky, and I used that weakness. We tied up the three guys on the outside, and only Christopher was with Mark. Once I breached the door, Mandi took the first shot and hit Christopher in the shoulder. Mark went unconscious as soon as their bodies collided, so I pray Christopher's bullet missed.

"Is he okay?" Jackson is frantic as he rushes towards us. "No! Is he?" Jackson can't even say the words. He steps forward and gets a glimpse at his body. "Holy fuck, he's—"

"He's breathing, but he won't wake up. We have to move him and get cleared out before the next part of the plan happens."

"You think you'll get away with this? You're done." Christopher yells from his position tied to the chair.

"Shut up!" I glare at him. Everything in me wants to kill him, but I'd much rather he suffer for his sins. Killing him would be a gift.

He chuckles. "I trained you better than this. Your father was an idiot, and so are you. You think you have this all figured out?" He laughs again. "I have friends everywhere. Friends who you think are on your side, but you're a puppet, and I hold the strings."

I walk forward and slam my fist across his mouth. "I said, shut the fuck up!"

He spits blood at my feet, but of course, he won't give up. "You'll end up six feet under."

Now it's my turn to laugh. "You couldn't find me before. You're weak, and I have what you want. What you'll never get is that I win." I rear back and punch him once more. I want to make him look half as bad as Mark. My foot lifts and I slam it into his stomach. The force of my kick throws the chair off balance, and he lands on his back. I step forward and press my boot to the side of his face. I use my weight to smash his face against the concrete.

"Your boyfriend gave it all up."

I lean down and punch him again. "That's not even a piece of what I want to do to you!" Jackson's arms wrap around my middle, and he drags me back.

"Stop, Charlie. We have to get Mark out of here." He reminds me why I can't beat the shit out of Christopher.

"Lucky for you," I sneer in his direction.

Jackson grabs Mark's arm and hoists him up and over his shoulder. As soon as he takes a step, Mark sucks in a deep, ragged breath, and one green eye flashes open. The other is swollen shut.

"No more!" Mark screams. "Fucking kill me! I can't take it. I won't tell you anything, so just kill me!" he continues as he slams his eyes closed.

Jackson lowers him to the floor, careful not to jostle him. I rush to his side and barely place my hands on his cheeks. "Mark, look at me. It's Charlie. I need you to open your eyes." I apply slight pressure and force his eyes on mine. "You're going to be okay. But we have to get out of here before the rest of the team figures this out. Our backup is coming, but I need you somewhere safe." His eyes well with moisture.

"You died," he mumbles.

"She's an illusion, Mark. Your mind is fucking with you," Christopher's voice rings from behind. This time, I don't have to punch him. Jackson takes the butt of his gun and slams it into his head. He slumps forward, unconscious.

I can't even imagine the things Mark believes are true. "No, babe. I'm here. I found you. Just us, Mark. It's just us."

My words seem to calm him. He stares at me and then his lip turns upward what little it can. "Took you long enough." Mark coughs and looks up at Jackson. "Always knew she'd save me. Good to see you."

"No, brother. It's good to see you. I'm going to carry you out."

He throws Jackson's hand off him. "Fuck you. I'll walk, just help me up."

At least he didn't lose any of his attitude. He struggles to stand, but his legs fail him. "He's too weak," I say to Jackson.

"You're not carrying me!" Mark grumbles as he tries again. "I'm walking out of this shithole on my own fucking feet."

Jackson throws one arm around his shoulder and holds onto his hip. I get on his other side and put his arm around my shoulder. Pain exudes from my side as I start to walk. I stumble a little but Jackson catches Mark.

Aaron rushes forward and takes my place. "You okay?" he asks.

"Yeah, just get him to the car."

Concern paints Jackson's face as I place my hand over my armpit. "Charlie?"

"Go. Mandi will handle the rest," I urge Jackson. "I'll be right there."

Mark, however, won't move. "What's wrong?"

"Please don't fight me. I need to give Mandi some instructions, and then we're going to spend some time together."

This plan is far from over. But right now, my biggest concern is Mark. Jackson knows why I need to get the hell out of dodge, and I need to move Mark quickly. We can't let anyone see me. Mandi and I have our team coming, but we had to move before the scheduled time. Christopher was going to kill him. "Charlie," Mark rasps. "I knew you loved me."

I fight the urge to give him some snide comment, but right now, time isn't on our side. There's no way Asher was keeping him here with only three others. And sure as hell not these three stooges. We move into the hall. Frank and Erik keep cover. They all nod as we pass, ensuring nothing comes at us from out of nowhere. It's so different when you work hand in hand with these guys. Like a well-oiled machine. They're anticipatory, smart, calculating, and alert—unlike times I've worked with other agents.

Jackson laughs. "Come on, Twilight. Let's get you in the car."

Mandi rushes to my side as I lean against the wall.

"Let me look," she says. She seems to know what I just figured out. I've been shot. She pulls my vest off and reveals a pool of blood.

"Oh, God." I start to feel it all now. The tissue burns where the bullet tore through. "How the fuck did I not notice this?"

"You know how," she says. "You were worried about him.

Your adrenaline was on high, but you're lucky. It's only a flesh wound. You, and everything, will be okay, but I have to stitch you up before you lose too much blood."

"Mandi," I say. I'm suddenly anxious.

"I know."

"I have to tell him. He has to know before anything."

"Let's get you two out of here." She tapes the bandage to my skin after packing it to help slow the bleeding. "Keep pressure on it. I'll drive, get you stitched up, and then we'll handle the rest."

Mandi is the only other person who knows I'm pregnant.

thirty-three

"I'M SORRY I FAILED him." I say to Jackson as I climb in the back seat with Mark. I needed to speak the words to his friend. I had no choices. If they smoked me out sooner, it would've been the end of all of us. I was so close to having the information we've been searching for, but when I discovered they took Mark, everything shifted.

Jackson's hand rests on my arm. "You did what any of us would do. He'll understand."

Did I? I hid. These men don't hide. They get caught because they think it'll save someone. They waltz into the face of the enemy and spit on him. I cowered in a corner until we had all our ducks in a row.

"Now, Charlie," Mandi says as she gets in behind the wheel. She's aware that we're wasting time. She's right, both Mark and I need to be treated.

"Be safe," Jackson says as he shuts the door.

I nod, and we race off to the safe house. I keep my hand on my wound, but I'm starting to feel numb. My head falls back, and I just want to sleep.

"Stay with me, Charlie. You need to stay awake." Mandi swerves through traffic as my vision fades. I'm coming down from my adrenaline rush, and my body is fully aware of the pain.

"What about the baby?" I glance over at Mark, who's asleep.

"As long as I get the bleeding to stop and you take it easy . . ." She stops herself as panic hits me.

"Oh, God."

"Relax. One minute and we'll be there. Just stay awake."

I fight with every ounce I have. I watch Mark, who was so strong and willing to endure much more than a small flesh wound. I can do this. I have to do this. All I keep thinking is that I hope he'll understand why I lied and pushed him away. Because he's all I care about right now. Not Mazir, not avenging my father's death, not what happens to Christopher Asher, just him and this baby.

We pull into the underground parking of the new safe house Mandi and I arranged. She and I are the only two people who know its location. She rushes to my door and puts pressure on my arm. "Shit!" I scream out as the pressure increases the pain.

I climb out of the car with her pressing right below my shoulder. "No one told you to get shot."

"I'll be fine. Let's get him inside. He's in far worse shape," I say as we move around the car and pull his door open. How the hell I'll be able to help carry him is beyond me.

I carefully reach around with my other arm and unhook his seatbelt. Mark's left eye opens. "Hi, blue eyes."

"Hi." I smile. "We need to get inside now. Can you walk with me and Mandi helping?"

His right eye is swollen shut, and I pray he doesn't suffer any permanent injuries. "I'm a tough guy."

"I know," I murmur.

We somehow extract him from the car. His pace is slow, but he pushes through. I count each step. We're getting close. I have to keep going and then I can sit. Sweat drips from my face, my legs keep wobbling from his weight and my blood loss, but all I can think about is the baby. We get up to the apartment, enter the codes, and I collapse against the door. I have nothing left.

"Charlie!" Mark calls out as he grabs my arm. I cry out in agony. He releases his grip and stares down at the blood covering his hand. "What the hell?"

I'm panting. "Calm down, you have to get inside," I say.

Mandi holds onto him. "I have to stitch her up, so we need to get inside right now. Let me treat her."

"How do I know you're not behind this?"

"Mark," I chide. "Inside."

He doesn't fight her, but he doesn't leave my side. "Her first."

Always has to fight me. I swear some things never change.

Instead of arguing with him, Mandi helps me inside before going back for him. I remove my shirt and everything is soaked through. Mark sits next to me, weak and bloody. "How bad?" he wheezes.

"Mandi!" I call her over. "I'm losing a lot."

"Shhh, everything will be fine. I need to work fast." She gives me her best comforting voice.

Of course, it does nothing for me. I can't lose this baby. Tears well in my eyes at the idea of having to tell him. "Please," I beg.

Mark's one eye stares at me as she removes the blood soaked bandage. "He fucking shot you."

He looks far worse than I feel. I hate that right now she's treating me instead of him. I'm not a medical professional, but I know enough to survive. The very little energy his body had stored, he's depleted. I need to get nutrients in him. It's been three weeks since he was taken from my apartment. Three weeks of God only knows what kind of treatment. Yet, I'm sitting here getting stitched up. I should be stronger than this, but the truth is—I'm not.

"It's just a flesh wound."

He growls and restlessly attempts to stand. "I could take it.

I could handle all the fucking hell they put me through, but he wasn't supposed to hurt you."

"Mark," I plead as Mandi gives me a look. "Sit down. I've had far worse injuries than this. We'll be fine."

"Yeah." He huffs. "We're all doing fucking peachy."

Mandi glances up, smirks, and then returns to the wound. She cleans it as a different kind of tears form. The burn is intense and extremely painful. This is worse than realizing I was nicked. "It just hit a weird place, that's why you're bleeding this much. I can't give you anything." Her eyes lock on mine and I nod.

"I can take it."

Mark shifts closer, taking my hand in his. "Take something for the damn pain."

"I can't," I say. I'm unable to look at him.

"Why the hell not? Why are you acting weirder than usual?"

My nerves are shot. My body hurts, and he's pushing me. I bite my tongue because there's no way I'm letting him know like this. He needs to be hydrated and preferably sedated.

"Charlie, you need to stay still, and calm." She lines the needle up to the skin. "This is going to hurt."

Mark pushes Mandi's hand away. "What is wrong with you? Take the painkillers. You've been shot!"

"Shut up and don't stop her again," I warn him. How the hell he's not passed out, I don't know. But neither of us has the luxury of arguing. "Either go in the other room, or sit quietly."

"Goddamn stubborn woman."

"They wouldn't kick in that quickly anyway. So shut up and let me do this so I can take care of you afterward. I don't need to be doped up when I'm trying get you stable. Would you like me to insert the IV in the wrong place?" I ask with hostility dripping from my words. I don't like this either, but there is more than one reason why me being anything less than alert is a bad idea.

Mark finally takes the hint and keeps his mouth shut. Once

I'm sure he's done, I nod to Mandi. "I'm ready."

"I'll be quick," she assures me.

Mandi starts and I slam my eyes closed. I count, singsongs, and think about the precious baby growing inside me. He or she is worth this. I need to stop the bleeding, and then I need to care for its father.

Once she finishes patching me up, we both move into action to get Mark cared for. Mandi has to get out of here, though. She could be tracked and then this house is no longer safe for us. She and I both know we have another ten minutes—tops.

"Get him set up. I have to go. I'll be in touch as soon as phase two is done. You have everything you need. Take care of you all." She smiles.

"Thank you. Find out who the son is," I remind her.

"I will." She hugs me gently before she leaves.

With no time to spare, I get an IV started in Mark. He lies back while I work on him. "Are you okay?" he asks. "And you think she can be trusted?"

I smile. "Yes, she's on our side. Mandi has proven her loyalty, and as for being okay . . . I am now." I stand beside him and touch his face. "I was worried . . . about so much."

There have been times in my life that I've felt true fear. One was when an asset turned a gun on me. I remember thinking it was the end, but he faltered. This day makes that look like a joke. This fear was paralyzing. It overtook every part of my soul. I couldn't think or find ways to keep my eye on the end goal. Getting Mark back was all I cared about. If others had to suffer from that, I didn't care.

"Once again, Charisma Erickson, you doubt me."

"Get some sleep. We have a lot to talk about when you're rested."

Mark reclines with ice packs on his face and several other areas of his body, but he doesn't complain. He keeps his gaze on me as much as he can. He dozes in and out, and each time he awakens, he searches me out.

Hours pass and I hear nothing from Mandi. I didn't think I would, but her silence is driving me insane. After we pinpointed exactly who was involved in Christopher's clan, we were able to make our move. Dominic contacted someone he trusted, and the mission began. The key is for me to remain underground until it's safe. I refuse to hand over my father's information until I know Christopher is detained.

I sit by Mark's side, hold his hand, and pray each time he falls asleep that he'll wake again. We stocked this house, prepared it for whatever condition he'd be in. I never imagined he would be this bad, though. I didn't think Christopher would ever go to these lengths. He must think there's more in that file than just a few photos and notes in some random code.

My heart rattles around in my chest as I envision what they had to do to cause this damage. I worry about internal bleeding, broken bones, and so much more. He needs to get to the hospital, but they'll kill us both before we get there. I just have to pray I know enough to get us through the next few days.

I check my phone again, but there's nothing. I worry about all the things that could've gone wrong. My type-A personality is spazzing out. I need some kind of news before I wear a hole in the floor.

Mark stirs a few times as I treat his wounds, apply arnica lotion, and ice the swollen parts of him, which is basically everywhere. The swelling goes down a little, then right back up once I remove the ice packs. After a round of clean bandages and a few hours of repeating the process, he appears a little better.

Observing him like this makes me hate myself. For the first time ever, I wish I were simply an antiquities dealer—not smoke and mirrors, no crazy job. Just a normal girl who doesn't have a death certificate waiting on her.

Everything inside me hurts—my heart, my head, my muscles. I need sleep, but I can't leave his side. If there's one thing I learned, it's that we're stronger as a team. When we're divided, there's weakness. There's nothing more I want than to curl up in his arms, but I can't. So I climb next to him, tangle my fingers with his, lay my head on his shoulder, and fall asleep.

I wake to him jostling back and forth. "Charlie," he moans my name.

"It's okay," I say reassuringly. "I'm here, Mark. Just open your eyes."

He opens them both, but the other closes immediately. "Tell me something only you know. I need to know you're real."

"I hate sharks, and you made me go in that stupid water."

He coughs. "Tell me what vineyard we went to." His eyes close as he fights exhaustion.

"Keswick," I say automatically.

"Glad you remember because I couldn't." He smirks.

The half giggle, half cry escapes my lips. He's still my Mark. They may have hurt him, but they didn't destroy him. Relief floods my heart as I gaze at him. I could've lost him. I almost did. It would've been my fault.

"I'm sorry for all of this." I brush his hair back as I break down. "It's just the way it had to be. I couldn't tell you anything. I was so lost, Mark. I was so intent on finding out more about my dad that I almost lost everything. I almost lost you." I press my lips to his shoulder as I let it all out. Years of pain and stuffing it down come bubbling up. "I didn't want to care about you. I knew this couldn't be good, no matter what, but you pushed me and pushed me. You made me look at you like you were everything. You have to forgive me. You have to understand why I did it."

"Charisma." His hand finds my wrist and he grips it. "Stop." My lips close as he struggles to open both eyes. "What is going on with you? You're crying, which I didn't know you could do, and you're going on and on about other shit, and you wouldn't take the medication. Why are you so worried? I'm here, I'm safe. You're here, you're relatively safe."

In this moment, three words fill my world. "Because I love you, and you have to love me. I can't lose you again. I don't want to do this alone," I say the words and all sense of time stops. I'm afraid he won't love me anymore. I'm afraid he never did. I'm terrified that I've broken my only chance at a life I never dreamed of. I don't know how to handle all these emotions. I don't like them, either, if I'm being honest.

"Do *what* alone?"

"The rest of our life."

"Then you should know how much I love you, Charisma Erickson." He tightens his fingers around mine. "I'd have died for your safety. When he told me they killed you, a part of me broke. When you pushed me away, I never knew pain like that. That beating . . ." He pauses and looks away. "Was nothing compared to the day I left you."

I know what he means. The three weeks he was away were torture. I've been starved and made to do unthinkable things, but not knowing how to find him was the worst time of my life. I couldn't *do* anything. I had to sit, wait, and hope to God the others found him. Mandi, Frank, and Dominic worked every angle while I fed them clues and remained completely hidden.

"You need to rest," I say. I press my lips to this forehead.

"Charlie," he rasps. "You've been shot. You need the same shit as me."

"It's nothing. I'm not bleeding anymore, and I took a Tylenol. You have to stay still. You have to listen to me."

"Bullshit. You were just as freaked out as I was. I'm in bad shape, aren't I?"

We both know that he needs a hospital. The extent of his damages could be far worse than we know, but for now, this is keeping him alive. It's like plugging a tire with bubblegum. I just pray this will be enough for now. As soon as Mandi calls, we'll be on our way there.

"It's beyond my training. I'm doing what I can, but you're covered in bruises, I don't know if you have any damaged I can't see."

"That's because I was their punching bag. I much prefer when you hit me." He tilts his head with a sly look.

He's unreal. Even after all of this he can still joke. "Princess," I say with love clear in my voice. "You can't handle my jabs."

"You hit like a girl."

"You act like one," I joke. This is normal. This is us.

"I'm tired again. What the hell did you put in this IV?"

"Pain killers, vitamins, and a lot of love."

Mark lets out a short laugh. "Look at you." His head falls to the side. "Being all romantic and shit. Maybe you should get shot more often."

Idiot.

The thing is that he doesn't see just how unnerving this all was for me. "You don't know how scared I was that he shot you. I don't get scared, Mark. I live this life, this job, and I've known it my whole life. It's all I've ever had. But everything is changing. Everything is different. You barreled your way into my world and forced me to love you against my will."

Mark closes his eyes and lets out a deep breath. "I thought you were caught by them. I thought you were being held, beaten, and then killed. I gave up at the end. I was willing to let them kill me because I failed you. Don't think this wasn't hard for me, baby. Don't think I wasn't the only one who didn't want to love. Because you aren't. I knew the risks, but you're worth the reward."

I smile as my heart accelerates. Everything inside of me beams. "I need you to make me a promise."

"Anything."

"No matter how hard it gets, no matter how much I drive you insane, no matter the cost, I need you to keep fighting. I need you to give everything you have to be okay."

His eyes both flutter open. "I'll fight to the end of the earth for you."

"Good." I kiss his cheek. "You should know something."

He gazes at me with apprehension. "I don't have a good feeling about this . . ."

"It's not bad, per se. It's just, well, a little . . ." I stumble on my words. How the hell do I tell him we're having a baby?

"What the hell did you do?"

"Me?"

"Yeah, you're stuttering and have that guilty look."

"I didn't do anything."

I'm not guilty. He was there for all this, too.

"I'm not the one acting like I did something wrong. Let me guess, you're going to do something while I'm stuck here? Just like the old Charlie, so much for a team."

Now I'm ready to punch him, but I clearly can't. Indignation rises within, and the need to set him straight builds. I wanted to be delicate before. Now I no longer care. So, I spit it out the only way I can think of.

"No, you giant asshole. I was going to tell you that you knocked me up."

He shifts to look at me better. "What?"

Not exactly how I planned this, but he should know. I start to tear up. Fucking hormones are making me a sobbing woman. I close my eyes, take a deep breath, and whisper the words, "I'm pregnant."

I wait for some sign of emotion, some form of hostility or disappointment. The reaction any man would have to find out his girlfriend—if that's what we are—is pregnant. I wait with nerves fluttering.

Instead, he does the opposite of what I expect. There's no anger, accusation, or even a word. He simply looks content. Mark grips my hand, presses his lips to the top, and falls back asleep wearing a smile.

Smug little shit.

W E MADE IT THROUGH the night with no major issues. I slept off and on, made sure Mark was comfortable, and kept an eye on my stitches. Mark slept like a log, and that grin never left his face. He hasn't said a word, but there's a sense of ease around him.

When I found out I was pregnant two weeks ago, I lost it. Apparently, the due date for my next shot was wrong on my calendar. I blame Mark for keeping me away from my house for so long, along with the ridiculous amount of sex.

Of course I freaked out and went into denial. Then something happened. I started to smile when I saw myself in the mirror. I'm having a baby. A tiny person is growing inside me, and it's ours. I then became even further obsessed with finding Mark. Mandi had to rein me in a few times because I started acting on pure emotion, but there was no way I was explaining to our child how his or her daddy never knew. No, I was finding him.

"Hey." Mark shifts and smiles, which causes his lip to crack open and bleed.

"Don't smile, you'll keep reopening it." I grab the gauze and clean him up again.

He nods as if he'll listen. "I'll take the pain if I get to see your face when it happens."

"Oh, good God. Now you're being all romantic and shit." I laugh and use his words against him.

He grips my wrist and stops me from cleaning the wound. "You can't fault me, Charlie. We've had a rough few weeks."

"Yeah, we have," I agree.

Rough doesn't even cover it, and we're not out of the woods yet. If Christopher escaped somehow or talked his way out of this, we're in grave danger. Plus, we now know that Christopher has knowledge of the person behind all of Cole Security's troubles.

I have no doubt that if they have Christopher, they're trying to extract the information. Aaron was going to handle the interrogation since he knows the most about Mazir and has the tidbits I provided. I hope by now Mandi is digging deeper because from what I was able to find, Christopher doesn't have children. He never married either, so this has been well concealed.

We won't even get into the crap I'm battling from being shot, and having a critically injured man. Oh, and I'm having a baby.

Seriously, you can't make this shit up, which reminds me that Mark still hasn't said a word about the baby. "Are we going to talk about this?" Does he remember what I said?

"I remember everything, Charisma." A thrill runs through me at the sound of my name from his lips. I never imagined how it would feel to share that with someone. "You're having my baby, you love me, we're getting married, and we're going to stop all the bullshit and be a team."

"I never said the last parts."

"Don't," he groans.

"You, don't. You're going to heal, Mark. This isn't me being difficult. This is me saying there's no way in your condition, you can do anything."

He starts to move and grabs for the IV.

My hand shoots out to stop him. "Are you crazy? You're not out of the woods."

"I need to go to the bathroom. See if I'm pissing blood. I need to make sure my kidneys are fine. They took a beating," he explains, and I lower my eyes.

"I should've gotten you sooner. I should've walked in there and given myself to them."

Mark grabs my hand and squeezes. "And what? Put yourself and our baby in danger? I'd never forgive you." He peels his lids open, and his eyes bear into mine.

"What?"

"You heard me!" he growls. "This isn't about just you or me anymore."

"Well, I'm not just sitting back while you get taken hostage and are beaten within an inch of your life. What did you expect me to do? Sit home and knit blankets? This isn't the 1920s."

"I expect you to take it easy."

I huff. "Don't get all alpha male on me now."

His pushes his legs over the side of the bed, grips my arms, and carefully pulls me close. "I've always been the alpha male. I just let you believe you had some say. Now that you're having my baby, you're going to stop this shit."

The temptation to rip my arms away is great, but I can't re-open my stitches. "Let. Me. Go." I enunciate each word. "Now."

He releases me, and I turn my back to him. I need to calm down. He's still processing everything, just like I am.

Mark makes a sound that stops my heart. I whirl as he tries to stand. Agony is splayed across his face. I rush to his side, slide my shoulder beneath his, and take some of his weight. "I can do this," he grits out from between clenched teeth. "I made it through that hell. I can walk."

I want to slap him. "Don't be stubborn. Lean on me. We have to lean on each other." My words mean so much more now.

Mark nods, and I help him lift up and balance. His legs are shaky, but for the most part, he holds himself steady. He's stronger than any man I've ever met.

I step in front of him, and his hand lifts to my cheek. "I love you, and I'm sorry."

"It's a lot."

"We'll find our way." His words reassure me that he's in it.

Not that I'm sure why I doubted him. Mark has proven more than anyone else just how much I mean to him.

"Charlie . . ." His voice is thick with emotion. "I need to kiss you, and I'm going to. I don't care how much it hurts. I don't care if my lip busts open. I'm going to kiss you because you're worth the pain. I'm going to kiss you because you're having our baby. And I'm going to kiss you because it's all I can do."

I smile, step closer so he can wrap his arm around me, and rest my hand gently on his chest. "I'm going to let you kiss me because it's been too long. I'm going to kiss you back because you're alive, and then you're going to get back in bed so you can heal."

"Bossy."

"You ain't seen the half of it."

He smirks. "I like bossy, and as soon as I'm better, I'm going to fuck the life out of you. Now, kiss me."

"Romantic. Now who's the bossy one?"

"Shut up, Charlie. Kiss me." His head dips down. I rise on my toes to shorten the distance.

When our lips touch, my world centers. Everything feels just—right. We're okay. I have him, and he has me. Together we have this new life. Something we did out of love, even if we didn't realize it. Even though I never wanted this, it's everything to me. His hands leave my face as he breaks the kiss. Mark shifts back slightly and presses his hand on my stomach.

"Just us."

My fingers touch the side of his face. "Next time someone says to leave somewhere, you should listen."

"Not if I think you are in danger. I will never leave you behind, Charlie. I'll bash through walls, take beatings, and give my life for you. That's love. That's how much you mean to me. Don't you get it? Without you in my life . . . it's worthless. You though," he pauses. "You are everything to me."

Tears pool in my eyes, "I love you, Marcus."

"My name isn't Marcus."

"Yeah, well, I owe you for the horrific names you came up with."

He laughs, kisses the top of my head, and slowly makes his way to the bathroom. Of course, he grumbles when he notices I'm behind him. But this is how it's going to go. I'll be here to catch him, just like he will be for me.

"SO WHAT'S THE PLAN?" Mark asks after his nap. He's eating a little, and thankfully, he seems to be doing okay. It's been forty-six hours since I've heard from Mandi. I can only take that as a good sign. If things were bad, she'd have called . . . at least I tell myself that.

My old self wants to tell him nothing, but that isn't how we operate now. Mark is my partner, and he deserves to know everything. Even if it's bitter to admit, I need him.

"What do you remember about your time with them?"

Mark steels himself with a deep breath. "I remember every detail. He said something about a son . . ."

"We're on that. We heard him."

"Who's we?"

"Mandi, Dominic, Jackson, and myself. That's everyone I trust right now."

Mark's eyes narrow. "I don't trust her."

"I know you don't, but she grabbed me off the train. She knew I was being tailed, so she took care of them and secured me. If it weren't for her, I don't know if I would've been able to hide." Mandi incapacitated two people and mixed up communications in the area so I could get to my safe house. She uncovered where Mark was, as well. Her loyalty is not to be questioned. I would've never made it to him without her.

"Okay, if you say so." He sits back against the couch. He looks much better today. The swelling has gone down significantly, and it's clear his eye won't have any permanent damage. He is eating a very restricted diet, walking a little sturdier, and has been able to wean a little off the painkillers. Both of us are able to take a deep sigh of relief.

"Just for now, don't worry about what's going on. Once we have something concrete, we'll talk."

"Damn right we will."

We settle in together and watch the news. There are always clues that the public miss. I await the story of the CIA Director stepping down. That will be when I relax. For now, I tuck my legs under me and curl up against Mark. He flinches but holds me so I can't move. I just want to be close to him.

"Charlie." Mark's voice has an edge to it.

I peer up at him. "Yeah?"

"I'm serious about marrying you."

"If that's a proposal, you suck."

"I'm giving you some time to get over whatever crap excuses you're forming. I'm telling you it's going to happen. I'm going to ask you, you're going to say yes, and we're going have a wedding."

I shake my head and turn my attention back to the television. "When will you learn that demanding me to do something doesn't work? Also, I'm not even sure I like you enough."

"You love me."

I sit up with my arms crossed over my chest. "I'm not denying that. I said *like* you. You're a pain in the ass, you're messy, you boss me around, you argue with everything I say—"

"And you're argumentative and frustrating, but it's going to happen. You'll get over all that crap you mentioned."

"So you say."

"Come here." He opens his arms wide. I scoot over and he pulls me against his side. "I'm done with games, babe. I'm not going to live the rest of my life without you here by my side. Our lives aren't a guarantee. So I'm going to marry you and impregnate you many more times. Also, we don't have to pay a minister."

I shift so I can see his face. "Oh, hell no. I'm not marrying you as my priest."

He rolls his eyes, "I'm not a priest. I'm a reverend."

"No, you're a jackass."

He smirks. "Keep it up, and I'll tell your mother you want her to plan the wedding."

My eyes bulge as I debate whether he's healthy enough to endure me beating the hell out of him. "I haven't agreed to marry you yet, and that's so not funny."

He leans forward. "Not joking. And you will agree when I ask you."

Before I can say a word, a noise at the door stops us both. Neither of us breathes or moves.

Knock, knock. Pause. *Knock, knock.*

Mandi is here.

"You're lucky. That's Mandi's code." I head to the door and check the peephole. *Thank God.*

I open the door and she smiles. "It's done."

"Done?"

"Yeah, he's in custody. He admitted to quite a bit, but Aaron really figured out the missing clues."

She enters the room, and I close the door behind her. We head to the couch and Mark shifts forward.

I'm dying to know how this all went down. Being sidelined hasn't been easy for me, but it was necessary. "What happened?" I nearly bounce in my seat. "I want all the details."

"After I got back, Christopher refused to speak to anyone until your father's old partner, Dean Tubb, showed up. He was working with Dominic to uncover some of the pieces you and I couldn't make fit. Like the photo your dad had of the building we couldn't place and the fact he had notes of dates and initials that you weren't able to decipher. Turns out Dean and Gerald used a code during their early years. As soon as he saw it, Christopher's tune changed."

She gives me a second to let that sink in. My dad and Dean had to talk in what was almost their own language back then. The CIA wasn't as advanced as it is now, but I never realized it could be a code. It makes sense that if my father had been suspicious of people, he'd revert to something that couldn't be traced. How the hell did I miss that? Oh, I know. The sexy blond next to me had my mind preoccupied. "What did the code say?"

"Well, as soon as Dean saw it, *he* knew, and wouldn't allow anyone else to speak. He took Christopher into custody and is now the Interim Director. I still didn't understand the connection with Mark, though. That was the part that kept tripping me up, and Dean still wasn't forthcoming with the meaning of the code." Her eyes come alive as she grows more excited. "But Charlie, when I mentioned how you were threatened because of the file, that Mark was taken, and that there was a correlation with Cole Security Forces, it all clicked."

"*What* clicked?" Mark snaps.

"Mazir *is* Christopher Asher!"

"What?" I'm confused.

"Don't you see it? It was obvious. You both had to be tied

to the investigation. There was a reason things got desperate once you joined Cole Security Forces. It's the only connection between Cole Security's stolen ammunition and your being the agent investigating Mazir, who was trading weapons."

Mark leans forward. "Meaning once we met, the fact that the arms dealer was an American would become clear to both of us. With both of our knowledge of the investigation, it would be easy to form conclusions."

Mandi nods. "But he was able to keep throwing you guys off and keep you looking for someone who didn't exist. He was able to keep you far enough away, but close enough that you kept working the case. The man is a true narcissist."

"And he was making a ton of money, taking out spies, and keeping a highprofile job at the same time," I muse aloud. "It really was the perfect plan. He was able to orchestrate everything from the confines of his office, line his pockets, and betray everyone he knew while we hunted a terrorist."

"Exactly," Mandi says. "Then he found out your father was looking into something fishy within the agency and keeping a file. Aaron was able to piece together the photo of the building. It was the site he was going to in Afghanistan where their shipment went missing."

Mark lifts his hands. "I had no idea. I never went there or was involved in that bid. We assumed that was where your father traced Mazir to."

My eyes drift out the window as I think it all over. All of this is Christopher's fault. My father must have pieced it all together and threatened to expose him. So Mazir had him killed and then claimed responsibility. All the while it was done by his friend, his ally, and his boss.

"It all makes sense. Each dead end was engineered at the hands of my boss. He knew where I was, if I was getting close to pertinent information—he was behind it all. He was using all of us to get what he wanted: money, power, and control." Every part of me wants to explode. My muscles clench as anger takes hold. "I should've killed him."

"No," Mark says. "You would've never figured this out. You would've spent the rest of your life looking for a ghost. This is all behind us now. We can move forward and find some normalcy. It's over, Charlie."

"Is it?" I ask. "Because regardless, people have lost their lives, you've suffered, I've suffered. Will it ever really be over? I can't trust my own agency. I can't go back to work there, and I can't bring my dad back."

Mandi shifts uncomfortably. "I think you guys need to talk. But it is all done now, Charlie. He's locked up, Dean is in charge, and everyone we could identify who was involved has been detained. And there is no son. We've dug and dug; he was just messing with us. He's a master manipulator."

There's no sense of ease and no feeling of accomplishment. My dad is still gone, and the agency I would've given my life for killed him. "I need to tell my mother who was behind my father's death."

She stands. "Dominic knows too. He's waiting for your call."

Mark gets to his feet. "I was wrong about you," he admits to Mandi. "I thought you were involved."

"I never betrayed her. The information I was giving was being monitored by Christopher. I didn't know it was him, but I suspected someone in the agency was watching. Once I started piecing together that something was wrong, I stopped inputting the correct info. It's why you guys were able to get out of the country undetected. I put a code on her file, and once it flagged me, I altered it. I was helping even if you never knew. I kept them off her back while you two were working."

Mandi has always had my back. She explained that she knew the agency was involved after my debrief. She was willing to destroy our friendship if it meant I lived. By having me taken off the case, put on leave, and kept out of the area, it allowed her to dig at the same time we did. Even with my cold shoulder, she was always there for me.

"Thank you," Mark says with his hand extended.

"She never gave up on you."

"She never gave up on you, either." He smiles.

"I'm going to walk her out," I explain to Mark. Honestly, I need to let all of this information settle away from him.

He seems to think everything is just great now, but this affects everything in my life. Every part of my life is tied to my job. I know things are different. I have him, and we have a baby coming, but I always thought I would still be an operative. Now, though, I don't know that I want to live this life. What kind of job am I doing, and for what?

"Why don't I feel that it's over?" I ask once we're out the door.

She leans back against the wall. "I think it's a mix of everything. You were so sure Mazir was obtainable and close, you couldn't take a breath without thinking someone was after you. And then the last few weeks were insane."

"But how did we not figure this out?"

"Let's face it—he's been doing this a lot longer than any of us have. Your father was on to him, but never got far enough to make the connection. But remember that Christopher is he's really good at his job. He was using an asset in Afghanistan to move things around, but he *is* Mazir. It's why you couldn't find him when you were there, because he was here. Plus, he was orchestrating a terrorist ring for God knows how long, Charlie."

She makes sense. The whole story does. Christopher Asher isn't an unknown. He has copious amounts of information to use as ammunition. He had many players and was making money selling arms. I remember the agents we lost from his antics. Any of us could've ended up taking the final bullet. I don't know that I'll ever feel completely at ease, but there's a small sense of relief knowing my father can rest in peace. His death wasn't in vain, and his killer will be dealt with.

"It just feels unfinished."

"I don't know, Charlie. I saw them take him away, and I'm not really settled. God only knows what will actually happen to him. I think you need to take a few days and let this sink in. Then come back to work. I miss my favorite pain in the ass."

I snort. "Maybe. I still haven't decided if I'll come back to the agency." I don't need to tell anyone where my head is, and right now, I'm emotional. Mark and I need to talk. I laugh a little at the fact he's already become a part of my decision making process.

"What?"

"That dumb man in there that I love. I need to talk to him."

"Never thought I'd see the day." She smiles.

"Me either." We both nod. "I still wish I could've interrogated Christopher. I wish I could've seen his face."

"Well, you have two things that are far more important to focus on now."

"Yeah." My hand automatically presses against my stomach. "He wants to marry me."

"I'm not surprised."

"I can't imagine being without him, but I enjoy making him think otherwise."

We both laugh. "I'm going to take care of some stuff at work. I have a lot of reports to fix, and I'm sure they'll require statements."

"Thank you for, well, everything."

"You never have to thank me. I care about you more than you know. You're my best friend."

I pull her into my arms. "I'm lucky to have you. Call me in a few days."

"You got it."

I watch her walk away as I lean back against the wall to give myself a minute. It's over. At least the question part is anyway. There will still be whatever action is taken against him, which most likely will never be made public. There's so much to be happy for. Mark is okay, we're having a baby, I'm fine, and we have closure for my father. I can live again. I don't have to psychoanalyze every detail; I can just be present.

I've finished cases before, but this feels different.

I turn to open the door when something presses against my back.

"Hello, Charlie," a deep voice gravels against my ear. "How about we have a little chat?"

I turn and lock gazes with a familiar pair of mud brown eyes.

I fucking *knew* this wasn't over.

thirty-five

Mark

WHERE THE FUCK IS she? I know girls like to talk and all, but Jesus Christ, they've been out there a long time.

I decide after another five minutes it's been enough time to do their girly shit. I've gone long enough without seeing her face.

When I open the door, I stop breathing. Every fear I've ever known slams into me.

"Erik? What are you doing?" I demand. He's holding a Glock to Charlie's head. "Dude, put the gun down. What the hell are you thinking?" I step out the door, looking for any reason he would be holding a fucking gun to my girl's head.

My mind runs through a million possibilities, but none of them makes sense.

Erik has been a member of our company for over three years. He's worked by my side. Something isn't adding up.

"Listen to him, Erik," Charlie says confidently as she catches my eye.

I'm not in any physical condition to fight, but there's not a chance this motherfucker is walking out of here. I step closer, but he grabs her and pulls her back. I don't know what the hell is going on, but he's not taking her anywhere.

"You're both so smug. So self-righteous. Do you know what I've gone through?" he yells, pushing the gun against her temple. "What I've had to live through the last few years? How I've watched you all live your lives—fall in love—while I suffer?"

"Lower the fucking gun," I warn. A part of me wants to plow forward, but not while she's in danger. "Why don't you put the damn gun down and come inside?"

"Fuck you." His eyes shift back and forth between us. This isn't the Erik Long I've had in my life. This isn't the same Navy SEAL who fought with us. No, this guy looks strung out. "This all ends today. You both are done."

His attention shifts back to Charlie. All I can think about is getting her away from him. There's not a snowball's chance in hell this will end the way he wants. No one is done here but him.

I need to keep this conversation moving and get her the hell away from this madman who I thought was my friend. "Why are you doing this?" I ask.

"Did you really think all the problems you and your stupid friends have dealt with were just from my dad?" And the final puzzle piece snaps into place. He's the fucker's son. *Well played, you dumb prick.* "Who do you think fed him all the intel about where you were?"

"Erik," Charlie says, and I glare at her. She needs to keep her mouth shut so I can handle this, not draw his attention. "Why would you involve yourself in this?"

My eyes don't move from her. I hope she understands my message to lie low. He's got a gun pointed at her head. The least she can do is be quiet and let me handle this.

He laughs as his hand shakes.

"Easy!" I say. She winces.

Erik then turns the gun to me. "Shut up, Dixon. I'm calling the shots now. Not you, so if you want your precious girlfriend to be spared, then shut up."

He has lost his ever-loving mind. "Fine," I agree with my hands up. I manage to shuffle a little closer. "You're in charge here, but if you hurt her, all bets are off."

"Don't threaten me. I'll shoot you both before you move."

"Why?" Charlie asks again.

Of course, she doesn't shut up. God forbid. I give her another look that tells her to stop.

"Why are you doing this?" she continues.

For fuck's sake. We're going to have a serious conversation about my facial expressions.

"Because he and his idiot friends don't know the first thing about being a team. They left those guys behind. They stood there while their friends died. Just so you know what you're dating—a fucking coward."

"What are you talking about?" I ask as I move a little to the right. My leg is screaming out in pain, but I keep my focus on Charlie.

"I stood by for years trying to get over it. I got out of the Navy, thought maybe if I was around you three I would see the leadership. But all I see are three assholes who are living while he isn't." Erik pushes the gun forward. It propels Charlie in front of me. The coward stands behind her, forcing me to observe her face.

I'm going to break his hand and every bone in his body. My jaw clenches and my fist balls. I'm close to fucking losing it. "I swear if you hurt—" I start to say but she stops me with her eyes.

"Mark," she whispers. "It's okay."

"No, it's not okay." I see the tears forming in her eyes as she stares back at me. I have to fix this.

"If you had only done what you were trained to do! If you'd saved your entire team, none of this would be happening!" Erik yells.

"Are you talking about the mission with Brian, Devon, and

Fernando?" I'm trying to draw a correlation.

He laughs and pushes her even closer to me. "The mission where Fernando was killed. The mission where you took everything that ever mattered in my life and destroyed it."

I must be high from the pain medication because I swear he makes no sense. Fernando was married with a kid. "Erik, I've had a really shitty few weeks. Now you've got a gun to my girlfriend's head, so spare me the fucking dramatics. Be a man and tell me what has you so fucked up that you'd go to this length."

"Just like you guys . . ." He glances away, and I scoot closer to Charlie. I could grab her, but before I can, he grips her shoulder. Her face contorts with pain, but she remains completely quiet. I see red. He hurt her, and I don't give a fuck what his reason is . . . he's dead. "You only see what you want to see. Everyone saw past the truth. No one saw how much I loved him. How much *he* loved *me*. No, you were too self-absorbed to witness the truth."

"Truth? You mean you and Fernando? Were *together?*" His grip tightens and a tear falls from her blue eyes. "Let her go. This is between us."

Erik releases Charlie and points the gun at my head. I yank her good arm and throw her behind me. "You're right. This is your fucking fault. Jackson, Aaron, and you are all the reason my life ended."

"So, you decided to go on some revenge mission? You need to put the fucking gun down before you can't get out of this situation. You're not this guy."

His eyes narrow. "I'm exactly this guy. I'm doing this for Fernando. I'm going to make his killers pay."

Jesus Christ, this is insane. "You weren't the only one who lost Fernando that day. He was my fucking brother. I carried his body out. I wore his blood and fought to save him. No one let him die."

"You did!" he yells out, wearing rage across his face. "You all did!"

I know how it feels to think you lost someone you love. Not even two days ago, I thought Charlie was gone. I felt there was nothing left that mattered. I was willing to lose my own life because a world without her held nothing. My life went dull, lifeless, and empty.

I also understand revenge, because if someone killed her, I'd be counting bodies too. This is going to come down to him or me.

"You have a choice here, Erik." I back up and push Charlie farther behind me. "You can turn around, walk out of here, and go get help. I understand you're hurting. I didn't know you loved Fernando like that. None of us knew. Hurting Jackson, Aaron, and me won't bring him back. It won't make this right." I try to push her closer to the door so she can get inside. If he shoots anyone, it won't be my pregnant girlfriend. "Or you can be prepared for what could happen if you choose wrong, because I can't let you kill me or Charlie."

He lets out a maniacal laugh. "I started this and I'll finish it. Each of you motherfuckers were supposed to die. But I failed each time, until now."

Charlie taps on my back. Erik moves forward, and I realize she's telling me something in Morse code. I have to focus since it's been forever since I've used it: *Gun on table.*

Well, that's great, but we're not close to the table. However, if we can get her inside, it could work.

I reach behind me and tap on her leg: *Go on three.*

That's all I can do. That, and keep him off-kilter. "I can assure you that this won't go down the way you think. I didn't survive the fucking hell your father put me through to let you kill me." I let him think I'm at the end of my rope. I have to play with his mind a little.

Erik points his gun right at my forehead. His anger is defined in his eyes. "You deserve to die the same way he did."

"How does that make it right?" I ask. I must try to keep him talking. We circle a little, and I maneuver Charlie so she can reach the doorknob. The gun sits right there. If she can open the door, we might have a chance.

Erik closes his eyes, and I use this moment to push Charlie back. She has one shot to get the door open and grab the gun. Or I die.

His demeanor shifts as he starts talking. "I did this because I couldn't take the pain. Then I saw how you struggled when one of you were hurt."

"Do you really think I'll stand by and let you do this? Do you think you'll be able to kill us and no one will know?" I'm grasping at straws, but I only need another minute.

Charlie taps my back: *Ready*.

She's in position, but this could go so wrong so fast. No matter what, I'll shield her. If anyone is going to pay for this, it'll be me. I love her more than my life, more than anything in this world. She won't pay for my sins.

I place my hand against her leg and tap.

One.

Two.

Three.

thirty-six

Charlie

I'VE ALWAYS WISHED I had a superpower. Such a valuable asset for a spy. There was the idea of course, of being bullet-proof, but I never thought that was relevant for me since spies aren't supposed to be seen. I checked that off. Then I considered invisibility—another great power—but I can already make my-self practically disappear. In retrospect, it might have helped. So would the lead suit, for that matter. What I always really wanted was the ability to suspend time. Such a cool trick. To stop the movement of life. Be able to fix what you wanted and then start it up as if it never happened.

However, I'm mortal.

I'm human.

I'm not a superhero.

One.

Two.

Three.

I spin, throw the door open, and reach for the gun. It all hap-pens in a split second. I'm thrown to the ground and Mark rush-es to cover me. Always protecting me, giving me his body as a shield.

This is love. He's the guy who will take the bullet. The man I've dreamt of being with.

"Mark!" I scream out with the gun in my hand. I lift it, but a shot fires before I can get one off.

I hit the floor with a thud and suddenly understand everything vividly. Love lets you see colors for the first time. It paints the world around you in vibrant hues, but once you think you've lost that love, it goes gray. Everything around me dims, and I'm certain my life will never make sense again. I'll know the pain my mother feels.

I've lost my perfect match.

Lost him in a way I'll never forgive.

I lift the gun and wait for Erik to charge. I'll riddle him with holes the way he's just done to me.

"Did you get him?" Mark asks while keeping me covered.

He's alive! "Where are you hit?" I attempt to lift him, but he won't budge.

"Charlie?" Mandi's voice rings out. "Are you guys okay?"

Mark rolls to his side and I get to my feet. "Is Erik—?" I ask with a shaky voice.

"He's down," she reassures me.

Mark's clutching his side. I rush to him. "Were you shot?" Mandi has Erik in the hall.

"No, but give me the gun."

I'm fully aware of what he wants to do. I want the same thing. I need to make sure this is the end of this shit. "I need five minutes with him."

"The fuck you do."

I don't respond. I just walk out the door and lift my gun to Erik's head, as he lies bleeding in the corridor. The piece of shit clutches his leg. "If there's one thing I've learned, it's that if you put a gun to my head, you'd better pull the trigger."

Mark comes from behind me, puts his hand on my shoulder,

and lowers the gun. "There's no way you're going to do this."

Mandi keeps her gun trained on him. "A bus is coming."

Sirens wail in the background. Mark crouches down, and his voice is cold as ice. "If you ever come near me, Charlie, Jackson, or Aaron, I'll rip you to shreds." His hand hovers over Erik's wound. He pushes his fingers inside the bullet hole. When Erik screams out, Mark twists his finger again. "If you think you've suffered, it will be nothing compared to the hell I'll make you live through."

He stands, and kicks Erik's leg for good measure.

"I . . ." he struggles to catch his breath. "Win."

"What?" Mark asks and glances my way.

This isn't over.

Erik reaches down, pulls out a gun, and places it to his temple. Before any of us can move or stop him, he pulls the trigger.

"Son of a bitch!" Mark screams out and pulls me against his chest. "*Fuck!*"

Now it really is over.

A sob breaks from my throat, and I start to shake.

"It's okay." He rubs my back. Every emotion I've bottled up floods forward.

My chest heaves, and I fall apart in his arms. "I can't . . ." I try to take in air, but it becomes too hard. "Breathe." Cries escape, and I mutter incoherently.

"I've got you, Charlie," he whispers against my ear. "It's all over now."

I've seen people die. I've witnessed executions, suicides, and gruesome scenes, but this was personal. This man tried to kill me and Mark. He could've, at any moment, taken all that's precious from me. He wanted to, but Mandi stopped him. I cry for the pain. I sob for the baby I protect inside me. I let go of all the hurt, pain, fear, and anger that has controlled me. I fall, but Mark keeps me safe. He holds me, just letting me feel it all as I soak his shirt.

And all I can think is, *he's got me and I'll be okay now.*

"HOW ARE YOU DOING?" Mark asks for the umpteenth time.

"If you ask me again, I'll punch you in the balls. Those weren't injured, right?"

He smirks. "You love my balls."

"Oh, dear God. I'm never going to marry you. I can't even stand you."

It's been eight days since the shooting at the safe house. Erik's death was ruled a suicide. Mandi corroborated our story by saying she found him threatening us and then he took his own life. It's been a crazy week, but I'm happy to be moving forward.

"Priscilla is expecting us in twenty minutes."

"Your point?"

"We have time for a quickie." His eyes are alight with mischief.

I swear that he's been trying to convince me for two days. When we took him to the hospital, weaving a story about how he was jumped trying to save my life, he stayed for all of two hours after they cleared him of any complications. Since then, he's deluded himself into believing he's ready for a sexfest.

"No."

"No, like final no, or no like push me up against the wall and have your wicked way with me? You could just help a brother out and give me a blow job."

Men.

"I could, but I've had this lockjaw thing." I open and close my mouth, making a chomping sound. "My bite is really strong lately."

His face is deadpan. "Funny. Don't ever joke about my dick in your mouth and teeth."

I grab my jacket and head toward the door. Mark catches up and cages me in. "Dixon, if you value your life, you'll step back."

His hand snakes around my stomach. A current runs through me from his touch. Mark may drive me crazy, but he's my kind of crazy.

"Marry me?"

I turn and face him. "Seriously?" I won't lie, I think about it a lot. Also doesn't help that he brings it up all the time. When we wake up, brush our teeth, go to bed—I swear, he even mumbles it in his sleep. If I marry him, I want the fairy tale—to some extent.

I want him to ask my brother and mother for permission and the grand proposal. I want the ring and the knee, too. Considering all we've been through, I think we both deserve a little bit of special.

"Nah, that was just a practice run."

"You're such a dick."

"Again with the giant cock talk. I think you miss him." He wags his brows like a villain.

My hand goes down, and I grab him in my hand. "What were you saying?"

"That I love you and you look beautiful, dear."

I release him. "That's what I thought you said."

He laughs, kisses me, and then we head off to my mother's. There's no way in hell I'm going to be late for dinner.

Tomorrow I meet with my boss, Tom, for my final debrief. Mark and I spoke a lot over the last week about our plans. He promised Jackson that once they settled the issues with Cole Security that he'd become part owner. I understand he wants to keep his word. He never once brought up my job, and not because I think he wants to push me either way, but because he knows it has to be my choice.

Dominic and I spoke at great length yesterday. He and I

sat with my mom and explained what we could. At the end of our story, she leaned back and smiled. I couldn't understand it. I thought maybe she'd finally cracked, but she said it was the feeling of peace. For her, knowing my father died was hard enough, but knowing he had business left unfinished was unsettling. She's always been a woman of faith, and she believed my father was home now.

That word stuck with me, though. Home.

"You're awfully quiet? Plotting your revenge?" Mark taunts on our way over.

"Just thinking about tomorrow," I admit for the first time. I've made my choice, and I'm really working on this team thing. If Mark is my partner in this life, then he should have a say, right?

"Is this a test? I really don't feel like dealing with whatever punishment you have for failing."

I ignore his jab. I need to hone that skill since I'm seeing my mother. "I'm going to leave the agency—permanently."

"Because?"

Mark keeps his gaze on the road, which hinders me from reading his expressions. I should've waited until I could watch him.

"You're my home, Mark." God, I feel like a dork. We've both been a little mushy, and it needs to stop. "Which can be burnt down."

He chuckles. "I love how you can't ever let one sweet moment pass. Your inner bitch just has to follow."

"Whatever." I cross my arms over my chest. "I'm all mixed up from being pregnant. I don't like this crying shit. Then there's the fact my boobs hurt."

"I like the new boobs."

"You're never touching them."

"Oh, I think you want me to play with those funbags."

"Did you seriously just call them funbags?" I ask. I'm slightly pissed, slightly turned on. I'm a host of contradictions.

"We're here."

"Yay!" I say with mock enthusiasm. We pull up to my mother's and she's waiting on the porch. Never a good sign. "Let's go before she lays into me for something."

Mark comes around the car and helps me out. He's been very sweet lately. Maybe he does deserve a little loving. Maybe.

"Hi, Mother."

"Charisma," she says with her arms open.

Ummm. I glance at Mark, and he shrugs. "Are you feeling okay?" I ask. She's never been a hugger. Public displays of attention are for married people, as she would say.

"There you are!" Dominic comes out and saves me again.

"See, that's how you do it," I say to Mark. If he's going to stick around, he needs to know how long I can handle Priscilla before I need to be saved. Being the daughter usually costs me greatly.

"Do what?" she asks while she heads toward Mark.

"Nothing."

"You need a haircut," she says before she reaches him.

Dominic pulls me into his arms. "Did you tell her yet?"

"Tonight," I say. I couldn't wait to tell him he would be an uncle soon. Plus, he won't judge that I'm not married or engaged. We then made a wager on how long it would take until Mom lost her shit. I've got six minutes, Dominic has three.

After a few minutes of Mom fussing over Mark, we head in for dinner. I swear that she likes him more than me. We talk a little about some of Dad's things and what she wants to do. She also takes this opportunity to inform us of another gala she's throwing.

"Charisma," she says in the tone that tells me this will be interesting.

"Yes?"

"I'm proud of you."

I choke on my food. Mark presses his hand against my back with a laugh. "I'm sorry, what?"

"Don't act so surprised." She sounds offended. "I'm proud of you. Your father would be proud of you."

Dominic laughs without shame. "This should be the best dinner in history."

Mom glares at my brother. "Why would you say something like that?"

"You both are ridiculous. When have you ever told her something like that?" Dominic is in rare form. He never talks like this.

"I'm proud of both my children." Mother puts the fork down and crosses her arms. "You both have made very good decisions."

Dominic snorts. "Oh, no, you have to tell her." My brother backs the bus up right over me.

He's going to pay for this. Maybe she would like to know he and Kristy Tubb starting screwing after the last gala she threw. I grit my teeth and contemplate my knife throwing skills. Mark grips my right hand, which counts that out.

"Tell me what?"

Mark clears his throat and stands, "I wanted to do this another way, but since Dominic is getting impatient, now works."

My mother smiles and Dominic grips her hand. Then it dawns on me. Sure enough, when I turn my head, Mark is kneeling at my side.

"Charisma Marcia Erickson, before you say anything, let me finish." He pauses as I bite my lip. "I loved you the day I first laid eyes on you. I saw you and knew. Somehow, someway, I would make you love me. And since I'm pretty fantastic, you did." I laugh as he winks. "But I never knew how much I would love you. I never knew that you would become the only person in the world who matters. We're the same in so many ways. Jobs were all we had, our careers were what counted, but you . . . you beautiful, insane, frustrating woman have shown me it doesn't mean anything without you." Mark pulls out a black box and places it on my knee. "So, I'm asking you, for real this time, to open the box. If you do, then you don't have to say anything. If you open it, you're opening your heart to me. You're going to marry me, and I'm going to make it my mission to make you happy."

Mark gazes at me with so much love and trust it makes my heart swell. His finger lifts, and he swipes the tear I didn't know had formed. I do as he asks. I don't say a word.

I grab the black box.

And for the first time, I don't want to wait.

I want my man.

I lift the lid as two sighs come from the other side of the table.

Mark doesn't make a sound. He just winks as if he had no fears.

Such an arrogant ass.

My arrogant ass.

Our lips touch, and I hear my mother's shoes against the floor. "Charlie!" she exclaims. "I'm so happy someone is finally going to make an honest woman out of you."

"Oh, boy." Dominic laughs.

What the hell is with him?

"Thanks, Mom . . . I think."

"Mark, come here." She embraces him. "Thank you for having the patience of a saint."

She is out of her freaking mind. Does she not realize the crap I deal with? "I wouldn't go that far. He's not exactly a walk in the park."

"Oh, hush. I lived with you for twenty years. You're no angel either." She heads back to her seat and Dominic lifts his chin with a smirk. "What the heck are you two giving each other looks for?" she snaps.

Here goes nothing.

"Mom . . ." I release a heavy breath. "There's more."

Her eyes narrow and I know I'm in for it. She's going to blow her top. On one hand, I've always taken joy in giving her a headache, but on the other, this might put her over the edge. "Out with it, Charisma."

"We're having a baby."

She doesn't say anything. Instead, her gaze shifts from me to Mark then back at me again. Her face is stoic, but I can see the wheels turning behind her eyes. "You're pregnant?"

"That would be how we're having the baby."

"And you're sure he's the father?"

My jaw drops as Dominic snorts. "Mom!"

"Well, I don't know what you do on these trips." She shakes her head.

"I'm not a whore." Mark grips my hand beneath the table. His thumb grazes my skin as I try to keep calm.

She stands and walks over as I turn my head to look over my shoulder. "Charisma," her hand presses against my cheek. "I never thought you were. You're going to be an exceptional mother."

Moisture pools in my eyes as she pays me the nicest compliment ever. "Thanks, Mom."

"Now . . ." her tone shifts as her hand drops. "You're to be married within the month. I won't have my unwed daughter traipsing around with her love child. I mean, what would people think?" She talks to herself as I watch the wheels turn behind her blue eyes. "We can't have a scandal, so you're to be married soon. It'll be grand so get your protests out now. You will not deprive me, and we need to have this happen quickly so we can explain you delivered early."

Mark laughs, Dominic leans back with a shit-eating grin, and I groan. She apparently has forgotten who I am.

thirty-seven

One Month Later

"HELLO, MRS. DIXON," MARK says as he strips out of his suit.

"No one can know we did this," I say with a grin. My mother was driving me crazy with this wedding. Mark didn't want to hear me bitching anymore, so he got the jet from Jackson and we flew to Turks and Caicos. Just us. We got married on the beach with no fanfare, exactly the way we wanted it. A couple who was walking along the beach stood up for us.

My mother will murder us, but since I'm pregnant, she may hold off. I'm sure people will be disappointed, but I don't care. This wasn't about them. This wedding was about us.

"It's our secret." He smirks and unbuttons his shirt.

I step closer in my tea-length red dress. I grabbed the first thing I saw, and threw it in the bag. I couldn't have cared less what I was wearing as long as it happened the way we actually wanted.

Mark's eyes watch me as I slide the zipper down the side. The dress pools at my feet. I was at least conscious enough to grab matching bra and sexy underwear. Since I still have my body for now, I decided to go a little skimpy.

"Well," Mark says as his eyes travel up and down. "I think my wife needs some attention."

"She does," I agree as I walk closer in my red heels. "She really needs to see that her husband still has it. That his old age hasn't affected a certain piece of anatomy I love so much."

I know how much he loves a challenge, and we've been having a lot of fun with my new sex drive. Not that we were tame before, but I can't get enough since I've been pregnant.

His arms slip around my back and pull me flush against him. "I'm about to blow your mind, wife."

"Prove it, husband."

I need him. I burn for him. I know he's about to make good on his promises. His lips hover above mine, and my breathing goes shallow. He toys with me, makes me earn his kiss, and I love it. I need the challenge, to be pushed for more, and Mark is more than happy to give it to me.

After a few seconds of breathing each other in, his lips collide with mine. I can't rationalize the passion between us, but then again, I don't want to. I just want it to always remain this way. I want the kind of love my parents had. One where after years of marriage, they still wanted each other.

His tongue delves into my mouth as he kisses me without apology. It's sexy, raw, primal—and he's in control. Our tongues tangle even as his hands roam my skin. My fingers dive into his hair to hold him where I want him.

Mark breaks the kiss. His eyes devour me as he pushes me back against the bed. "Let me see you."

I lean back, lift one leg, and call him over with my index finger. "Touch what's yours."

His eyes flame and my body ignites. "That's right, baby. Say it again."

"Touch me."

He shakes his head, "Don't play games, Charisma." My head

falls back as he climbs up on the bed, keeping his weight off me. "Say it. Tell me who you belong to."

I look up with a grin. "You. I belong to you. And you, my husband, are all mine."

"Oh, yeah, I am." He pulls me against him and unhooks my bra. He slides it down.

His tongue circles before he pulls my nipple into his mouth. My eyes water from the pleasure he extracts from my sensitive breasts. Everything is heightened since the baby. I feel it ten times more intensely. My orgasms are like a drug, and I can't get enough of them.

Mark slides down my body, trailing his tongue on his way. I squirm beneath him as he makes his descent to my core. "You ready for number one? What do I get if I get it in under a minute?"

"Let's not forget you still have to give me a Charlie Day." I remind him of his obligation.

"I say you give me at least two blow jobs whenever I want them."

"We're not negotiating now, Mark!" I groan as his fingers lightly trace my opening. I squirm. I need his touch, his mouth, his cock. "I need you."

"If I blow your world in a minute, you can blow mine."

"Fine!" I yell out in frustration.

I hate him sometimes.

As soon as my head hits the bed, his mouth goes to work. He licks, sucks, and bites softly against my clit. Motherfucker is relentless. I climb but try to hold off. I focus on anything to not let him win, but I'm so sensitive. I'm so horny, and I'm so in love with this man. My breathing becomes labored as I try to count past sixty. I don't want to lose, but really . . . I'm far from losing here.

I count to fifty-eight and any grip on my control slips away. I fall into the black hole as colors flood my vision.

"God, you're good," I say, trying to catch my breath.

I flip him over and smile at the memory that hits me. Not too long ago, we did this on a plane. It was that moment when my life changed. I gave up a part of myself to him and never got it back. He and I shared something that night. We gave each other something we had never shared with anyone else. It bonded us. I press my hand against his cheek and my two-carat princess-cut diamond shines between us.

My lips press against him as I try to convey my love to him. I arch up and sink down on top of him. He moans in my mouth and I rock back and forth.

There's no hurry. I want to feel him. I want him to feel me.

"I love you, Mark."

"I love you more," he says against my lips.

We move in unison, slowly, but then we pick up the pace. I orgasm and Mark grunts as I squeeze him.

He follows me over after the second time. We lie here, naked, with limbs tangled together. The breeze off the ocean floats through the room. The salt air comforts me. It reminds me of him. Fresh air and salt. "I'll always think of you and the water."

"Because you're warming up to surfing?" he asks. He rolls over to face me.

I get on my side to see his eyes. "Did you eradicate the sharks?"

"No, but for you I might try."

"Aww." I touch his cheek. "You're so cute . . . sometimes."

Then, in true Mark fashion, he reminds me how not cute he is.

"I'm going to miss these." He grabs my boob.

I smack his hand away. "Well, they're not going anywhere."

His green eyes darken. "And neither are you."

"No," I say with a smile. "I'm not. You knocked me up and

married me. I guess we're stuck."

Mark pulls me on top of him and kisses me. "I guess so."

I roll off him, sit up, and look around. "I think it's how it was meant to be. We're exactly where we should be. You, me, here on this beautiful island. Just us."

His hand rests on my stomach. "All of us. Forever."

"Well . . ." I pause and then shake my head. "Nah, Forever and always."

epilogue

Five Years Later

"WHERE ARE THE KEYS?" I yell out as Makenna runs around in circles in her walker. She's the spitting image of her father—blonde hair, green eyes, and his attitude. In other words, she's a giant pain, but awfully cute.

"Where you left them!" Mark calls out as he tries to get our oldest corralled. Cullen is a handful. He literally has the worst traits of both of us. Stubborn is an understatement. He refuses to even look at the potty, won't eat anything that's green or brown, and sleep isn't in his vocabulary. Mark and I cherish each second with him, mainly because we're on nanny number six.

Yeah, six. He's the devil. No, he's his father. He's forced me to become a work-at-home mom because we can no longer get anyone to respond to our ads. I swear kindergarten can't come soon enough.

My pregnancy was easy, but his birth was far from it. I went through twenty six hours of labor, only to be rushed in for a C-section. I ended up hemorrhaging, and Cullen spent eight days in the NICU for difficulty breathing.

"Cullen!" Mark yells, and I laugh. He hates his name, but when Mark was gone for the night getting some sleep, I filled out the birth certificate, and Mark signed it in his sleep deprived haze. Thus, Cullen was named. "Charlie! You can't leave me with this kid!"

"I have to go, and he's your kid!" I look over at Makenna, thankful I'm bringing her in the car. She's so easy.

When I got pregnant with Makenna, we agreed not to even attempt natural birth again, but she had other plans. Nine days before my scheduled surgery, Makenna decided it was time to make her appearance. I was crowning by the time we got to the hospital.

"My mother is going to kill me!" I continue tossing over everything in the kitchen, hunting for the damn keys.

"It's a four-hour drive. You should've been on the road a while ago," Mark says with Cullen hanging upside down with no pants on.

"How is it that you can't handle getting a four-year-old dressed? Aren't you supposed to be all badass?"

"Badass!" Cullen repeats. Of course.

I crouch down as he hangs like a bat. "That's a bad word, baby. Don't repeat what comes out of Mommy's mouth."

Mark laughs. "We should have another kid."

I stand slowly and glare at him. "We're never having another child. You can't even handle the two we have."

"Says the woman who has 'go get your son' on repeat."

"He listens to you more," I say, still searching for the damn keys. I stomp my foot as I grow more aggravated. "We have to go, now."

Mark pulls me against his side as Cullen giggles. "Mommy, I go to Mamma's?"

I lean down and ruffle his hair, "Not this time buddy, but Mommy isn't going anywhere unless I can find the keys."

"Potty!" he says.

Mark looks at me and we both close our eyes. "He put them

in the toilet," I grumble. This kid.

I head into the bathroom, and sure enough, sitting sub-merged are my keys, along with a few other items I'll never touch again.

"Mark," I say sweetly.

"No."

"You owe me!"

"Cash that fucking day in, because I'm tired of hearing about it."

Never. I'll hold on until the day I die. It's my one bargaining chip.

Mark and I took this week off to head to DC. Dominic is be-ing sworn in to Congress tomorrow, and of course, my mother is throwing a party. Once we realized we'd need to have the oldest spawn out in public we reevaluated and decided to leave Mark and Cullen home.

We don't see my family as much as I would like, but I love our home here in Virginia Beach. Mark sold his bachelor pad on the beach for more money than we could've ever imagined, plus my apartment sold for top dollar. We bought a piece of land and built the perfect home for us. Full of toys, technology, and baby proofing.

I work from home most days, thanks to the demon I love so much, tackling various intelligence projects for Jackson and Mark. The California office exploded in the last year, so I do work for both sites. Mark made an effortless transition as co-owner, and the pay raise helps.

Everyone handled Erik's betrayal differently, but Jackson and Mark stepped up and kept everyone calm. Aaron was by far the angriest. He lost the most, thanks to Erik's betrayal.

"Mark!" I call for him again. "Please! I'm willing to bargain."

Some things never change.

He comes in behind me. "I don't get you. Slaughtering,

torture, and spying was good, but fishing some keys out is an issue?"

"And I have to kill the spiders," I counter.

"Let's not even talk about your fear of sharks. The insanity *that* is. Cullen is going in the damn water this year."

"He's welcome to the beautiful saltwater pool in the backyard. As much as he drives me insane, I like him enough not to get eaten."

"Charlie," he grumbles.

"Mark."

"Charisma." He kisses me quickly.

"Such a charmer."

"You know it, beautiful."

He reaches down and tosses the keys at me. "Asshole! I hate you," I say since I have to change my damp shirt and be even later to my mother's.

This is our life. It's crazy, fun, messy, and chaotic. We fight a lot, but we have even more fun making up. Hence, why Makenna came so soon after Cullen.

"You love me, baby!"

"Love to kill you."

"You'd miss me."

"Not this time! I have better aim than you," I call out. He laughs.

When I get back downstairs, Mark is sitting on the couch with both kids nestled in his sides. I stand against the wall just watching them. He reads as Makenna stares at him with a smile on her face, and Cullen touches the pages.

Moments like this, getting to see the most wonderful husband and father, make everything we've been through worth it. While we may have gone through a whole lot of hell, we found our heaven—together.

the end

about the author

CORINNE MICHAELS IS THE USA Today and Wall Street Journal Bestselling Author. She's an emotional, witty, sarcastic, and fun loving mom of two beautiful children. Corinne is happily married to the man of her dreams and is a former Navy wife. After spending months away from her husband while he was deployed, reading and writing was her escape from the loneliness.

Both her maternal and paternal grandmothers were librarians, which only intensified her love of reading. After years of writing short stories, she couldn't ignore the call to finish her debut novel, Beloved. Her alpha former Navy SEALs are broken, beautiful, and will steal your heart.

www.corinnemichaels.com

books by
Corinne Michaels

THE BELONGING DUET

Beloved (Book One)
Beholden (Book Two)

THE CONSOLATION DUET

Consolation (Book One)
Conviction (Book Two)

DEFENSELESS
INDEFINITE *(coming soon)*

acknowledgements

MY ATTEMPT TO KEEP this short and sweet should be interesting.

My readers: I can never fully explain what it means to me that you not only took a chance on me, but that some of you have stuck with me. I know I tend to keep leaving you with these crazy cliffhangers and you still love me. The support that you give me is astonishing and humbling. I love you so much!

My beta readers: I don't think anyone truly understands the sacrifice you make by dealing with me. You drop everything, read my drafts over and over, and put up with my insanity. Jennifer, Melissa, Katie, Holly, Michelle & Kristi . . . thank you will never be enough.

My early readers: Melissa & Alison, once again you give me the insight I need. I can't express my gratitude.

Christy Peckham: You're an asset in my life. We laugh, cry, and you keep me sane.

Melissa Saneholtz: The word publicist doesn't seem fitting for what you do. You run my life pretty much and I couldn't imagine anyone else doing this with me.

Stabby Birds: You guys are the best people I know. You're my sisters through and through. We laugh, cry, and bond together like nothing I've ever seen before. I love you!

Claire Contreras, Laurelin Paige, Mia Asher, SL Jennings, Whitney Gracia Williams, Mandi Beck, Kristy Bromberg, Kyla Linde, Tillie Cole, Leylah Attar, Kennedy Ryan, SL Scott, EK Blair, Lauren Blakely, CD Reiss, Pepper Winters, Elisabeth Grace, Rebecca Yarros, Livia Jamerlan, &—thank you for making me smile, laugh, talking through one of my crazy ideas, and just being my friends. I'm truly blessed to have you in my life.

Jesey: I haven't been able to do this until now. Thank you. Because of something we dreamt of two years ago, look where we are. It's amazing to think the friendship we've had has somehow twisted our worlds to this place. I love you!

My editor: Brenda, thank you for loving my characters as much as I do. Your feedback made this book everything I could've hoped for.

My formatter: Christine, you are first-class in this business. Your professionalism and attention to detail are above and beyond. You work tirelessly and it doesn't go unnoticed.

My cover designer: Sarah, thank you for making probably my favorite cover of this entire series.

My photographer: Nicole, seriously! You nailed this shoot. You were an absolute dream to work with!

My proofreader: Ashley, my comma loving friend! You crack me up with your notes and you're a dream to work with.

Lisa from The Rock Stars of Romance: THANK YOU! Your support has meant everything to the success of this series. I can't begin to thank you enough. I love your face!

Bloggers: I don't think you guys understand what you do for the book world. It's not a job you get paid for (well, not nearly what you deserve). It's something you love and you do because of that. Thank you from the bottom of my heart.

To my husband and children, I'm so lucky to have you. You probably bear the worst part of this process. I love you three more than anything in this world. Thank you for putting up with all that you do. I know I need to put the computer and phone down more because you deserve that. Thank you for being here and supporting me day after day. Thank you for letting me cry when my feelings are hurt. Smile when something amazing happens. But mostly thank you for loving me and believing in me.

CPSIA information can be obtained
at www.ICGtesting.com
Printed in the USA
BVOW03s1254071216
470066BV00021B/416/P